THE RAT KING

By

LP HERNANDEZ

THE RAT KING

"Night Feeding" originally appeared in *The Monstronomicon*

"Daddy Longlegs" originally appeared in *A Monster Told Me Bedtime Stories*

For more information, including links to other published works and audio productions, please visit www.lphernandez.com.

The cover and interior illustrations are © Brett Bullion. Please visit his website at *https://www.brettbullionart.com.* Thank you, Brett! It has been an absolute joy working with you!

This release of The Rat King is distributed by Sleepless Sanctuary Publishing, a sister company of The NoSleep Podcast. You can find out more about them here: http://www.thenosleeppodcast.com

ISBN: 978-0-578-75815-2

CONTENTS

* Some stories featured on The NoSleep Podcast have been edited from their audio versions.

For Miranda, the other half of me.

Bad Apples

Bruce lived in the house next door to mine for more than a month before I first saw him. The house sat vacant since the previous summer when its occupant, Mrs. Kingsbury, passed away. She was older, but not elderly, and so her death was surprising only because we tend not to think about things like that. There was an estate sale within a month of her passing and then a realtor's sign was erected on the front lawn. A few contractors and repairmen visited, but then the activity stopped. The grass of the front lawn grew, to my father's great annoyance, until it obscured the name of the real estate agent at the bottom of the sign.

It was the week before school began and the neighborhood kids were doing their best to squeeze the mirth from each minute of those long summer days. We skipped rocks across the pond in the park a few streets over. We climbed trees until we reached the thinnest branches that sagged beneath our weight. We raced down searing sidewalks and displayed our skinned knees with pride.

The laughter tapered off quicker than it had in June, when summer was a wide-open field of possibility before us. We went through the motions, but there was a theatrical quality to our actions, as if we were thespians in the final performances of a long-running play.

As I pedaled up the hill I heard the roar of a lawnmower and assumed my father cracked from the injustice of the overgrown lawn next door. He only mowed our lawn on Saturday mornings after a reasonable breakfast of eggs, an English muffin, and coffee. It was Monday evening and the sun had just disappeared behind the line of trees, its light an electric orange that reminded me of the popsicles with the ice-cream center.

I crested the hill and saw that it was not Dad but the neighbor, a new neighbor. There was a moving truck in their driveway, men with sweat-soaked shirts ferrying a bookshelf into the house. The man mowing the lawn paused to dab at his brow with a handkerchief, then tucked it into the pocket of his jeans. I guided my bike to the front door and waved at the man, who offered a smart salute. I craned my neck to see if there were any toys in the truck, something to indicate the presence of a kid my age, but saw only a slice of a table with a dark cherry finish. I had many friends in the neighborhood, but my particular street was mostly populated by retirees.

My mother introduced herself to the neighbors on behalf of our family, offering a pecan pie as if that was a normal choice for the summer. She reported that the couple did, in fact, have a child, and at ten years old he was only a year younger than me.

"Sadie, don't get your hopes up just yet," Mom said.

"Why?"

Mom shared a quick glance with Dad.

"The boy, Bruce, has some medical conditions. Sounds like it's mostly related to his diet. He's a bit small for his age and might not ever be able to keep up with you. Not to say you can't be friends, but it will have to be on Bruce's terms. He spent much of his life in hospitals and has mostly associated with adults in his life."

"What's up with his diet? Allergies?" I asked.

"Dan and Grace made it seem like it was more severe than that. Just be patient, honey. He'll come around in time."

Summer concluded to the teeth rattling sound of my alarm clock. I stood at the bus stop, devastated, demoralized at the sight of the approaching bus. My days were soon filled with homework and after school sports. I forgot about Bruce until that Saturday in September.

The lawnmower's engine died and I heard the familiar sound of my dad stomping on the entryway mat. He passed me in the hallway, pointing at his white New Balance sneakers that were now streaked with forest green.

"Super cool, Dad," I said, rolling my eyes.

The freshly mowed grass littered the backyard in sticky clumps that threatened to make my shoes a companion to my dad's. I climbed the rope ladder to my lovingly crafted but rarely visited treehouse. I rummaged through comics, their pages yellowed and brittle. I munched from a bag of Doritos whose expiration date was too faded to read.

Wiping my orange fingers on my shorts, I gazed upon the roofs of houses. I noticed the mask in the second story window of our neighbor's house and thought it a bit early for Halloween decorations. It was a rudimentary thing, like a paper plate with eyeholes and a mouth cut out. Then it vanished, and I realized it was a face, the face of Bruce, the unseen boy. He was so pale he practically glowed.

I watched the window for a few minutes but detected no new activity. I dismissed the apparition and stacked my comics back on the shelf. As I reached for the rope ladder a voice called up to me.

"Hello?"

I screamed from the shock and pressed my hand to my chest. He stood in the shade of my tree, though on his side of the fence.

"You scared me!" I said, to which he shrugged.

"My name is Bruce."

"Sadie."

"What are you doing up there?"

I hadn't really been doing anything but made something up on the spot.

"Keeping a watch on the neighborhood. Looking for strangers," I said, casting my gaze over the roofs again.

"Do you ever see any?" he asked, burying his hands in the pockets of his pajamas.

"Once. There was a man in a dark suit who walked down the street. Had a briefcase with him. A minute after he reached the end of the street he would appear at the beginning of it again. I watched him for two hours," I said, then glanced at him to see if he bought it.

He looked toward the street but likely could not see much beyond the top of his fence.

"I'm kidding! I'm just hanging out, reading comics and eating chips," I said.

He smiled and mimed wiping sweat from his brow.

"Want to come up?" I asked.

He looked over his shoulder and I noticed the figure in the sliding glass window. It was Grace, his mother.

"Well, I do, but…"

"Do you need to ask permission?"

Grace stood at the window, watching, her arms relaxed by her side.

"I should probably stay in my yard," he said.

I nodded, "That's okay, I can talk to you from here."

4

"Really?" he said, smiling.

"Sure."

His Batman pajamas looked as though they were borrowed from an older brother, though I knew him to be an only child. His voice was small but confident, like a cartoon mouse that always manages to gain the advantage over its fumbling feline rival.

I remained in my perch until Mom called me inside for breakfast. He issued questions almost faster than I could answer. I understood he was home schooled and had fleeting contact with children his own age. I empathized with his curiosity and attempted to paint an elaborate picture for him. He did answer the few questions I proposed, though he looked over his shoulder as if he feared his mother would hear through the glass.

"Most foods make me sick. I can only eat what my parents prepare for me," he said, tracing light patterns in the grass with his bare toes.

"Sick like how? Like you'd need an ambulance?" I asked.

He glanced over his shoulder. Grace had not moved from the sliding glass door, though she appeared to be engaged in conversation with someone in the house.

"Just sick. It sucks because there's so much I never got to try."

My ears perked.

"Got to try before what?"

I expected him to say before he was diagnosed with his condition, which had gone unnamed to that point.

"Before I died," he said.

I sputtered.

"Well, I didn't stay dead," he said, presenting his small body as evidence.

"You died?"

"For a bit. When they brought me back the food thing came with it."

"Did you see anything when you were dead?" I asked, leaning so far out of the treehouse a gust of wind would have sent me crashing to the earth.

He nodded, "Yes, but I don't remember. It comes back in dreams sometimes."

I had a million questions to ask, but my mother chose that moment to announce breakfast was ready.

"Can you come back out later?" I asked as I reached for the rope ladder.

"Maybe. My mom's pretty protective of me. I'm surprised she let me talk to you this long," he said.

"Hey! I have an idea! I have walkie-talkies we can use. They're cheap plastic ones, only go about a hundred feet. But that would be plenty between our houses."

He nodded, smiling.

"I'll leave yours on your side of the fence."

Mom called again, agitation creeping into her voice.

"Nice to meet you!" I yelled as I sprinted to the house.

"You too," he called, his voice tickling my ear and disappearing like a puff of smoke.

I did not see Bruce again for a week, but we were in constant contact via the walkie-talkies. His was a worldview I had never known. Much of his life was lived in an antiseptic white room, his breaths ushered in and out of his lungs through the labor of machines.

He was equally fascinated by the relative normalcy of my life. He requested I recount the details of a particularly contentious soccer match. Perhaps he imagined himself on the pitch in my place, his miniscule frame darting through defenders as I had done. Inevitably, the conversation returned to him and that simple, staggering fact of his death.

"So, you were at home and your heart stopped?" I said as I lay in my bed, eyes fixated on the ghostly streaks of paint on the ceiling.

"For a couple of minutes."

"And the doctor just showed up?"

"Yeah, he was my new doctor and wanted to introduce himself. I feel like I kind of remember him. Like I was outside of my body when he came. But, he's just sort of a blank space. I can see my parents react to him but can't see him."

"That's so crazy! You die and one of the only people in the world capable of saving you shows up at your house," I said, eyeing the yellow slab of light beneath the door. I was supposed to be asleep, but it was a Friday and I doubted my parents would mind. They encouraged my blossoming friendship with Bruce.

"I guess it is. But, it's only crazy because I lived. If he hadn't brought me back it wouldn't be that interesting. Sad, but not interesting."

I learned more about his family and what inspired them to settle in our small town. Dan, his father, was a pilot. He commuted one-and-a-half hours to Denver and was often gone for two or three days at a time. He had one day off at home and then was back in the air. He recently completed a purchase on a small jet, preparing to transition into becoming a private pilot.

"Why not just live in Denver?" I asked.

"Bad memories. Hospital life took a toll on everyone, not just me. Plus, I died in that house, you know? I think my parents just want me to have a normal childhood. As close to normal as I can get. We don't really think about my condition as much out here."

By the end of September, we had each changed the double A batteries in our walkie-talkies twice. Bruce and his family came over one Sunday to watch football. Dan appeared relaxed, slapping my dad on the back and loudly bemoaning the play-calling when his team did not benefit from it.

Grace hovered near my mom, but her eyes seldom strayed from her son. I imagine she had once been a striking beauty, but the years of witnessing her only child deflate before her eyes had robbed her of something. She covered her mouth when she smiled, which was a rare occurrence. She molded herself into as small a physical shape as possible, her arms glued to her torso, her knees slightly bent. It was as if she had tightly coiled springs for bones.

Over the course of the previous week Bruce and I devised a plan that we executed that day.

"Mom, can I go trick-or-treating with Sadie on Halloween?" Bruce asked.

Grace fumbled the plastic cup in her hand, some of its contents spilling onto the tiles. Her jaw was slack, eyes swollen in disbelief.

I stood next to Bruce, my chin about level with the crown of his head.

"It would only be for a few hours," I said.

Grace looked first to the living room. Dan was on the edge of the couch, a corn chip hovering a few inches from his lips as he awaited the verdict of a challenged play. She then looked to my mother, whose

8

countenance began to mirror the woman's obvious concern.

"Bruce, honey, I think that's something we should talk about at home. You know you might have trouble keeping up. We certainly wouldn't want to interfere with Sadie's fun," she said, clearing her throat to punctuate the statement.

His head drooped on cue.

"She's the only friend I've ever made," he whimpered.

I draped an arm around his shoulders and he leaned his small body into me.

Grace's eyes darted from her husband, still unaware of the unfolding catastrophe, to my mother, who seemed unsure if she should smile or frown in that moment.

"What if we just did our street? I'll walk with Bruce around the neighborhood and bring him right back to you. Thirty minutes, tops," I bargained.

Grace nodded, the intensity of her anguish diminishing.

"But, honey, your diet," she said.

He dabbed at the corner of his eye and, in his tiniest voice said, "I wouldn't eat any candy. I would just give it to Sadie. I just want to be a kid on Halloween."

Grace relented to the pressure of the moment and we darted back to my room to finalize our plans.

That night I chatted with Bruce via walkie-talkie. His excitement over Halloween, still more than a month away, had not diminished. We said our goodbyes at about 9 o'clock and I settled into bed.

The walkie-talkie fizzled and popped on the nightstand. A light voice sang the theme song to a cartoon. This had happened a few times previous. The walkie-talkies were cheap toys and sometimes the button on Bruce's got stuck, meaning he broadcasted inadvertently. The week before I listened to his mother tell him a bedtime story before the button released and the transmission terminated.

That night was different.

I suspected Bruce carried the walkie-talkie in the pocket of his pajamas because there was a constant scratching sound of the fabric rubbing over the microphone. I heard the sound of a sports show as Bruce walked past the living room. His father lamented, "That wasn't even close!"

Bruce giggled and kept walking.

The sound of the television faded and there was a series of knocks.

"Come in," Grace said.

"Mom, I'm hungry," Bruce said as he shuffled forward.

The sound of movement stopped and Grace's voice was louder.

"Oh, honey, we're all out. You know that," she said.

I imagined her running thin fingers through his chestnut hair.

"I know. I'm just really hungry," he said.

Grace sighed.

"I just fed you a little while ago, honey. You can't wait until your father gets back?" she asked hopefully.

"I don't think so," Bruce whispered.

There was a period of silence.

"Okay, but just a bit, honey," Grace said.

A drawer opened. After a delay there was a hiss of air passing through teeth.

Then there was a sound of wet swallowing interrupted by soft moans of satisfaction.

This persisted for a minute. I held the walkie-talkie to my ear.

"Bruce, that's all tonight," Grace said, her voice stern.

"But Mom, I'm still hungry. It doesn't fill me up like it used to."

She sighed, "Give it a couple of days."

The transmission ended as the button popped back into place. I placed the walkie-talkie on the nightstand and reclined in bed. In a matter of weeks, Bruce had become my best friend. We did not speak often about his dietary restrictions. It simply wasn't interesting conversation. I knew he could not eat most foods.

What *did* he eat?

Autumn descended on the front range of Colorado. Flurries of golden leaves skittered through the streets until the rain came. In the week leading up to Halloween a blanket of clouds the color of dryer lint obscured the distant Rocky Mountains. The dancing leaves were molded to the earth, held in place by cold, fat drops.

Bruce confessed that his mother had threatened to cancel our Halloween scheme if the weather did not improve. She tolerated the idea of her only child being out of sight for half an hour, but he would not be cold and wet. Fortunately, the clouds dispersed two days before Halloween and an Indian summer took root. By Halloween our air conditioner thrummed.

I could not convince Bruce to change his costume. He had no interest in the macabre and was stone-faced at my suggestions for a humorous alternative.

He was a cat.

Of all of the possible costumes he went as a cat.

I am almost positive Grace found the costume in the girl's section of the Halloween store. But, he was ecstatic with it. He wore the tail and

11

ears for days. He randomly meowed through the walkie-talkie. More than once I pressed my face to the glass of my window in search of a stray cat outside.

Had I believed he was serious about the cat costume prior to selecting mine I might have chosen a companion, a dog or rat. Instead, I was a zombie. Dad sacrificed a flannel shirt to the cause and I was given permission to tarnish a pair of jeans which were a size too small.

Grace escorted Bruce to our front door. I answered the knock and found her staring at the sky as if willing the clouds to reassemble.

I lurched at Bruce with arms outstretched and he scurried away. He whipped his tail at me and hissed.

"Don't get yourself worked up, honey. And remember…" Grace trailed off, allowing space for Bruce to finish the thought.

"No eating candy," he said.

Trick-or-treating began at six o'clock when it was still fairly light out. Bruce and his mother congregated in our entryway for fifteen minutes until the porch lights came on.

We skipped down the driveway. My mother took pictures while Grace propped herself against the doorframe and cradled her stomach. Bruce grasped my hand as we turned onto the sidewalk. I glanced over my shoulder to wave at my mom and saw that Grace was smiling. Somehow, she still looked sad.

Bruce pulled me forward like a stray dog on a leash. We scaled the driveway to a house with the porch light on and he was nearly breathless from the effort.

"Trick-or-treat!" we shouted in unison.

"Oh my, Sadie, I hardly recognized you! And who's your little friend?" Mrs. Chapman asked.

"I'm Bruce. I'm new in town!" Bruce responded and snapped his pillowcase open.

"Well, welcome to the neighborhood, Bruce," Mrs. Chapman said with a wink, releasing a handful of miniature chocolates into each of our bags.

As we walked to the next house Bruce said, "I can't believe it really works like that. You just walk up to someone's house and they give you candy? I kind of thought it only happened in movies."

Bruce delighted at every Halloween decoration. He giggled at the goofy epithets on Styrofoam tombstones and squealed at the blinking red eyes of a plastic Dracula. As we neared the cul-de-sac at the far end of our street I picked up the pace a little.

"What's the rush?" Bruce asked, jogging to catch up to me.

"Mrs. Dubois, my old babysitter. She makes candy apples for Halloween but only two dozen. If we don't get there quick the other kids will get 'em!"

There were four children at her front door and no telling how many had already visited. We dashed up the driveway, passing the kids as they departed. They held their candy apples aloft like torches, Tootsie Rolls and Jolly Ranchers forgotten for the moment.

Mrs. Dubois stood in the doorway, her brown hair streaked with gray and piled atop her head in a loose bun.

"Hi Mrs. Dubois! Are we too late?" I said.

She held an empty tray in her hand.

"Sadie I…" she began.

My head drooped.

"Of course not!" she said, then stepped aside to reveal a second tray with a dozen bright red candy apples.

13

Mrs. Dubois swapped the empty tray for the full one and lowered it slightly so that I could take my pick.

My fingers danced over plastic stems. The candy apples didn't look real. They were too perfect. Thin, white fingers brushed up against mine and liberated an apple from the tray, which canted for a moment until Mrs. Dubois stabilized it.

"Wow…" Bruce said as he retreated two steps.

Mrs. Dubois winked, "You're welcome, little cat."

I claimed an apple with the largest pool of hardened candy coating at its base.

"Thank you, Happy Halloween!" I said and joined Bruce.

His lips glistened with saliva that threatened to spill out of his mouth. He beheld the candy apple as if his mind did not understand the concept of its existence.

"Did you ever eat candy?" I asked.

He nodded his head and peeled his gaze away from the apple.

"Yes, before I died. My parents didn't give it to me much, but I did have some. Sometimes the nurses snuck it in."

"What was your favorite?"

He beamed.

"Jolly Ranchers."

I nearly dropped my apple as Bruce opened his mouth and sank his teeth into the ruby red, candied surface. He closed his eyes and wrenched a chunk of the apple's flesh free. He chewed slowly and moaned as he did.

"Bruce! Your diet!" I said.

He swallowed and his half-lidded eyes found mine.

"It's so hard, Sadie. So hard to live like this."

14

He buried his teeth into the apple again, juice running down his chin in twin streams.

"Your mother is going to kill me! She's going to kill us!" I protested, glancing at our houses in the distance.

He swallowed again and uttered, "She said no candy. She didn't say no candy apples."

I nodded, the adrenaline leveling in my body.

"What's going to happen to you?" I asked.

He shrugged his shoulders and took a third bite, then began to walk toward the next house.

We did not have to wait long to find out.

The apple toppled to the earth, its candy façade cracking as it rolled to a stop in the grass. Bruce hunched over and I rushed to his side. His body trembled as he gasped wetly.

"Bruce, what do I need to do?" I asked, my hand pressed against the small of his back.

He shook his head, stood a bit straighter, then opened his mouth. A torrent of red exploded with volcanic force. It splattered on the sidewalk and then the grass as he turned slightly. Within the rapidly growing red puddle were crimson clots of apple and fractured bits of candy. A smell of old pennies washed over me.

His little chest heaved during a brief respite. Then he groaned, his cheeks puffing out with gore that he tried to keep within. His head whipped back and forth like an unsecured firehose. I pivoted and scanned the houses near me. There were no trick-or-treaters within earshot, no open doors.

The word *help* bubbled in my throat, but I did not utter it.

Bruce spat one final time and then stood erect. He wiped his thumb

15

across his lips and a shudder wracked his body for half a second.

"Worth it," he said, and retrieved his pillowcase, which had fallen behind him.

"Ready?" he asked, smiling.

I looked to the red soup on the sidewalk. It didn't seem possible that so much liquid could fit within such a small boy.

"Bruce, what happened to you?"

He cocked his head to the side and smirked, "Allergies."

I imagine the puddle of what I assumed was blood would likely be dismissed as spilled juice by passersby. I jogged to catch up to Bruce, not comprehending how he was so unaffected by what transpired.

The next ten minutes passed normally. Bruce showed no ill-effects from the episode and I said nothing because I could think of nothing to say. We reached the houses on the opposite side of the street from ours and he proudly offered me the contents of his pillowcase.

"That was better than the movies. Thank you so much, Sadie," he said.

He skipped across the street and ran to greet his mother, who waited in the doorway. Prior to reaching her he stopped, turned, wagged his tail at me and meowed.

"How did it go?" Mom asked as I entered the house.

"Um, good. Bruce gave me all his candy so I think I'm okay for the night."

Mom arched an eyebrow.

"Not going back out with your other friends?"

I hefted my sack over my shoulder.

"Not this time. Think I'll head upstairs."

I held a rag beneath a warm stream of water and stared at myself in the mirror. I replayed the scene in my head on a loop, Bruce's cat ears askew on his head as it thrashed about. I saw the candy apple, its white handle stained with streaks of red on its side in the grass. I saw Bruce lurch and the gush of crimson. The sound of was like a saturated mop slapping a tiled floor.

I wiped the gray and green makeup from my face, wanting to put Halloween behind me as quickly as possible.

"Sadie?" the walkie-talkie hissed.

I draped the rag over the faucet and ran to my bedroom.

"Sadie?" Bruce called again.

"I'm here."

"Sadie, I just wanted to tell you that tonight was the best night of my life. Sorry for the stuff earlier. Don't worry about it. I'm okay," he said.

"I had a good time, too, Bruce."

I waited for more but he said nothing.

"Bruce? Was that blood?"

He sighed and then said, "Good night, Sadie. Thanks again."

When I pressed the button to transmit I was met with a steady tone that meant Bruce's walkie-talkie was still triggered. I heard the springs of his mattress as he bounced off his bed and the whisper of his bare feet over hardwood floors.

I returned to the bathroom and removed the rest of the zombie makeup. At two to three-minute intervals our doorbell rang. Within ten or so seconds the voices of children echoed within the house.

Trick-or-treat!

I tossed the shredded shirt into the laundry hamper. Maybe next year I would just hand out candy.

"Mom! I'm hungry!" Bruce whined, startling me out of my sleep.

The walkie-talkie had been silent over the past hour or so. I fell asleep without having realized it. His voice was not clear, likely originating in the hallway outside of his bedroom.

"Your father will be home soon, dear," Grace called, her voice barely intelligible.

"But I'm hungry now," Bruce muttered, clearer now.

I heard his footsteps padding across the floor of his bedroom and the sound of light clattering. I imagined him playing with his toys, but there was a blank space in my thoughts. I did not know what kind of toys he played with. I had never been inside of the house, much less his room. Bruce didn't talk about himself much.

I sat up in bed. If I had vomited blood I would likely not be thinking of food for some time. I saw the images again, heard the wet mop sound.

The springs of my bed squealed as I flipped over and rested my chin on the top edge of the headboard. I parted the blinds with two fingers and saw the milky yellow glow of a lamp in Bruce's room. I watched for his silhouette but realized the light source was too near the window.

Light flooded the alley between our houses and I recoiled, the blinds snapping back into place. I imagined Bruce in the window, his pale face staring out as when I first saw him weeks ago. I clenched my fists and eased another few inches away from the window.

The garage door opener thrummed to life and I realized the light was from the headlights of Dan's Jeep. I parted the blinds again and watched the Jeep vanish within the house.

"Finally," Bruce whispered, the sound barely picked up by the walkie-talkie.

There was nothing to see but vinyl siding. No windows with the curtains errantly parted. Bruce skipped down the stairs, the sound fading to nothing after a couple of steps.

And then I heard the screaming.

It was faint through the miniscule speaker, and quickly cut off by the slamming of a door.

It was a baby crying.

The blinds snapped back into place again as I abandoned my post. I sagged beneath the implications of the sound. I could think of no reason, no good reason why a man would retrieve an infant in the middle of the night.

Perhaps the baby was family?

Sure, but why the midnight voyage? And where was the child's family?

And why had Bruce whispered that single word?

I replayed the sound in my head as I stared at my ceiling. As I did its texture changed. It was less harsh, less desperate.

It was an animal.

Had to be.

I rolled on my side and stared at the walkie-talkie, silent then. Bruce was no longer transmitting.

It had to be.

I avoided Bruce for the next week. He attempted to contact me via the walkie-talkie, but I did not respond.

"Sadie? Are you mad at me?" he asked.

I stared at the walkie-talkie.

"Did I do something wrong?"

The Indian summer relented to the winds of autumn. One frosty November morning I opened my blinds to let light into my room. Bruce was in his backyard, his figure consumed by a puffy red jacket. He walked the inside border of the yard, head down and hands buried in his pockets. And he walked. And he walked.

I watched him for ten minutes and his pace never wavered. In the previous week I convinced myself that Halloween had been a misunderstanding and nothing more. Bruce was allergic to just about everything. It was the first thing we were told about him. If vomiting blood was the result of eating outside of his diet it made sense that Grace hovered so protectively over him.

As for the screaming…

There was nothing to rationalize. Either I misidentified the sound or there was an explanation for it.

Bruce stopped, turned, and withdrew a gloved hand. He waved and I found myself waving back. How long had he known I was watching? Then he resumed his solitary march, hands in pockets, head bowed.

Here was a little boy, isolated from the world, walking infinite laps within the confines of his own backyard. I was his only window to the outside, a sliver of normalcy in a life that had been anything but. I shrugged into a sweater, donned my jeans and skipped down the steps.

"Bruce?" I called.

Through the narrow gaps in the wooden fence I saw him pause.

"Sadie?"

He jogged to the fence, his torso twisting awkwardly as his arms

20

were not free to move.

He pressed his nose into the gap between the slats.

"I thought you were mad at me."

I sighed.

"Just confused, I guess. The vomit thing was pretty scary."

He withdrew his nose a little.

"Not for me. It took months before we figured my diet out. I threw up everything."

So, what do you eat?

I didn't ask the question.

"Sadie, can I tell you something?"

My heart beat faster.

"Of course."

"I lied to you about when I died. I *did* die. But, I lied to you about one part of it. When I died I was outside of my body. That part was true. I mentioned the doctor that showed up at our front door. That was also true. But, I said I didn't remember him, what he looked like. I do. It's just something I don't like to think about."

"What did he look like?"

"Not a doctor," Bruce said in a somber voice.

"Why are you telling me?"

His nose peeked through the fence again.

"My mom's waving for me to come inside. We have to go back to Denver for a couple of days," he said.

"Okay."

"Sadie, can we be friends again when I come back?" he asked in his smallest voice.

"Sure, Bruce."

He dashed to the sliding glass door. I climbed up my tree a few feet so that I could see over the fence. Bruce clenched a glove in his teeth and pulled it off his hand. He plucked something from the soil of a potted plant and returned to the sliding glass door. After he opened the door he returned the object, a key I assumed, to the dirt. The curtains fluttered behind him as he disappeared inside his house.

A chilly wind gave life to the dried leaves fastened to their branches by brittle stems. They shuddered, sounding like a den of angry rattlesnakes. I watched the house from my perch, a hard, plastic stool designed for a toddler one-third my weight. The curtains twitched as an unseen person walked by, but otherwise the house was still.

Not a doctor...

I shivered. It would be at least a couple of days before Bruce could elaborate on his story. A couple of days that his house would be unoccupied...

The potted plant was like a beacon. The garage door hummed open and Grace's white sedan backed into the street. There was a glare on the window and so I could not see if Bruce was waving at me, but I waved anyway.

A couple of hours later I paced my room; the idea in my mind was like an itch that I could not reach. It demanded all of my energy. I glanced through the partially opened blinds as if I expected the house to sprout legs and sprint away. Of course, it did not, but I watched anyway.

"Mom, I'm going to the playground!" I shouted from the backdoor.

"Which one?" she called from the kitchen.

"The big one with the blue slide. If I'm not there I'm at Kelsea's house," I said and closed the door behind me.

In the few hours I had been indoors the day had grown colder. My breath issued in little spectral puffs. I scaled the fence that divided my yard from Bruce's and landed on grass still billowy from the early autumn rains. I padded across the yard to the potted plant and spied the top edge of the key in the soil.

As I turned the key I wondered if the house might have an alarm system. I never heard an errant chirp in the background of my walkie-talkie conversations with Bruce. It was a safe neighborhood, almost depressingly so. Having an alarm system might arouse more interest than not having one.

I opened the sliding glass door and eased inside, tucking the key into the front pocket of my jeans as I did.

What was my purpose here?

To be honest, I did not know.

I explored the first floor, which was handsomely decorated in muted tones of gray and black. I surveyed the pictures on the mantle above the fireplace and along the walls. The sadness I felt manifested in my chest as a swelling sensation. In all but the most recent pictures Bruce was in a hospital setting.

In one picture he sat on Santa's lap, a wisp of a boy in a Christmas sweater that threatened to consume him. His parents stood off to the side, smiling practiced smiles. A nurse in pistachio-green scrubs was visible in the background, shattering the façade.

There were a dozen similar pictures. Birthdays. Easter. Thanksgiving served on a tin tray from the hospital cafeteria. And then there was me.

"What?" I whispered.

The picture was taken less than two weeks ago, yet here it was.

Bruce and I posed in our costumes, his tail a blur of motion.

I felt like an intruder.

I reached inside my pocket for the key. And then I recalled what happened after the picture was taken. I remembered the scream cut off by a door slamming.

I placed the key back in my pocket and resumed my search. Exiting the living room, I was confronted by a door that was slightly smaller than the others. There were minor layout differences between that house and mine, the same parts rearranged slightly. I guessed this was the door to the basement. I kneeled before it. There was a padlock affixed to a safety hasp. Judging by the chipped paint around the hasp this feature had been recently added.

The padlock was secure, but the hasp had been left open. I turned the knob and the door opened. A wooden stairwell descended into darkness before me. There was a light switch just inside the entrance. I flipped it on and the basement flooded with light, phosphorescent bulbs buzzing audibly. I closed the door behind me and walked down the stairs.

My attention was immediately drawn to a wall-mounted desk. Ancient books populated its shelves. One was open on the desk. Its title, in flaking gold letters, read *Germanic Folklore During the Black Death*. I found an entry with a dog-eared page.

There was a simple sketch of a figure wearing a black cowl. A plague mask emerged from the hood, but few other details were visible. Below the illustration was the title *The Healer*.

Versions of this legend predate the era of the Great Plague. It seems the Healer is a popular character in myth, in various guises, across the globe. He arrives at a time of intense peril, typically at a moment of life or death. It is obvious, then, why his presence would be associated with the Black Death, as peril was the permanent state of much of the European continent.

The name is a misnomer, to an extent. The Healer does heal, but at a cost. In essence, he is more of a trickster than a healer. Alleged to arrive right at the moment of passing, The Healer targets loved ones of the departed, offering them a unique opportunity. The Healer will return the dead to life, with no debt owed to him. But that does not mean there are no consequences.

The newly living come back different, in unpredictable ways. One tale recounts a young mother who returned from the dead and believed herself to be a rat. She was often found naked, swimming through garbage with her furry brethren. Her forlorn and frightened husband moved to another town, an effort to protect his child. One night he awoke, suffocating beneath the weight of a thousand rats and saw, in brief glimpses, the ghostly pale shape of his wife as she fastened her teeth around the baby's neck and ferried it into the night.

In another story a mother wakes from a deep sleep to find her recently resurrected son has nibbled off three of her toes. She screamed and hobbled out of the room, leaving the boy to lap at the small puddles of her blood.

I stopped reading.

I had no issue with the possibility of apples making Bruce vomit. I could not accept, however, that his body's allergic response would be to immediately eject a quart of blood. The body doesn't work that way.

But, what if the blood was already in his stomach?

There was a map of North America plastered on the bare, brick wall. Three penciled lines connected Denver to three towns in northern Mexico. Written above the lines were distances in miles followed by weights in pounds, the meaning of which I did not understand. Did it have something to do with Dan's job as a pilot?

The key was in my hand again, though I did not recall retrieving it. I left the desk to explore the rest of the room. There were metal shelves with spare light bulbs, canned goods, and the like. Translucent tubs of holiday decorations were stacked against the wall.

In the center of the room were relics from Bruce's baby years. I glanced a second time at the bassinet. There was a metal grate on top, secured shut with a padlock.

"What the…"

The changing table next to the bassinet had also been modified with the addition of three leather belts.

Restraints.

The sound came back to me. The scream that ended at the slamming of a door.

The key was hot in my hand. My elbow bumped a rolling tray table, tipping its contents, rubber tubing, IV catheters, and opaque blood bags to the floor.

I walked backwards, away from the baby items and medical accessories. My extremities tingled and it seemed the oxygen had been syphoned from the atmosphere. I collided with a standing freezer and grunted in surprise.

I had to know.

My hand grasped the long, white handle of the freezer. I pulled but the freezer door remained shut. I pulled again and the entire appliance rocked, but still did not open. I jammed the key in my pocket, gripped the handle with two hands and wrenched.

The freezer tipped forward several inches but was prevented from crushing me by the open door, which contacted the floor. The contents of the shelves toppled free.

The garage door hummed to life overhead.

I heard it but could not move.

The baby inside the plastic bag was frozen with its small hands balled into fists, covering its face. A thin layer of frost had grown over the thick mane of ebony hair. There was more that was wrong about it than its frozen state. Its legs were malformed, like the tail of a seahorse and they curved toward its spine. It also seemed compressed.

Deflated.

Drained.

There were other bags, their contents coated with frost. My stomach lurched but I had nothing to expel.

I heard a door shut in a room above me, breaking my trance. I uprooted my legs from the floor and sprinted to the other end of the room, hiding behind the metal shelving unit.

Heavy steps clomped down the hallway and into the kitchen. I crouched and clamped a hand over my mouth as the door to the basement opened.

"Hello?"

The lights. It was Dan.

"Honey?"

My vision narrowed. My limbs felt weighted with blood as my adrenaline surged. Bruce said *we* have to go to Denver. He did not state which *we* that entailed.

"Bruce?"

He would see. He would see the still open freezer door and the frozen baby in the bag. Then he would search. And he would find me.

28

"Hey, Grace, did you leave the lights on in the basement?" he spoke in a lower voice.

There was a pause.

"Maybe it was Bruce. You guys in Denver yet?"

He was on the phone. I peeked around the shelves. He stood with one hand on the wall, staring at the map.

"Okay. You said you'd be there two days?"

If he stayed like that for ten seconds I could sneak behind him.

"I know. I just don't want the doctors getting too nosy."

He would eventually turn and see the open freezer, the blood bags on the floor. And the baby.

"I get it. He has other health concerns. I just don't want them getting too close, or running a test that might give it away."

I stepped around the shelves and into the main body of the basement. If he turned his head to the right he would see me.

"It's what we have to do right now, dear. Maybe it'll be different in the future. You know I hate it too."

I was within ten feet of him. I never realized how tall he was, even bent over at the waist. I took an exaggerated step over a surgical blade that had fallen on the floor.

"I think I have one in Sonora. $800. Sixteen weeks old."

I gritted my teeth. I was directly behind him as he stood upright.

"I know, Grace, but they're going to die anyway. These aren't healthy babies. Nothing else works for Bruce."

I took two more steps and was now to his left. He placed a finger on the map.

"I would do anything for him. Yes, I know you would too."

The stairs were half a dozen steps to my left. Had the wood popped

29

or squeaked earlier? I didn't remember. My muscles vibrated.

"Okay, well, let me know when you guys get there."

I placed a quivering foot on the first step, never taking my eyes off him.

"Tell him I love him."

Dan turned around and might have seen me if he was not immediately distracted by the mess on the floor. He ended the call and stepped forward. I was likely an unmoving blur in his peripheral vision.

"Oh shit," he said.

I waited, afraid to breathe.

He looked to the right at the shelving unit that had been my hiding place a minute before. I bolted up the stairs, not caring about the noise. I knew he would look to the left next.

"Hey!" he shouted.

My body was electrified. I burst through the door and darted down the hallway. The front door was a mile away but I covered the distance in three seconds. I fumbled with the lock as Dan exploded into the hall.

"Stop!" he yelled, voice ragged with hysteria as I slammed the front door closed and raced across the lawn. The distance to my house was too great. I knew he would see me before I reached it. Instead, I hooked to the right and leaped at the fence to the backyard. I was weightless. It was an effortless, fluid motion. I landed on the grass and resumed my sprint.

I locked the sliding glass door behind me, stumbled into the dining room, and collapsed into a heap on the floor. I wretched but only spittle trickled from my mouth.

There was a knock at the front door. Quick and timid. I wanted to cry out to my mother to not answer it but was certain he would hear it.

I pushed myself off the floor, kicked off my shoes, and padded through the kitchen. There was a dark silhouette visible through the narrow window of pebbled glass. He cupped his hands around his face and peered through, but would only see vague shapes.

The form left and the breath straining my lungs rushed out of my mouth as if I'd been punched in the stomach. There was a note on the kitchen island.

Sadie,

Dad and I went to grab a bite for dinner. We will be back before dark.

Love, Mom

I lifted the phone from its cradle. How would I explain it to the police? The story was ridiculous. Unbelievable. How could I convince them to check the basement?

I cleared my throat, took a breath, and dialed 911. I crafted a story about screams coming from the basement next door. The operator yawned as she repeated the address back to me.

"We'll send someone out. Try to have a good night," she said.

I watched from the safety of my bedroom. A patrol car arrived forty-five minutes later, flashed its lights once, then parked in the driveway. A single officer emerged from the car and was greeted by Dan.

He nodded his head vigorously and motioned for the officer to follow him. My parents arrived as I watched the house, chirping curiously about the police car in the neighbor's driveway.

"I hope everything's okay with Bruce," Mom said.

The cop appeared in the driveway as the sun dipped behind the mountains to the west. He was smiling. Dan waved as the car backed out of the driveway. It left in silence, headlights stabbing yellow cones in the gathering darkness.

I returned my attention to Dan, who was looking directly at me.

I squealed and dipped beneath his sightline.

Hours later I lay in my bed. I decided not to tell my parents. They would not have believed me anyway.

"Sadie," a voice hissed through the walkie-talkie.

I sat up in bed.

Spoken through clenched teeth, Dan said, "I would do *anything* for my son."

I never saw Bruce or his family again. By midday there was a moving truck in the driveway. By Monday morning there was a For Sale sign on the front lawn.

My last contact with Bruce of any kind happened during the Thanksgiving holiday. Stuffed with turkey, mashed potatoes, and pie I clambered up into the treehouse to get away from the noise of barking uncles and whining cousins.

The walkie-talkie, Bruce's walkie-talkie, was on the plastic stool and beneath it a note.

I never wanted to be like this. I never wanted to come back.

In the Valley of the

Headless Men

"If you won't take us, we'll just find someone who will," I said, withholding a grimace at the B-movie line.

This was a lie for many reasons and the man standing in front of me seemed to know it. There were only two other pilots flying people into the Valley. If he refused my demand my options were cut by one third. His ice blue eyes, half-lidded with disinterest, locked onto mine. I retreated a step without having realized it and fixed my gaze upon the amber shot glass in my hand. The celebratory drink still burned in my belly.

The pilot looked to my friends at the bar as they relieved themselves of their newly acquired Canadian dollars in exchange for another round. His eyebrows, wild and multi-toned like lichen on a tree branch twitched, betraying his annoyance. We were living up to every stereotype of traveling Americans.

"You really want to go?" the man asked.

His lips curled around each consonant so that his sneer never wavered.

"I do."

"Why?"

I didn't have a simple answer to that question. Perhaps it was just the name, so seductive to my teenage mind when I discovered the legends years ago. My instincts told me Pilot Bob, as he introduced himself, would not be entertained by my story. It wasn't really a story at all.

It was an obsession.

"To see something I've never seen before."

His cheeks were perpetually red from exposure to sunlight reflected off of snow. Maybe he saw some of himself in me, a naïve desire to experience something *other*. When he smiled his face transformed. He could easily have passed for a department store Santa Claus.

He grasped my shoulder.

"Son, you may see things you've never dreamed before."

He motioned for me to rejoin my friends and accompanied me to the bar. Our arrival was justification for another round of shots and the bar filled with cheers once again. Vince Gill, of all people, serenaded us through a single speaker that fizzled and popped as though one of its connecting wires was loose. The trio of First Nations men in the corner of the room sipped beer as they watched us, speaking in low voices a language I would not have understood.

The Valley of the Headless Men. I first encountered it during a late-night Internet odyssey while a freshman in high school. Although it was a well-known legend, it seemingly suffered from little embellishment. Each website recounted the same compact story.

The Nahanni Valley, as the region is labeled on the map, is a remote wilderness in Canada's Northwest Territories. Evidence of habitation dates back ten thousand years, though this was sporadic. The tribes shared legends of evil spirits and strange creatures. The *Dene*, whose territory bordered what would eventually be named Nahanni Valley, recounted massacres at the hands of giant men. These *Naha* warriors, it was said, decapitated their enemies and vanished into the wild, rugged expanse. Although the region is mostly unexplored, no evidence has been discovered supporting the existence of giants.

Despite its northerly clime, in isolated pockets the hot springs of the Nahanni River support nearly tropical vegetation. It is a virgin land of staggering vistas, roaring rapids, and a waterfall that dwarfs Niagara. Some say it boasts all of Canada's natural beauty in one place.

And, as recently as the 1900s, trappers and prospectors died in this far-flung Canadian wilderness, their heads cleanly severed. These grisly discoveries tapered off in the 1940s, which is not to say the slaughter subsided. Most of the gold found was incidental, nothing worth dying over. Solitary prospectors gave way to wilderness tourists, who also died. An average of one soul a year enters the park, which is only accessible via plane, and never leaves.

I entranced my high school friends with descriptions of the Valley. It became a sort of touchstone for our group. After nights of passing around a lukewarm bottle of beer liberated from my dad's mini-fridge we would build the lore in our minds. It was the last refuge of Sasquatch, the entrance to the inner-earth, or a land forgotten by time itself. Did some remnant of Naha warriors endure the introduction of European diseases?

"Imagine seeing a giant. A real giant. It would change human history," I offered.

"I don't know why you're talking about it like it's a good thing.

What are you going to do if you see one, take a selfie?" Gabe replied.

In our senior year of college we rejected the temptation of Panama City or South Padre and instead saved our money. Two weeks after the last among us received a diploma we were on our way to Canada.

Russell had the height for basketball but never played competitively. His arms and legs were as thin as reeds, not suitable for any competition that could not be conducted from a couch. He stood next to the bar, shivering despite many layers of clothing, and blew hot breath into his hands.

Gabe was his body opposite. He was squat, fair-skinned, and could often be found at the end of a trail of discarded clothing. He draped a bare arm over Pilot Bob's shoulders as the man recounted a story about a mysterious green orb that pursued his plane for half an hour.

And then there was Jess. At some point each of us had fallen in love with her. After nearly a decade as friends, though, she really was just one of us. I no longer felt a twinge in my stomach if she dropped an offhanded comment about a date or boyfriend. The woman had cupped a fart and disposed of it in my open mouth on more than one occasion. She was the little sister of our group.

The bar was only open during the summer months when the meager tourist season was at its apex. The Native men discussed something among themselves while nodding toward Gabe. The bartender disappeared into a side room as Vince Gill's Greatest Hits began to repeat. Journey was next, meaning Gabe would soon be drunkenly crooning along, pulling at his clothes as if they were made of ants.

"So, Pilot Bob, what time are we meeting you tomorrow?" I asked during a lull in the conversation.

36

Russell, now wearing Gabe's discarded jacket, sleeves terminating mid-forearm, pressed a closed fist into his lips and bolted out the bar. He expelled the contents of his stomach, whiskey and airport food that was several hours old.

Pilot Bob laughed, "If we're going by his timeline I would guess about noon."

Jess offered, "Take it easy on him. He just graduated from Smirnoff Ice this year."

Pilot Bob laughed furiously, the fit culminating in phlegm-filled coughs. He patted his pockets as mucus trembled on his lips.

"Need a handkerchief? Take this," Gabe said, removing his shirt.

The sun was up before we were, but night was short at that time of year. We peeled our sweaty bodies free from woolen blankets and adorned ourselves in layers we could later discard if necessary. Pilot Bob mentioned that snow was possible at any time of the year this far north. The forecast for our five-day trip projected intermittent rain with low temperatures in the 40s and highs barely a few degrees warmer.

The "airport" was a strip of weather-worn asphalt a couple of blocks from our room. Frosty clouds of exhaled breath trailed behind us like dialogue bubbles in a comic strip. Each of us suffered in varying degrees from the libations of the night before. Russell had not spoken a word, seeming to be capable only of walking and massaging his temples.

"I hope we see a bear!" Gabe said from his position at the head of our group.

"You do know we can all outrun you, right?" Jess said.

Gabe stopped and adjusted the straps of his backpack.

"I have a plan. I'm going to shove a fistful of edibles in its mouth," he said.

"Not much to look at, is it?" Russell muttered as they neared the plane.

Pilot Bob was just out of earshot then. He lifted an arm and waved, which Gabe took as an invitation for a hug that lasted a second or two longer than was comfortable for the man who spent nearly half the year in isolation.

"I kind of like the weathered look. It's made it *this* long," Jess said.

Pilot Bob, still recovering from Gabe's embrace, cleared his throat and offered a hand for me to shake.

"My American adventurers!" he said as we approached.

My gaze fell upon a silver strip of duct tape on the wing, flapping in the breeze.

"Just decorative!" he assured me, slapping me on the back as I passed.

The flight was equal parts terrifying and exhilarating. The constant drone of the plane's engine made conversation next to impossible and so we quickly abandoned the effort. I pressed my face to the cold glass of the circular window and watched a herd of caribou meander near a glittering river. The buzz of the plane overhead spooked a few dozen who galloped away from the herd.

Stubborn patches of snow were visible here and there, like little pieces of white lint on a green quilt. There were no cars, no roads. We were not even in the Valley and it was already everything I hoped it would be.

"Getting close!" Pilot Bob yelled.

What Bob and I agreed to the night previous was not that he would take us into the Valley, but that he would take us to a remote corner of it. I had a decade of curiosity and five days to exorcise it.

"I'm not allowed to," was his response.

After more failed negotiations I delivered my ultimatum. Together, we looked at a map and reached an agreement. "This is where I'm planning to drop you off. It's near a ridge above the valley. You can descend into it from there. Should be a fantastic view. And, so you know, there isn't *one* valley. There's dozens. So, when I say *the* valley I mean the one I'm taking you to. If the weather turns bad the valley can flood pretty quick, so best to camp at a higher elevation and away from water. Water also attracts animals, many of which you'll want to avoid. You might go in thinking about wolves or bears, but you're more likely to get trampled by a pissed off moose."

"Or Bigfoot?" I asked.

Pilot Bob slapped him on the back and winked, "He hates that name."

As the plane's tundra tires contacted the ground it jolted back into the air, springing each of us out of our seats. Pilot Bob laughed, spittle flying, as he wrestled the plane to a stop. Russell, Jess, and I panted, our limbs rigid. Gabe woke from his nap smacking his lips.

"We there?" he said.

We unloaded our gear and solidified arrangements with Pilot Bob.

"I'll come right back here in five days exactly," Pilot Bob said, looking at his watch. "That dead pine tree will be my landmark. I suggest you set up camp nearby. If for any reason you need to abandon camp do your best to lead me to you. Make a giant arrow out of sticks. Stick a note on the tree. Do whatever you have to do."

I nodded and blew warm breath into my hands.

"Now, if you get in there and get lost, always follow the water. There might be a handful of tourists out here with you, a few guides, but it would be a needle in a haystack to find them. Follow the water. There are a couple of ranger stations, probably not manned and thirty or more kilometers away from where you stand right now, but there should some provisions and maybe a radio. They'll be within sight of water. Otherwise, Fort Simpson is about 150 kilometers that way," Pilot Bob said, flicking his fingers toward the southeast.

"What if we get hurt?"

Pilot Bob sighed, "Well, if it's bad better hope it's bad enough to kill you right off. That ain't a place you want to have a broken leg."

After handshakes he was back in his plane and skyward bound. Once the buzzing of the engine died I became aware of the absence of all other sounds. It was just us, the whisper of unseen water purling, chirps rising from the lip of the valley. I could not stop smiling.

Russell scratched his head, failing to penetrate both the hood of his parka and his wool beanie. He clenched a finger of his winter glove with his teeth and pulled his hand free, then scratched his head properly.

"I thought it would kind of just pop out," he said, frowning at the unpacked tent with its array of structural components.

Gabe stood beside him, "They do. If you buy them that way."

Gabe unzipped his tent's carrying case and dumped it on the ground. After a moment's hesitation the tent unfurled in an electric orange flourish.

"Like that!" he said, patting Russell on the back.

After the tents were assembled we loaded our backpacks with gear, much of it likely unnecessary, and walked toward the edge. The world spread before me, distant ridges of hidden valleys like open arms. It was a primitive sort of beauty, and that particular view was one perhaps only a handful of people had ever before seen. Beneath my boots the ground sloped in a severe, downward angle. There were rocky outcrops to my left, looming over the coniferous terrain below. In the valley itself, flashes of red and yellow, like miniscule fireworks frozen in time, emerged through the velvet green.

The air in my lungs was painfully pure, cool but not cold. Sweetened with pollen, I could nearly taste it. At the limits of my vision were snow-capped peaks and sheer rock faces. All of it felt alive. Life pulsed through this place. It hummed in the trembling pine needles, in the vibrating bodies of bees relinquished from their winter quiescence. Its language was the babbling stream, slipping over rocks and around boulders, destined for deep lakes miles away.

"Well, now what do we do?" Gabe asked, his moon face beaming.

Each of us was affected by the valley in some way. I cannot guess what sort of emotions stirred in my friends, but the near permanent smiles on their faces revealed much.

"Pan for gold. Catch a fish. Find some mushrooms?" I offered.

"Shall we?" Russell said, gesturing with his trekking stick.

We nodded, but found no easy paths before us and so walked for a few minutes, searching for a gentler slope, but none of us really knew what that looked like. We started more avalanches with their trekking sticks, testing the stability of potential paths into the valley.

Russell paused, "I guess this'll work. We can use those trees on the way down," he said, pointing at pine trees that followed the gradient to the valley floor.

"I'm not going first," he said, slowly.

Gabe hopped off the ledge and landed on an exposed, flattened boulder. He turned to us, "It's solid."

Jess entered next followed by Russell and then me. Despite the extra pounds he carried, Gabe was the most athletic among us. *I'm the fastest man within ten feet*, he claimed many times throughout our friendship. He surveyed the potential obstacles with knitted brows, working through a math problem in his head. Then he nodded, eased off the boulder, and turned his body as if on a surfboard. Pebbles tumbled before him, but he was able to reach the first tree with relative ease.

"Come on you pieces of shit!" he yelled.

Over the course of the next half hour we descended, grasping trees, planting our trekking sticks into earth. Gabe was like a pinball, seldom alighting for more than a moment before jaunting to the next landmark. Russell followed a foot or two behind me, colliding with my backpack more than once, sending us both tumbling to the ground.

"Jesus, Russell, you might need to take one of Gabe's edibles. This is the easy part. We still have to climb out!"

Russell looked over his shoulder, through the boughs of conifers, his eyes like a child just realizing he jumped into the deep end of a swimming pool.

"I think I can fit into Gabe's backpack," he said, a smile eventually betraying his serious tone.

Gabe reached the valley floor first and sprinted through the calf-high grass, trampling poppies and punting arctic bumblebees with abandon. He smiled with a wide open mouth, pollen speckling his teeth. In the valley was every color of the rainbow and those in between, only slightly enhanced by the remnants of the edible he downed on the walk to the plane. He assured his friends it was the last, or at least that he did not remember where he'd packed the others.

We caught a fleeting glimpse of a wholly black mountain goat.

"Guess it's like a reverse Spirit Bear," Jess said, which made sense to us.

The stream swirled over smooth, earth-toned rocks that reminded me of dinosaur eggs. Despite the water's movement there was an almost oppressive silence. I manipulated my jaw in an effort to pop my ears and witnessed my friends repeat the exercise.

Gabe was the first among us to sample the water, discarding his gear and pressing his lips directly to the stream.

"Shit that's cold!" he said, then drank more.

"Kind of metallic. But refreshing," I said, wiping the water from my chin.

"So, no one's worried about bacteria?" Russell said.

"Cold water and free diarrhea? What's not to love?" Jess said.

We stayed near the stream for a couple of hours. I retrieved my gold panning kit and we each took a turn. Russell found a nugget the size of a lima bean and tucked it into a pouch of his backpack. My cheeks throbbed from smiling. It was all that I had hoped for. It was more beautiful than any picture I had seen.

Jess walked ahead of the group and found a sandy area. We joined her and retrieved various snacks from our backpacks. Furry bumblebees the size of my big toe floated past, aiming for a cluster of poisonous wolf's bane on the steep slope of the canyon wall. Life so near the Arctic Circle was a fleeting thing, a yearly cycle of death and rebirth consolidated into three months.

Russell stood as if he'd been stung, crackers spilling from his lap.

"No one else hears that?" he demanded, a nervous smile on his face.

"Hears what?" Jess asked.

"That sound? It's like a box fan right next to my head."

Jess, Gabe and I exchanged confused looks.

"Have you tried popping your ears?" I said, moving my jaw in demonstration.

Russell scratched the back of his neck and returned to his seat, "Yeah. Yeah, I tried that. Just feels a bit off, like the air pressure is different here."

He collected his crackers and dusted the dirt off, then sat in silence. After lunch we resumed our exploration of the Valley.

"It's just like you said it would be," Jess observed in a dreamy voice.

"Well, we haven't seen Sasquatch yet. But it *is* incredible," I replied.

Gabe drifted off to the side some, nearing the bank of the stream. He viewed the sun through his plump fingers.

"You should see it on edibles. It's like…everything," he said.

The staggering vistas purged my mind of all thought. I was a vessel filled to capacity and stumbling forward. Russell lagged behind the group. When I turned to check on him he was often standing still, burying knuckles into his ear canals.

"You okay, Russ?" I asked.

"Of course," he said, his smile showing too many teeth.

"Do you think there's actually enough food to sustain a Bigfoot here?" Gabe asked.

"Could hibernate like bears do. Apes are herbivores for the most part unless an opportunity for easy meat presents itself. And there's plenty to eat here," Jess said.

"I wouldn't imagine they're the ones cutting off heads, though," I said.

Before any of us could reply, a scream cut through the air. It resonated like a gunshot.

"What the fuck was that?" Gabe said.

We waited, listening for more. But there was only the single scream.

"A goat, like one of those mountain goats? Maybe a bear got it," Jess offered.

She stroked her mouse brown ponytail and looked to us for confirmation.

"Only one problem with that. If it was a bear then that means there's a bear nearby," I said.

"A well-fed one," Gabe offered hopefully.

I looked to Russell, who removed a finger from his ear and grimaced at the sight of blood. He wiped the blood on his jeans and then noticed I had seen.

"Mosquito," he said, showing teeth again.

Over the course of the next few hours we ventured deeper into the Valley. There were pockets of trees here and there, flowers in every color. Rumpled gray clouds paraded across the sky, dulling the sun's light. We encountered a bull moose wading in a deeper portion of the stream, his antlers dripping with emerald green leaves. A trio of bald eagles inspected us from sturdy perches. We posed for pictures, but our smiles grew forced over time, extensive travel coupled with physical exertion catching up to us.

We walked in a silence occasionally disturbed by the sound of someone slapping a mosquito. The little bastards were voracious and seemed not at all put off by the insect repellant we showered ourselves with.

"Probably time to turn around," I said, looking at my watch.

Russell was behind the group by twenty or so paces. He wiped his hands on his jeans and I noticed the area around his pockets was stained with crimson. Jess had drifted away and popped her eyes when I spoke, almost as if she'd been sleepwalking. Gabe nodded but said nothing. He opened and closed his mouth as if still affected by the change in air pressure from the flight hours ago.

"Night's only four hours long at this time of the year. Actually a lot later than it seems," I said, checking my watch.

Jess, in her traffic cone orange parka, stood in a field of flowers and stared up at the sky.

"It's so beautiful here," she said in a slurred voice.

I suppose I should have noticed the change in my friends, but I cannot say I was in a proper head space myself. I hardly thought of anything at all. More than once, however, I turned toward the sound of my name and discovered that no one in my group had uttered it. We spoke little, but I attributed this to the environment, which was no less beautiful even as my ability to appreciate it dwindled. Jess was determined to experience the Valley on her own terms, slogging through more challenging terrain fifty feet away from us. Russell, now leading the group as we had turned around, cupped his hands over his ears and said nothing. Gabe giggled a lot, but that might have been the edibles.

The stream narrowed and Jess suggested we cross it at a shallow point.

"Let's see what things look like on the other side."

We obliged in an area of the stream where a log, stripped of most of its branches, had become wedged between boulder-sized stones.

Russell nearly lost his balance as he scratched furiously at his left ear while crossing.

"Are we okay, guys?" I asked the group when we assembled on the other side.

Jess nodded but scanned the meadow ahead and seemed anxious to depart in that direction.

"Regretting not having second breakfast," Gabe said, giggling into his fist.

"Fucking mosquitoes," Russell said, wiping blood on the hips of his jeans.

I wanted to ask if anyone had called my name but held my tongue and gestured for my friends to continue. The ground was softer on the opposite bank. We found a cluster of wolf paw prints in a muddy area as well as a sun-bleached bone floating on cloudlike tufts of spongy grass.

Jess tracked a couple hundred feet ahead of us, arms in constant motion as she increased that distance. Within an hour I had to strain my eyes to pick out her parka from the surrounding green. I surveyed the patches of pine and readied myself to sprint if I saw anything emerge from the foliage. Not that my presence would have affected her fate if a grizzly bear or wolf attacked.

"What?" I said to Gabe, who trudged through the mud a few feet to my left.

"Huh?" Gabe said.

"You didn't say my name?"

Gabe frowned and twirled his barn-red beard.

Jess shouted before Gabe could speak, though the concern in his eyes cut through any lingering effects of the edible. We both attempted to sprint but the effort was thwarted by mud suctioning our boots. Little information was conveyed in the texture of the shout, but we powered through the mud as if we might have to break up a bear attack. Within about twenty seconds we saw that Jess was jumping up and down, beckoning us with a windmill motion.

"Hurry!" she yelled. Gabe collapsed upon arrival, his chest heaving. He smiled, appearing to enjoy the pain. I looked over my shoulder and saw Russell plodding along with his hands cupped over his ears.

"Look what I found!" she said.

It was a battery-powered AM/FM radio that was very much a relic of the 1980s. There were faux wood slats across the front and a cracked, black plastic carrying handle.

"What's it doing out here?" I asked.

Jess' eyes were wide and slightly wild.

"Don't know, but I knew if we walked on this side of the water I would find something. "She plucked off her gloves.

"You don't think…" I began.

She twisted a knob and the radio fizzled to life. From the speaker came, of all the ludicrous possibilities, calliope music like from a carnival merry-go-round.

"There's no way this should be receiving a signal," I said.

Jess held a finger up.

A voice spoke through the speaker, robotic and monotone. I interpreted it as an English woman but later learned the others heard differently.

3-7-4-1-5 , 3-7-4-1-5 , 3-7-4-1-5

Beep Beep

6-6-4-7-5 , 6-6-4-7-5

Beep Beep

48

The calliope music began again and the pattern repeated itself.

"Holy shit," Jess said.

I ripped my beanie off of my head and ran my hands through my hair as the pattern continued to play from the radio, fizzling and popping at times. I stared at the canopy of gauzy gray clouds overhead, searching for the sun. It was impossible to place.

"It's a numbers station," Russell said.

"What?" Jess said.

I hadn't realized Russell was there.

"Anyone's guess what they are for, but most believe it's governments communicating with agents in the field. They've been around for a while. If you believe the conspiracy sites they could be responsible for political assassinations. An agent might have a cipher of some sort that corresponds to the numbers. Impossible to crack if the agent is the only person with the cipher."

"We're almost in the Arctic Circle. How is this picking up a signal?" I asked.

I noticed Russell wore earmuffs over his beanie.

"Well, typically you'd use a shortwave. AM travels far, couple hundred miles under ideal conditions, but I don't know how it's picking it up."

We crossed the stream again. Jess held the radio in her arms as if it was an infant. I quickly grew tired of hearing the English woman's voice as well as the calliope music and asked her to turn the volume down. Rather than honor the request she jogged ahead of the group.

Derek...

It was impossible to know if the voice calling my name originated from anywhere other than inside my head. Suppressing the urge to respond was like denying a reflex. I allowed Gabe and Russell to track a few feet ahead. They were talking and joking again, which brought me some relief. Conversation throughout the day had been sporadic and I had begun to wonder if some of the wilder theories about the Valley might be true.

"Yes?" I whispered in response to the voice calling my name.

Derek, you are so close. So very close. But you're walking the wrong direction. I stopped and pivoted, scanning the clusters of trees nearest to me. Pine needles trembled in a light breeze, but otherwise all was still.

"So close to what?" I whispered.

To the answers. The answers to all of your questions.

"What questions?"

But the voice did not speak again that day.

We neared our point of entry and Gabe was the first to notice our new admirers. Three black mountain goats looking as if they'd been taxidermied. They stood on the outcrop, unmoving except for their heads, which turned to follow our passage up the incline to our campsite.

"Kind of unsettling," I said, maybe too softly, as my companions did not acknowledge.

Climbing out of the valley was arduous compared to descending into it. The muscles of my legs twitched with every unsteady step and pebbles as slippery as ball bearings hid beneath thin layers of pine needles. We emerged, sweating from the ascent despite the cool temperatures, exhausted beyond the point of speaking. The clouds fragmented, allowing shafts of airy, yellow sunlight through. Though the light felt like mid-afternoon my watch revealed it was eight o'clock. Sunset would not come for a few more hours, and there would not be full darkness this night.

"Firewood?" I said.

"I'll go," Jess replied, and she hurried away, the relic of a radio perched on her shoulder.

I returned to the precipice overlooking our portion of Valley. A few thousand years ago the trumpets of wooly mammoths would have broken the brittle silence. Perhaps in some isolated pocket a small collection of the beasts survived. Unlikely, but I smiled to think of it. It was the least gruesome possibility of the Valley's legends.

Jess dumped a few loads of wood and pine cones. Russell and Gabe used a flint kit to get a fire going. We sat on our backpacks and cooked canned dinners over the fire, which popped hissed, spitting scalding embers.

I broke the silence.

"So what did you guys think?"

"It's beautiful," Jess said without hesitation.

The radio was underneath her outstretched legs, the volume on the lowest setting. Every now and then I heard the faintest tinkling of calliope music.

Russell and Gabe nodded in agreement.

"I mean I kind of feel like something is happening. Something strange. My mind was fuzzy at times down there. Thought I heard some things too," I said.

Russell slurped down a mouthful of beans.

"Yeah I heard something. Driving me nuts down there. Almost like the sound was coming from inside my head," he said, scratching his hidden ears.

"You guys really think there's bad shit in the water?" Gabe asked.

For a while everything felt normal. We chatted for an hour, rebuilding the fire as the kindling dwindled. When the physical toll of hiking and slogging through mud superseded our desire to commiserate about our experiences we retired to our tents, Gabe and I sharing one and Russell and Jess in the other.

I do not know if I ever slept or simply drifted in and out of awareness of my consciousness. The sun kissed the horizon after midnight and the world was twilight for a few hours. All was still except for the fizzle and pop of the radio, the muted sound of calliope music.

I roused, groggily, scraping grit from my eyes. Gabe was not in the tent though I did not recall hearing him depart. I stretched and crawled toward the tent's opening.

Gabe's back was to me and he was bent over at the waist. His body lurched and there was the sound of something wet slapping the earth.

"You okay, Gabe?"

He looked over his shoulder, his eyes terrified and dancing in their sockets.

"Gabe?"

He smiled and blood cascaded from his mouth, running through the coarse hair of his beard.

"What's going on Gabe?" I said in an unsteady voice.

I took a few hesitant steps toward him, my heart rate increasing. Thin ribbons of steam rose from a puddle of gore on the grass.

He attempted to speak but sputtered, choking on his own blood. Gabe spat a fresh clot atop the puddle and wiped his lips.

"Parasites, man. From the water. I knew they got in. I could feel 'em all day yesterday. Little worms like spaghetti noodles crawling through my gums."

He spat again and smiled. His gums were crisscrossed with slashes, patches of bone visible near his canines. I noticed the pocketknife in his left hand, a globule of blood trembling on its tip.

"It's all good now. I got rid of 'em," he said, aiming the toe of his boot at the puddle.

I swallowed and inspected this handiwork.

"I don't see anything there, Gabe," I said.

He sighed, hands resting on his hips, "Yeah, they went back into the ground. Squiggly little fuckers."

Russell and Jess emerged from their tent, both looking like they slept poorly if at all. Russell shivered beneath a fleece blanket; his ears were still covered by both his beanie and earmuffs. Jess held the radio in front of her body, twirling it unconsciously.

The battery compartment was open.

There were no batteries.

3-7-4-1-5, 3-7-4-1-5

"Guys, what's happening to us?" I said, my voice weathered from lack of sleep.

"What do you mean?" asked a smiling Gabe as blood trickled from his mouth.

"You just cut your fucking gums open because you thought there were parasites inside of you. Jess is holding a radio with no batteries that is playing carnival music."

I faced Russell, "At this point I wouldn't be surprised if you'd cut your ears off."

He frowned but broke eye contact.

"Well?" I demanded.

53

Russell hesitated, then lifted his beanie, which caused his earmuffs to fall. His ears were intact though not unblemished. Scabs of black blood adorned his earlobes like bloated ticks.

"What about you?" Jess hissed, the radio now hidden behind her back.

I stammered, feeling the weight of my friends' eyes. If the Valley was responsible for their actions the same was true for me. No point in disguising the truth.

"Someone or something is talking to me. Inside my head. Directing me somewhere. The voice says it will lead me to the answers to all my questions."

"About the Valley?" Russell asked.

I shrugged my shoulders.

Before we could further explore the matter, Jess gestured with her radio at something in the distance.

"Is that smoke?" Jess said.

We shuffled on timid feet toward the edge. The outcrop of rock that formerly hosted the black goats was now occupied by a man. He stood when he noticed us and waved. The smoke was from the meager fire he'd built.

"Hello!" he called, his voice washing over us in diminishing waves.

We were too stunned to speak. We were supposed to be alone. Either one of Pilot Bob's competitors secretly flew the man into this remote part of the Valley or the man had walked there. If he had walked he had done so through hundreds of miles of wilderness, an easy target for anything with four legs and sharp teeth.

"I'm coming over!" he called.

Gabe spat blood and muttered under his breath, "What the fuck is

54

happening?"

Part 2

He introduced himself as Bill, smiling broadly and pushing aside our outstretched hands in favor of vigorous hugs. The stench of his body was like sulfur or milk left in the sun. Bill informed us that he was entering his third week in Nahanni, though skillfully averted questions as to how he came there.

"Lots of ways to get here," he said, smiling so widely we accepted it without further inquiry.

Bill stood a few inches shorter than Russell. His clothes, a red plaid button-up and flared jeans, hung loosely over his light frame. Perhaps he'd lost weight during his time in the Valley, but I didn't think so. Despite his thin body his face was cherub-like, with only a hint of stubble in patches on his cheeks.

"What are you doing out here?" I asked after the uncomfortable hugs.

"Oh, I imagine same as you. See if the legends were true. And if they were, to find the source," he replied.

He was never not smiling.

"The source of what?" Jess asked.

"Of the mystery. What beheaded the Natives and prospectors? The UFOs, Bigfoot, giants. All of it."

"Did you?"

"Find it? Oh yes. Oh yes I found it."

I shared a glance with Jess, who shrugged but seemed intrigued.

"Yeah right," Gabe whispered as his fingertips traced the skin of his cheeks.

Bill placed his hand on the back of my neck and squeezed briefly.

"I can take you there," he said.

We asked for a few moments to discuss the prospect and Bill obliged, sauntering to the precipice with his hands on his hips.

"I don't like this. Look at him. Where did he come from? Where's his gear?" Russell said. He held his hands over his ears again.

I realized then that Bill had only a simple backpack, certainly not large enough to contain a tent. How had he survived three weeks in the wilderness? Had he slept outdoors and foraged for his food? Nothing, from his out-of-style jeans to his lack of survival gear suggested he had been in the Valley for three weeks.

"It's pretty weird," Gabe giggled, fluctuating from annoyed back to amused.

I was about to speak when Jess interjected.

"What are we doing out here then? Isn't this why we came? Strange guy shows up out of fucking nowhere in the middle of fucking nowhere and tells us he can show us the source of everything," she said, her voice strained and undulating.

I found it difficult to maintain eye contact with her. None of the men spoke.

"I'll go alone, then," she said and began to walk away.

"No, Jess, I'll go. *We'll* go," I said, nodding to Russell and Gabe.

Bill assured us that we would be back before night, or what passed for night in the Valley. We packed a light lunch and a few snacks but left most of our gear with the tents and hung our food from a branch of a nearby tree in case a bear wandered through our camp during our absence.

Our journey began. Bill led the way, his persistent glee showing no sign of abating. An endless torrent of words spilled from his mouth. I was often two or three sentences behind and attempting to catch up. He recounted the wondrous things he saw in the Valley. None of it was particularly believable, but it was fascinating to listen to.

"There is a cavern about half a day's walk from here. The deeper you go the warmer it gets. I tell you, I was just about naked after an hour. And there was some light in the cavern. It was never dark. There were plants in there, ferns and miniature palm trees. There were citrus trees too! The fruit was like nothing I'd ever had, so sweet. I never found the source of the light, though. I heard a roar from deeper in the cavern that sent me running the other direction, holding my balled up jeans like a running back!"

"So, what brought you here?" Bill asked over his shoulder.

"Huh? Me?" I said, out of breath.

"Yeah. This was your idea, right?"

"Yeah. Yeah it was," I said, and stopped and placed my hands on my knees for a few seconds, "I've always had these thoughts about cryptic places. So much of the wild world has been destroyed. There are just these few patches left. I guess I thought there must be a reason for it. There must be a reason people stayed away. I wanted to find out why people stayed away from here."

"Some of us can't stay away, though, huh?" Bill said, smiling over his shoulder.

Bill practically danced over the terrain as we slipped and stumbled. My lungs were desperate for oxygen and I soon found myself disoriented. I had no idea where we were in relation to our camp. We trekked through copses of trees, disturbing birds of prey into flight. We crossed over streams, hopping on river rocks to stay dry. Although my head was mostly down, fixated on the few square feet in front of me, I realized we were trampling over our own boot prints at points. I chased after Bill's voice as he continued his stories, pulling Gabe along with me.

I lost track of time, lulled into a watery fugue, propelled forward like a rat pursuing the pied piper. His words washed over me like waves of sand, filling my ears until I heard nothing else. There were other things I should have noticed but didn't at the time. Amid the grass and flame-colored wildflowers was the flotsam and jetsam of prior explorers. There were leather shoes of indeterminate vintage, a lantern, spools of wire, and other assorted materials. I had no time to consider the objects or the people that had left them.

You're so close now, Derek.

I did not know if it was Bill speaking or the voice inside my head.

"Wait guys," Russell said, drawing me out of my stupor.

We were in a meadow. I had no idea how long we had been walking. My legs ached and my clothes were soaked with sweat.

Bill stopped as well, his face betraying annoyance for the briefest of moments.

"What is it?" he asked.

"Where the fuck is the sun?" Russell asked.

We craned our necks skyward and searched. There were no clouds. All was blue, infinite and uniform.

"It's daylight. Where the fuck is the sun?" Russell asked.

Jess lowered the radio, which had been perched next to her ear. Gabe inspected his fingernails. There were bloody claw marks on his cheeks and forehead. He grimaced and began to scratch at his skin again.

"Where is the sun?" I echoed, directing the question at Bill as he seemed to have an answer for everything else.

Bill trotted back to the group. I had been staring at the back of his head for I didn't know how long. The man that stood before me was not the man that had introduced himself to us that morning. His face was drawn and gaunt, jaundiced yellow in color. He smiled and displayed crowded teeth the color of old ivory. He appeared to have aged thirty years.

"You're really in the Valley now," he said, and then walked away, his arms hanging loosely at his sides.

I assessed the group. Gabe fingered the open wounds in his mouth. Jess nodded as the radio broadcast something only she could hear. Russell once again wore his dual layer of ear covering but seemed the most present.

"Russ, what do we do man?" I asked.

We watched Bill's form diminish as he trudged up an incline leading toward an earthen ridge. His pace was slow but deliberate. There was no sun above, yet there was daylight. I inspected the meadow and found strange trees mixed in with the expected foliage. They were tall and thin with broad leaves. There were insect noises as well, sounds I would not expect to hear so near the Arctic Circle, buzzing and whirring like the cicadas back home. I shrugged out of my flannel shirt and tied it around my waist. Over the course of our journey we'd encountered alternating pockets of cool and warm air. The warmth appeared to have won out.

Russell removed his beanie and twisted it. Sweat dappled the ground at his feet. He sighed as if to steady himself and then removed the earmuffs as well.

"They don't help. I can hear it all the time and it's not a drone anymore; it's a voice or several voices. It's getting louder, which means we're getting closer. I don't think we really have a choice but to follow

59

him now. We can't make it back to camp on our own and we don't have enough food to sustain us for more than a few days if we ration. Whatever the fuck this is, man, we gotta see it to the end."

Follow…

Gabe grabbed me by the wrist and whispered through clenched teeth, "They're in my skin, Derek. I don't know how much more I can take. It's driving me insane."

Bill stood at the edge of the ridge and faced away from us. He pointed toward something beyond our sight.

I found it difficult to make eye contact with Gabe. He was in near hysterics, blood streaming from a dozen self-inflicted wounds on his face. A flap of skin the width of his ring finger rested on the bridge of his nose. I placed my hand on his shoulder in a supportive gesture and flinched.

Something moved beneath my fingers. I retreated several steps, colliding with Jess who seemed not to notice. She pressed the radio to her ear and nodded her head, mouthing words she did not actually speak.

"You felt it, didn't you?" Gabe asked in a defeated voice.

Before I could reply the buzz of insects was temporarily halted as another, much louder sound took its place. Through a childhood of watching nature documentaries I never heard a similar bellow. It resembled both the curious cackle of the hyena and the jungle-clearing wail of New World monkeys. Its distance from us was impossible to guess, however we did not consider the matter long. The initial call was echoed three times from different points in the meadow.

We sprinted toward Bill, who was frozen in place at the top of the ridge, gesturing with a trembling finger. Gabe tripped over his feet and did not seem to have either the strength or the will to regain his footing.

Russell and I ducked beneath his arms and hoisted him off the ground. As we ran in short, fast steps I felt writhing on the back of my neck where the skin of Gabe's arm was in direct contact with my own. He moaned, head lolling as pink spittle spilled from his mouth.

Jess held the radio in her teeth as she clambered up the incline toward Bill. Russell and I arrived with Gabe a few moments later. I chanced a glance at the meadow and saw patterns carved in the tall grass, the paths of unseen creatures. They filled my ears with their maddening call but refused to venture beyond the protection of the tall grass. In the shadows I saw dozens of yellow eyes, glowing, unblinking.

At once the calls ceased and the eyes retreated. Russell paused to catch his breath. His eyes were frantic, like two little brown beetles trapped in a jar. I assumed he felt the same movement beneath his fingers. He nodded and we resumed our ascent.

We lowered Gabe to the ground when we reached Bill. Jess stood off to the side and stared in the direction Bill's slender finger indicated. From this vantage point I could see for miles around, but it did not hold my interest. I followed Jess' gaze and saw the entrance to a cave a hundred yards or so distant.

Bill finally lowered his arm. He was another decade older at least. More than that he appeared deflated, of his prior happiness and vitality in general. His face sagged as if the fat and muscle had been siphoned away, leaving only the skin behind. He cupped his hands beneath his chin and spat.

"Not much time left for me here, I'm afraid," he slurred, then offered the contents of his hands.

Three teeth rested atop a hillock of gore, a deep crimson, pulpy mass. He nodded toward the cave.

"I'll tell you what I can but know that I can only guess at much of it. Don't waste your curiosity on the mundane details of who I am or how I came to be here. There are bigger mysteries than that."

We walked beside him. The movement beneath Gabe's skin became frenzied, almost as if the muscle itself was vibrating. Russell shook his head and I saw that there were tears in his eyes. Jess walked with almost ceremonial deliberation, like a bride approaching her groom.

"Shut up!" Russell whispered.

"I do not know if it is sentient, but it might be. I do not know if it has an agenda, but it might. I do not know if it has a purpose greater than existing as it does. There is some underlying logic to it, though I cannot say that it was designed as such. For any one thing that enters, one thing will return. The exchange is not necessarily equal. Toss a grain of sand into it and it may eject a boulder," Bill said.

Gabe writhed beneath my grasp and became increasingly difficult to hold.

"Most *things* that come out of it do not survive long. Those that do tend to stay nearby. But not all."

"Sasquatch?" I questioned.

Bill looked over his shoulder and smiled, displaying loose and bloodied teeth.

He stopped before the mouth of the cave.

"And here we are," he said

Russell dropped Gabe and pressed his palms to his ears. His eyes pleaded with me, but I had no window into his suffering.

The cave was perhaps thirty feet tall and ovular in shape. Daylight poured into the cave but was blocked by a structure I could not comprehend. It was like an upright, shimmering pool of solid black water. It perfectly conformed to the walls of the cave and rippled ever so slightly, as if touched by a wind I did not feel. At the crest of each ripple there was a brief glint of light, giving the impression of ten thousand stars winking in and out of existence all at once.

"I stood in this cave as a young man in 1972. I walked into that darkness and it took me to another place, another reality. It-it's like a dream now, though. Can't remember it well. Suppose my years have caught up to me," Bill said, looking at the depleted skin of his arms, "I remember taking that step into the darkness and then I was back in the Valley on that outcrop of rock. The memories of what transpired between the day I walked into the void and this morning have come back to me in fragments as I came closer to this place."

He looked to me, his smile apologetic, "I was supposed to bring you here. It's a thing you know and don't *know* all at once."

Gabe sat up screaming. He ripped at his clothes, tearing his shirt from his body with a strength I could not imagine he possessed. He was rabid, spittle flying, eyes rolled back so that only the whites were visible. His flesh was alive with movement.

"Gabe? What's happening man?" I yelled.

His eyes found me for a second and he just shook his head. He opened his mouth but not to speak. He vomited a torrent of thin, white worms that slapped the floor of the cave and slithered toward the black pool.

"Told you...they were...inside," he choked.

His scream filled the cave as the white worms burrowed through

64

soft spots of his flesh. His eyes quivered in their sockets, dancing from the motion of the worms within. They emerged from his eyes like snaking bean sprouts, leaving wet holes in the wake of their escape. He opened his mouth again as the worms broke free from his gums and coursed through his tongue, popping from the flesh and plummeting to the ground.

Gabe stumbled forward toward the black pool with its infinite points of starlight. The thin worms shredded his insides in their maddened attempt to return to their point of origin, carving thousands of narrow canals through the gray matter of his brain. They erupted from his torso and then his legs and struggled to break free to be swallowed by the darkness before them. Gabe gurgled, the worms bursting through his throat, his body appearing as though it had been forced through a fine cheese grater. He stumbled over the trembling white mass and slid on puddles of his own blood. He hesitated before the black pool and then took one step and was enveloped by it.

His scream echoed in the cave for a moment after he disappeared. I watched as a small, rodent-like creature emerged from the black pool. It scurried toward the light at the mouth of the cave, but at once its scuttle slowed. It collapsed a few feet before us, its tiny chest heaving one final time. Although its body was very much that of a rat its face was nearly human. It died gasping for air, its tiny pink tongue resting on the floor of the cave.

"I am sorry for your friend. I no longer belong to this world, though. It's time for me to go," Bill said.

He ambled forward, arms outstretched to steady himself as he stepped over the oily carnage. Bill did not hesitate but fell into the embrace of the black pool, which rippled as it accepted his form, starlight sparking as the constellations reassembled. A gray slug-like creature wriggled free from the darkness. It was the approximate length and width of a man. There were no distinguishing features other than its mouth, which gnashed at the air. Within its mouth were concentric rows of conical teeth that extended as far back into its throat as I could see. There was motion within, as if each row of teeth rotated in the opposite direction of the row in front of it.

It lumbered like an inchworm, its mouth sucking an atmosphere it did not recognize. As it neared the mouth of the cave we moved to the side, though it seemed unable to sense us. Its motion slowed when it reached the grass. It lifted its head as if to survey the new land around it, then slumped in a wet heap. Its flesh began to bubble as the body reacted to the elements of the air.

"What the fuck?" I whispered, burying my nose into the crook of my elbow.

I turned to my friends and saw that Jess was no longer among us. She stood directly before the black pool.

"6-6-4-7-5," she said in a monotone voice, the second half of the code.

"Jess?" I called.

She looked over her shoulder at me then back at the void. did not, in that moment, see the face of my friend, the girl who was my first real crush. Her emerald eyes were unpolished stones, devoid of vitality. She returned her attention to the rippling mass before her.

"6-6-4-7-5," she said again.

Jess allowed the radio to fall from her grasp and it clattered to the ground.

"Jess, don't..." I said.

She mimicked the calliope music and then stepped into the black pool, which thrummed like the skin of a drum. At the moment of her vanishing the radio metamorphosed into a bundle of sticks fastened together with twine. This *thing* was of the same dimensions as the radio, leading me to believe there hadn't been a radio at all. Had she made it herself? And why did we see it as a radio?

Russell was in the fetal position on the floor of the cave. He cradled his head and hummed in an attempt to drown out voices only he heard. I waited for the black pool to evict some new horror. The possibilities were limited only by the evolutionary constraints of a particular plain of existence. Perhaps the black pool was just a mile marker along the highway of the universe. Perhaps it was the highway itself.

I clenched my hands into fists and crouched into a ready stance. I knew I could not carry Russell and would have to leave him behind. Something stepped out of the black pool, a presence I felt but did not see. I sensed it as a slight disturbance of the air, a shift in atmospheric pressure. It glided over the pink slime, the sinuous mass of worms and stopped before me.

Unseen tendrils slipped through the creases of my brain. It dissected my memories, my fears, and my hopes. It sought to understand me, and by extension, humanity. Amused or entertained by what it gleaned, it recalled its tendrils and glided toward the dusky light. My senses reported none of this information, yet I knew it all to be true.

3-7-4-1-5, 3-7-4-1-5

6-6-4-7-5

The bundle of sticks was reformed as a radio once again, a more modern version than the one Jess found the day previous. I abandoned my consideration of the lifeform that dismantled and reassembled my consciousness in a matter of seconds. The radio was about two feet away from the black pool, much closer than was comfortable for me. I kept a wary eye on the rippling void as I retrieved it.

The calliope music blared again followed by the numbers. The woman speaking did not have an English accent.

It was Jess.

3-7-4-1-5

You're so close, Derek.

6-6-4-7-5

I cried out as something gripped my shoulders from behind. The radio tumbled from my grasp and crashed to the ground.

"It knows, Derek. It knows what I did. It knows what I did, man," Russell said, then sobbed.

His grip tightened on my shoulders, vicelike as I attempted to face him.

He cleared his throat, "You would never allow me to do what I need to do. I'm sorry, Derek. I love you, man."

I did not feel the impact. My world went dark.

The air was cool on my skin. My eyelids fluttered open and, for one blissful moment, I did not recall the events of the previous hours. I lifted my head, which required some effort, and saw that Russell's backpack had served as my pillow during my forced slumber. The memory came back in a rush and I sat up.

I was about halfway between the black pool and the mouth of the cave. It was nearly full dark now, which I knew was impossible at this time of the year.

"Russell?" I half whispered and half yelled.

There was a dull throb on the left side of my occipital bone. I touched it with my fingers and found a small lump.

"Russell?" I called again.

I looked to the black pool and strained to recall the words Russell spoke before he struck me. Something about *it* knowing what he did.

From outside the cave I heard a short grunt of effort. In the fading light I saw Russell stagger forward a step, his body shuffling on loose limbs, as if controlled by an amateur puppeteer. After two steps he slumped to his knees. An arterial spray of blood spurted from the ragged stump of his neck and painted the wall of the cave.

Of the horrors I witnessed that day, this was the sight that truly corroded my spirit. His body slumped to the side, the blood gurgling in a steady stream. I crawled to within a few feet of him, my mind devoid of thought. If not for the carnage of his ruined neck he could have been napping.

Swaying at the mouth of the cave was a crudely-fashioned noose. Russell was behind me for most of the day's journey through the Valley. He must have collected the wire we passed amid other refuse abandoned by prior travelers, perhaps anticipating its future use. A few feet beyond the entrance to the cave his head stared into the black distance.

I stepped over Russell's body, a scream burning in my throat. The wire was secured to a rocky nodule at the top of the mouth of the cave. In order to generate the momentum necessary to sever his head he must have leaped from that point with the noose fashioned around his neck.

He was a gentle boy, a quiet and good-natured teenager, and had been as dependable a man as I had ever known. Whatever betrayal he buried in his past he did not deserve this end, to die in isolation. To die with sorrow in his heart.

Outside, strange constellations winked above me. Planets that did not belong in our solar system were faintly visible. A sea-green gas giant rested between two bright stars, one red and one white. Other lights streaked across the sky, tearing through the inky canopy.

In the Valley the nocturnal beasts began to chatter. The distant yowl of the yellow-eyed creatures was consumed by the resounding roar of something much larger and much closer to me.

I shivered, my breath issuing in misty clouds that quickly dissipated. I returned to the cave and had no choice but to walk through Russell's blood, which continued to spread across the floor.

Nietzsche said, "And if thou gaze into the abyss, the abyss will also gaze into thee." The intent behind his words did not conform to my situation, yet I *did* believe the abyss gazed into me. Its eyes were ageless, its ambitions unknowable. Maybe God wasn't some bearded ghost silently judging His creation from a throne of clouds. Maybe God was an infinite black pool in a forgotten part of the world, transcending time and space with neither malice nor love woven into its composition.

The cacophony outside was rabid, a frenzied chorus of hunger and anguish. A sound emerged above the others as it projected into the cave. I looked over my shoulder and saw a black silhouette of a bipedal figure that was likely twice my height. It emitted a curious, almost questioning chirp followed by a series of rapid clicks. I discerned none of its features beyond its basic shape.

It crouched over Russell's body, prodded and sniffed at it, chirping and clicking. I do not know if it was aware of my presence or if it would have considered me prey. It scooped Russell's body up and hoisted it over its shoulder, sent a few chirps and clicks into the cave, and then walked away.

3-7-4-1-5, 3-7-4-1-5

Derek, we're all here now. Gabe is here. Russell is here.

6-6-4-7-5

It's so beautiful here.

6-6-4-7-5

I faced the black pool. I gazed into the abyss. touched it with my fingertips. Ripples spread from the point of contact.

Behind me was a world I did not recognize. I could likely survive on my rations for a few days. I could wait for daylight, hope that daylight would come again, and possibly retrace my steps. But I didn't think so. I had scrutinized the map of the Valley for years, had scoured the satellite imagery for some anomaly, something that would explain the mystery.

I don't believe I was on the map any longer. I was in the overlap, where the fringes of another reality bled into the fringes of ours.

I allowed the black water to envelop my hand.

Before I could recall it, another hand grasped mine…and pulled.

LP Hernandez

Night Feeding

Ruby watched the sea foam kiss the pelt on the beach and reached for a tree to stop herself from falling. The white hide, besmirched by sand and seaweed, was unmistakably her dog, a Great Pyrenees named Ralph. He had been missing for two days and had never previously been out of her sight for longer than the eight hours she spent at school. She had lost so much in the previous two years; the worn stitches that held her heart together strained against the pain.

"Dad!" she shouted, falling to her knees.

She called for him again, but he did not come. Ruby bore the pain alone until the evening when he strolled through the door, whistling and bouncing as if there were springs in his shoes.

Ruby, her face mottled with red, eyes puffy and burning from tears, sat at the dining room table.

"Where have you been?" she asked.

His smile quivered.

"Hey, honey. I was on a walk with Sookie. Told you we had a date this morning," he said.

Ruby gritted her teeth as the name spilled out of his mouth.

"Ralph is dead. He's on the beach. I told you it was not *okay*. I told you something was wrong."

He rushed to kneel before her, but she put the chair between them.

73

"Oh, honey, I'm so sorry. It's not that I didn't believe you. This is a big island with a lot of places to explore. I'm so sorry."

The pain in his eyes was real. The dog was as much his as it was Ruby's, but it was also a connection to her mother. Ralph was specially trained to assist Marilyn as the disease corrupted her organs and settled into her bones. He cuddled beside her in bed on the night she took her last breath. And now he was dead, a feast for the translucent crabs that littered the beach.

"Bury him nearby. I can't look at him again. Make sure to mark it," Ruby said and skipped up the stairs two at a time.

Before she entered her room, she called down, "*She* did it, Dad."

The idea to move to this remote island off the coast of British Columbia bounced back and forth between her parents like a tennis ball in a match that persisted for years. Marilyn's diagnosis expedited the plan and Randy retired from the United States Air Force a couple of years prior to schedule. In one week, they abandoned Alabama, their home for the previous four years, and settled into a weathered wooden domicile that had only been wired for electricity in the past decade. Seventy acres of old growth forest surrounded the house and from it a trail led to a sandy beach from which they sometimes watched orcas migrate in the cove.

By the time the cancer was recognized for what it was there were only therapeutic options available. During their first weeks Marilyn walked to the beach nearly every day. Within a month, the journey was aided by a walking cane Randy purchased from the First Nations craft store in town. The next month she needed two canes. And then she was gone, a dim candle extinguished during the quiet hours of the night.

For a year it was just Ruby and Randy. It was not a life either would have designed for themselves, but they settled into their roles and leaned on each other when the grief was too heavy a burden to bear alone. Then Sookie showed up.

Ruby returned from school one day and found her father seated at the dining room table with a woman she did not recognize. Randy stood and jammed his hands into his pockets. He smiled too broadly, hints of pink creeping up his neck until it touched his cheeks.

"Honey, this is Sookie. We met on the beach," Randy said.

Ruby slammed her books emphatically on the counter. Her eyes fell to the mug of steaming tea in front of this mysterious woman with rust-colored hair and lips as red as a poison apple.

World's Greatest Mom it read.

"Nice to meet you, Ruby. Randy told me all about you," she said in a husky, leathery voice.

She wrapped a smile around each syllable. Ruby avoided her extended hand and retrieved the mug.

"Ruby, honey, don't—" her father said.

She dumped the contents of the mug into the sink and then placed it on the counter.

"Ruby..." her father attempted again.

The wooden steps popped beneath her boots. She stood on the landing, her body trembling with rage.

"Well, that didn't go well," Sookie said and chuckled.

Randy divided his life in two from that moment. He visited with Sookie during the day while Ruby was at school, then spent the evening with his daughter, peppering their conversations with casual references to the woman whose perfume still polluted the air.

"I think you would like her if you gave her a chance. She loves the sea just like you."

Ruby removed her father's arm from her shoulder.

"Well, Ralph isn't a fan. How did you even meet her anyway? There's like three-hundred people on this island." Ruby said.

"Honey, Ralph hates anyone who isn't you or me. She was walking on the beach. I told you that."

Ruby crossed her arms.

"Yeah, but from where? Walking from where? We know all our neighbors. If she was a tourist she should have gone home by now."

"She has a home, honey. Don't be silly," Randy said, crossed arms mirroring his daughter.

"I'm not, Dad. It's not about missing Mom. It's about not trusting her."

"What reason has she given you to not trust her? You've only been around her for a couple of hours."

Ruby recalled the dinner from the previous week. Sookie moved the meal from one side of the plate to the other and spoke reverently about Randy's cooking prowess. She consumed none of it. After each bite she wiped her mouth with a napkin. By the end of the meal there were four napkins in a small hill next to her plate.

After Sookie left Ruby retrieved one of the napkins and found a mouthful of mashed potatoes and corn tucked secretively within.

"A feeling more than anything. Mom always told you to trust a woman's intuition," Ruby said.

"Fair enough."

"But there's something else. She smells. It's not the perfume. It's what the perfume is covering."

Randy sat up, arms still crossed and eyebrows furrowed.

"What do you mean? What is the perfume covering?"

Ruby broke eye contact to stare at Ralph, limbs dancing in the midst of a dream.

"It's like the ocean at low tide. It's salt. It's sulfur. It's natural but not."

Randy smiled to hide an emotion he wished to hide.

"Honey, don't be silly," he said, then left to pour himself a drink.

Later that night, as Ruby read in her bed, Randy knocked on the door.

"Honey, is it okay to talk a moment?" he asked.

He stood in the doorway, hands clasped behind his back. He wore his glasses all the time now, and the streaks of silver at his temples were slowly overtaking the rest of his hair.

"Of course."

He padded forward silently, moccasins sliding over the hardwood floors.

"I don't know if Sookie and I are meant to be together. I honestly don't believe we are. But she's helping right now. I'm not trying to forget your mother. It's just so quiet when you're not here," he said, eyes dancing around the room but never landing on his daughter.

"Okay," Ruby said with no inflection in her voice.

"If our...friendship lasts for another week, a year, or evolves into something more I just need to know that it isn't going to be at the expense of my relationship with you."

"Dad, nothing could ever come between us."

He nodded, smiling, "Thank you, honey. I needed to hear that."

They embraced and he mussed her hair. As he left her room he called out over his shoulder, "Oh, she may be staying at night sometimes."

He closed the door before she could respond.

Sookie often came late at night, well after Ruby had gone to bed. Ralph's barking would wake her from a deep slumber, followed by Randy's increasingly antagonistic admonishments of the dog. Eventually, Ralph was relegated to the porch.

Ruby found sleep difficult to come by on these nights. Sookie's laughter was like a blade on glass. She took to sleeping with her headphones on.

One September night Ruby woke to discover her headphones were silent, the charge having died at some point. She sat up in bed, searching for the noise that interrupted her sleep. She cocked her head to the side.

It was Ralph growling, a bass-heavy sound from deep within his throat.

Shhhh…

Sookie hushed him, or attempted to.

The screen door of the porch closed with a barely audible click. Ruby scampered to her window and watched as Sookie dashed, barefoot, along the path that led to the beach. Ruby donned her own moccasins and skipped down the stairs, avoiding the noisy steps she knew by heart.

She shivered as the damp night air enveloped her. The ground was wet, the discarded leaves heavy with moisture. Ruby moved in near silence over the terrain, with even the snapping of a branch producing only a muted crunch.

She spied Sookie ahead, glowing against a black backdrop. There was something odd about her posture, bent at the waist with arms splayed as if in pursuit. She stopped and lifted her head, sniffing so loud that Ruby could hear it even at a distance of a couple hundred feet. Steam issued from her nostrils as she exhaled.

They both remained as still as the trees that surrounded them, the only sound the perpetual patter of heavy dew drops upon the forest floor.

Sookie crouched, disappearing from view. Ruby strained her eyes, but there was foliage between them.

"What the..." she whispered.

A minute of silence followed and Ruby feared Sookie would suddenly appear behind her, breathing her saltwater breath on her neck.

Instead, there was a quick grunt of effort followed by a bleat of surprise. The pale shape wrestled with something dark, its silhouette mostly absorbed by shadows. Other dark shapes sprinted into the forest, and Ruby caught enough of a glimpse to understand that they were deer.

Sookie disappeared again and Ruby seized the opportunity to close the distance to her by fifty feet. She spied her wispy nightgown, the spill of her crimson hair across the body of the dying animal like seaweed. Sookie was on all fours with the deer beneath her. She held its neck in her teeth as puffs of steam exploded from her flared nostrils.

The deer's body slumped and Sookie released her hold on it. Ruby bit the pad of her thumb as Sookie ushered the streak of blood on her chin into her mouth. She stood and stretched, bones popping in quick succession, sounding like a fireworks display at crescendo. Then she slinked out of her nightgown and stood nude in the path, towering over her kill.

Ruby wondered if her father would hear her if she screamed.

Sookie sniffed the air again and took a step forward. She glared down the path to the precise area where Ruby hid. The girl willed herself to become smaller, to melt into the tree itself. She pressed her back to it, lungs aching for breath.

A minute passed and she chanced a glance. Sookie was almost gone, her white form nearing the border between forest and beach. Yet, she was no longer all white. There was a dark band around her calves that seemed to be growing.

The house behind was visible in narrow gaps between the leaves and pine needles, but Ruby walked in the opposite direction. She stepped around the small puddle of blood, appearing black in the darkness, that pasted the fallen leaves to the earth. Ruby reached the point where the path opened onto the beach, the crash of waves weighing down all other sounds.

She found the nightgown folded on a boulder, its front stained with the cooling blood of the dead deer. The moon and stars were hidden behind gray clouds like strips of smoke bundled together. Ruby scanned the beach and saw a black shape dragging a smaller form of a lighter color, half on the sand and half in the sea. Two tentacles encircled the carcass while others beneath undulated like snakes, carrying the creature and its prize into the water.

Ruby ran across the shifting sand to the place where it was wet and as hard as concrete.

The creature mewled and the call was echoed by other black shapes bobbing in the waves.

"Hey!" Ruby called.

The creature, half-submerged, turned slowly.

There were elements of the human form still present. The prominent breasts were now hidden behind a fine black down. The eyes were larger, but still recognizable as Sookie. It was the mouth that removed the strength from her legs. It opened wide in an affectation of smile, conical teeth dripping blood and seawater.

The black shapes in the water drew nearer, sea spray issuing from searching nostrils. Ruby ran on legs that forgot their purpose. She ran out of her moccasins and did not stop running until she reached home. She roused her father out of his sleep and convinced him to follow her to the beach.

There should have been blood on the path, but the gentle rain that began during her flight washed it away. The nightgown should have been on the boulder, but it was not. As Ruby gestured at the strange canals in the sand her father replied, through a series of yawns, that there were many beach-dwelling animals that could carve the same paths.

In the days that followed Ruby began to doubt her memory. She convinced herself that the event had been an amalgamation of a nightmare and sleepwalking.

As autumn's grip on the island tightened Sookie came around less. After the first snowfall Randy reported that she would be gone for a while. She *would* be back, he assured her, likely after winter. Ruby nodded, wanting to appear neutral to the news.

Life resumed its normal pattern after that. Ruby sometimes sojourned to the beach and watched the waves for an errant tentacle. Other than the black fins of migrating orcas, which electrified her nerves for a moment, there was nothing.

Except Ralph still growled at night, the threatening grumble previously reserved for black bears. It wasn't every night, and never when there was snow on the ground.

And, her dad asked a strange question after they had finished opening presents on Christmas.

Had she ever wanted a little brother or a sister?

Ruby assured him that she was happy with just the two of them and he nodded, then turned his gaze to the window.

The week Ralph disappeared had been warm. Green buds dotted the barren trees like little acorns. When Sookie returned the dog greeted her with gnashing teeth and flying spittle. From her bedroom window, Ruby watched her father rush to greet her.

After they embraced Sookie said, "I don't want that dog around my children."

The Rat King

There were many questions we never asked about him, Rat King. His name, for one thing. He was Rat King for the most obvious reason you could guess. He ferried a pet rat, often curled into a slumbering ball in the slope of his neck, everywhere he went. Affixed to the rodent's head was a tiny felt crown, fit for a king. As a society we have decided to sidestep the topic of mental health like a splatter of red vomit on the sidewalk. Best not to ask questions. Hopefully it was just tomato soup.

I did not know the Rat King's specific affliction. No one in town was interested in exploring the topic. My father suggested that, though he was harmless, it was best to keep a respectful distance.

Rat King was background noise throughout my childhood, pedaling up to my group of friends on his bicycle, brandishing a camera. We posed with our tongues out or flashing the peace sign. He would snap a few pictures while saying *Cheeeeese* in that high-pitched voice of his. I doubted there was actually film in the camera. As far as quirks go it seemed harmless enough. He was a fixture of the town like the broken fountain on Main Street, filled with leaves and murky water, forgotten but ever-present.

As a boy of twelve, Rat King quite literally towered over me. I was small for a twelve-year-old and he was a large man for any age. Another of his quirks, and equally harmless, was his love of candy. Its effect on his body was evident both in his considerable bulk and haphazard arrangement of brown teeth in his mouth. He smiled often, and without

85

reservation, despite the fact that he looked as though he had always just finished chewing a Tootsie Roll.

It was the week of Halloween. The rain that threatened to thwart my trick-or-treating goals finally dissipated, the steel-gray clouds bringing misery and dashed hopes to the kids on the east coast. I walked out of the school well after the last bus left, having endured an additional hour of in-school suspension.

Mrs. Duffy, my homeroom teacher, was the most beautiful woman I had ever seen. Her hair was candy apple red and smelled as sweet. Unlike most teachers in the school, her profession was not evident in the clothes she wore. Mrs. Kimble, my math teacher, wore a vest with cartoon rulers on it every other day. Mr. Martin likely kept the novelty tie business afloat with his various, science-themed accoutrements. But not Mrs. Duffy. My suspension was strategic as I knew she had that specific duty that day. My hope that we would spend the hour alone was realized.

I gripped the handlebars of my bike, mind recalling the errant glimpse of Mrs. Duffy's emerald green bra as she kneeled to retrieve her purse. I did not hear Rat King approach and nearly screamed when he barked his greeting at me.

"Hello, friend!" he snapped a picture.

I lowered my arms, which had been shielding my face.

"Oh, hello," I said, instantly out of breath.

"It's almost Halloween!" he said, flashing muddy teeth.

"Yes, I can't wait."

He snaked his plump thumbs behind the straps of his overalls. The rat on his shoulder walked in a small circle and resumed its nap. Its crown canted to the side.

"Is this one new?" I asked.

Rat King frowned, not understanding my meaning for a moment.

"Hm? Oh, him? Yeah, he's the new king. He don't even have a tail!" he said, giggling.

I needed to make it home within the next fifteen minutes to arrive there before my dad. Otherwise I would be forced to explain the in-school suspension.

"Cool, well, have a great day!" I said, straddling my bike.

Rat King dismounted his bike and sprinted, much faster than I would have given him credit for, to me. I was eye-level with his chest as he spoke.

"Oh! I'm having a haunted house for Halloween! You have to come. You have to. Last year nobody came and I waited all night," he said, face wilting.

There was no affect to his words. They were a bit soft around the edges but wholly coherent.

"Well…"

"You have to come! I got all the stuff for it! Promise me you will?" he pleaded.

He clasped his hands together as if in prayer. His padded knuckles, browned by the sun, hovered over my head. Knotted together they were the size of a small cantaloupe. Rat King closed his eyes and mouthed the word *please* in rapid succession. I quickly glanced up and down the street and saw no outlet for escape.

"Okay, I'll go," I relented.

He cheered, thrusting his fists in the air. The rat that had been sleeping on his shoulder buried its claws into the denim of his overalls, its eyes frantic.

"I'm gonna go work on it some more. I got all the stuff," he said, then ran to his bike.

I soon forgot about my obligation, distracted by the lure of Halloween and then Christmas just over the horizon. During the school day I invented a future in which Mrs. Duffy and I were in love. At night I finalized the trick-or-treat route with my friends. Rat King was not in my thoughts as Josh, Zac, and I began our pursuit of candy that day.

We coordinated our costumes, hoping their kitschy appeal might inspire generosity among the houses we visited. Josh went as take-out Chinese food. Zac was a fortune cookie. I was a bottle of soy sauce.

"You're sure these aren't racist?" I asked Josh as we left my house, empty pillowcases flapping in the wind.

"Well, I'm like half-Chinese so it's okay," Josh said.

"Next year we're going as Mexican food then," I said.

"That's fair, but what about me?" Zac asked.

"How about mayonnaise, white cheddar macaroni and cheese, and skim milk?" Josh asked.

"Okay, now that's racist," I said.

The sun descended toward snow-dusted peaks of the Rocky Mountains to the west, casting gossamer shadows behind us. Clusters of children darted past, most accompanied by adults transfixed by their cell phones. A small boy dressed as a cat hissed as we approached, twirling his tail and curling his fingers into claws.

"It's his first time," his zombie companion explained, a girl I thought I recognized from school.

The cat high-fived us as we passed.

By the end of the second hour our bloated trick-o-treat bags floated

88

an inch or two above the concrete. Josh, who had worn his father's dress shoes, limped as the stiff material abraded his heels. There was a hint of chill in the air, the onset of autumn one frosty morning away. One by one the porchlights extinguished just at the streetlights turned on, collecting hordes of anxious moths.

"I think I'm about done," Josh said as we meandered down a street with only a single porchlight left burning.

"Me too," Zac agreed.

"Good haul this year," I said, hefting my pillowcase.

My eyes were drawn to the light a few houses away from where we stood. It was only then I realized which street I was on. The house had been in a perpetual state of disrepair as long as I could remember. Ivy snaked across its wooden façade, gradually shifting the color of the house from white to forest green. There was a lone figure there, seated on the steps leading to the porch.

"Oh shit," I said.

"What is it?" Zac asked as he yawned.

"Rat King. He asked if I would visit his haunted house tonight."

"And you said yes?" Josh asked.

I shrugged, "Didn't have much of a choice at the time."

"Count me out. I was supposed to be home a half hour ago. My mom's gonna beat the mayonnaise out of me," Zac said.

We shared a laugh.

"I'm gone too. My socks feel wet and I don't think its sweat," Josh said, grimacing at his shoes.

They inspected their haul as they walked away, leaving me alone in the phosphorescent wash of a streetlight. Crickets screeched as I shuffled my feet, a rush of windborne leaves skittering past. Rat King's head sank beneath the weight of his sorrow. It was nearly full dark and there were no potential customers for his homemade haunted house.

"This'll be quick," I assured myself.

Another thing I did not know about Rat King was his living situation. I was aware of the fact that his parents had passed away, perhaps many years before my birth. Rat King had a sort of youthful exuberance about him that distracted from the sprout of fine lines at the corners of his eyes and flecks of silver at his temples. I did not know how old he was or how long he had been living alone. And whatever his handicap was, he *did* live alone, subsisting off of his inheritance and government assistance I would imagine.

I leaned against the white picket fence. The paint peeled away in long strips, giving it the appearance of stripes. In the yard, which was recently mowed for likely the first time that year, were various dollar store props. There was a cemetery of Styrofoam tombstones with pun-infused poems. Cardboard cutouts of movie monsters leered from a patch of grass between the large oak tree that dominated the yard and the sidewalk. Clumps of wispy cotton adorned the bushes in an artless fashion, indicating Rat King's impatience at setting up his little haunted house.

"Am I too late?" I asked.

Rat King looked up. His rat wore both its crown and a fur-trimmed robe.

His face quivered into a hopeful smile. He wiped his meaty arm across his nose.

"No. You can come. Do you want to see?" he asked, getting up.

As he stood he nearly punted the tiny boombox blaring spooky noises into the yard.

"Of course," I said, and walked through the gate.

Rat King wore a carnival barker outfit, which was probably the largest size of the costume offered but still too small for him. The buttons of his striped shirt strained against the thrust of his belly, like a brittle a dam holding back a river. The slacks ended a few inches shy of his shoes.

He slipped into character, "Come one, come all! See the greatest haunted house on Lotus Lane!"

He gestured to the open door and I walked into the house.

I expected more dollar store crap, perhaps a bowl of eyes that were really grapes, brains that were really spaghetti. I stood in the entryway, which had not been decorated for the holiday. It was bare except for a small table that held a bowl of keys.

"Yes, this is really something. You will be *so* scared, Christopher," Rat King said, closing the door behind him.

He flipped the porchlight off and I cocked an eyebrow.

"So we're not interrupted," he said, winking.

I did not immediately notice the shift in his language skills, but the sound of his voice was different, lower, more fitting a man of his size.

"Where is it?" I asked, glancing through entryways into other rooms.

"Before we begin, I took the funniest picture of you the other day! Do you want to see it?" he asked, clapping his hands together.

"Um, sure."

He took the lead and I followed behind. I peeked into the living room and saw that it was well-furnished with modern fixtures, including a flat screen television mounted on the wall. If I anticipated anything it would have been a fatback TV, something his deceased parents purchased from Sears in another decade.

There were no cheap decorations, nothing to indicate that it was Halloween.

We walked down a darkened hallway, the sound of his shoes like minor explosions in the stillness of the house. The fine hairs along my neck pressed against the rough fabric of my costume. The hallway seemed to extend forever and Rat King became a silhouette of man-sized smoke.

"It's really something," he said indicating the door at the end of the hallway.

I looked over my shoulder, a difficult task in such a cumbersome costume. The front door was miles away.

"After you," I said.

He nodded, flashed his chocolate teeth, and opened the door.

"Quick!" he ordered.

We stood in a room that was completely dark save for a single bulb off to the side. I squinted, searching for meaning in the black shapes. He closed the door and stood behind me. His sour breath washed over my neck. It smelled of peppermints and nougat but with an acidic tinge.

"What is this place?"

I retreated a step and collided with his massive body. I began to turn but he stopped the motion, gripping my shoulders through the costume.

"It's a dark room. It's where I develop my pictures," he said and gave me a little push.

I stumbled forward but stopped as soon as I was able. The candy in my belly floated on a rising tide of digestive juices. His vernacular mirrored mine, the voice at its much lower natural octave.

"Grab those two pictures hanging there. You're going to be so surprised," he said, his hot breath in my ear.

I shuffled forward, my fingers flexing into useless fists. I sensed him tracking behind me with each step.

There were two black and white pictures hanging from a line above a tub filled with some solution. Above it was an amber bulb that cast a pool of reddish light. I retrieved the first picture and held it under the light.

"That's you! Standing in the bushes outside of your teacher's house. Isn't that funny?"

The picture shook and stomach juices coated the back of my throat. "This isn't..I-I-I…"

"I thought it was funny. Look what you're doing in that picture! Funny how I saw you but you didn't see me! Grab the other picture. You're going to love it!"

His hands gripped my shoulders again and squeezed like pincers. That brief effort demanded little of his strength but made my knees week from the pain. I plucked the other picture from the line.

"You left before it got interesting. That's some teacher of yours. I understand why you'd want to stay after school with her."

The picture was through the blinds, the same I had peeped through that evening. Mrs. Duffy stood naked, her back to the camera, with a towel wrapped around her head.

"I wasn't looking. I wasn't. I wasn't."

He squeezed again and I pressed my face into the crook of my elbow as my stomach lurched.

"Even if you weren't, out of context it looks pretty bad, right? You know what else looks bad out of context?"

I shook my head.

He relieved the pressure on my left shoulder for a moment and handed me two more photographs. I recognized myself in the first image. I was a year or so younger judging by the haircut, which had changed since then. I held a rock in the air, my attention directed at something below me not captured in the picture.

"Look at the next one."

It was a baby bird, its head smashed, the contents expelled like an exploded grape.

"No! No! The bird was injured. It was being eaten alive by ants! I did this to save it!"

"Maybe. Now, you can probably bounce back from the Peeping Tom pictures. You'd be surprised how common a pastime that is in this town. But killing little animals? Christopher, that really is surprising," he said.

"But I was trying to help it," I moaned.

"Probably true, and I don't judge you for it even if you weren't. You know, I have some very interesting pictures of your father when he was about your age. Very similar in nature. I don't know if he was *trying to help*, though."

I shook my head, not understanding. My eyes, now adjusted to the dark scanned the room. There were no fine details, but I saw dozens, perhaps hundreds of pictures hanging from lines along the walls of the room.

"Oh, it's not so bad, Christopher. I have lots of pictures of people doing surprising things. Tell you what, you can keep that picture of your teacher. I have my own copy."

I knew he was smiling when he said these words. I imagined his stained teeth and shuddered knowing I was alone in the dark with them.

"What do you want from me?" I finally asked.

"That comes later. This is a haunted house, remember? I wasn't lying about that. Although, you might think of it as more of a modern art piece. Let's go upstairs."

His heavy hands led me to the door. The murky hallway light was painfully bright. He shoved me again and my weakened legs gave out. The pillowcase with my Halloween haul fell to the floor, some of the candy spilling free.

"Sorry about that, Christopher. Sometimes I don't know my own strength. Just leave the candy," Rat King said, then hoisted me back to a standing position.

He guided me to the stairs with gentler pushes. I gazed up into darkness, fear blanking my mind of any thoughts.

"Up you go Christopher."

He flipped a light switch on and the darkness retreated.

The stairs squeaked beneath my weight and shrieked beneath his.

"People call me Rat King. Isn't that right, Christopher?"

I did not reply.

"I don't mind the name. It's better than Francis. But, did you know rat kings are a real thing? When groups of rats live in tight quarters their tails may become intertwined. This can be aided with the addition of some sticky material, sap, or syrup. Rats aren't the cleanest of animals. The tails form a giant knot and the rats eventually starve. Well, they don't starve right away. The rats will eat their neighbors until there is nothing left to eat."

We reached the second level of the house, which offered doors on either side of a long hallway. He moved me to the side and stood before a nondescript door that was cracked open.

"Now, there aren't many examples in nature, some reported sightings and a dozen or so mummified specimens. But, you don't need nature to produce a rat king. If the tails are long enough, you can tie them together like shoelaces! Might have to rupture some tendons but, hey, they're just rats," he said, shielding his mouth as if telling a secret.

I smelled it then, the feces and urine. He opened the door releasing a tidal wave of putrescence. I turned my head and vomited on the wall, red from the candy apple I could not resist eating earlier that evening.

Rat King frowned, "Just leave it. I'll scoop it up and feed it to the rats later. That'll be a treat for them. *They* love candy, too," he said.

He gripped my shoulder and pulled me into the room, which was alive with squeaks and movement. There were forty or so glass enclosures, rats of various sizes within.

"Look on the table there. That one is fresh, only a month or so old. It was fascinating to watch," he said.

There was a table in the center of the room and a mass of fur on its surface. I approached, seeing no other option.

"I tie them together, you see. It's a bit messy. They shit and piss on me. They bite, but I wear gloves. Then I watch. Sometimes it takes days, sometimes weeks. Sometimes they scurry around as a unit, looking for food. But, I don't feed them. Soon enough they realize the only food available is directly in front of them. They always go for the brains, maybe as a mercy. It's a quick death except for the burrowing into the skull part."

I held my hand to my belly, which undulated with nausea. There were nine rats, some partially eviscerated. Their tails were clumped together in a confused knot of pink flesh and wiry hair. An additional tail, not connected to a rat carcass, jutted from the cluster.

"Philip was a bit of a cheater, but he survived. Chewed through his own tail, can you believe that? Killed the rat in front of him first, though. Regardless, he survived and that makes him the king," he said.

Rat King nuzzled the animal on his shoulder and adjusted its crown.

"After doing this with rats for so long I began to wonder it if was possible with people. What if I broke their legs just so? Could I tie them together like the rat tails?"

"I don't know," I muttered.

"Well, your father has been helping me figure it out. Very fortunate that he has that hospital job. I have so many surprising pictures of your father! Hey, do you want to see what I've come up with so far? It's only a prototype and it smells awful, but I'd love to show it to you!"

He pointed across the room. A canvas material was draped over a strange shape with odd angles. There were brown blotches where whatever the shape was pressed against the canvas.

"No, please don't," I mumbled.

"Had enough? I understand it's a lot to take in. Let's head downstairs and discuss the terms of our arrangement."

Rat King led me out of the room and I half jogged and half fell down the stairs. He stomped behind me, testing the strength of the wood with each step.

"You're young, Christopher, so tonight's tribute will be easy. Just leave your Halloween candy. That's it."

"Tribute?"

We stood at the base of the stairs. He slapped a frying pan-sized hand on my shoulder, the shock only partially absorbed by my costume.

"That's what I call them. I am the king after all. I get lots of tributes. I have so many surprising pictures!"

The knot in my stomach loosened. If I escaped the house only having sacrificed my candy I would consider myself lucky.

He squeezed my shoulder again. I imagined his thumb and index finger bursting through the skin and connecting within.

"Next week, though, I want something different. Did you know that the window to your teacher's house was unlocked? I'm too big to get inside, but you aren't! She is a beautiful woman, Christopher. She's really something. For next week's tribute I want you to bring me something of hers. Something worn. I think you know what I mean. If they're stained, even better."

He licked his lips.

"I can't..."

"But you *can*, Christopher. If you can smash a baby bird with a rock you can sneak into your teacher's bedroom and take a souvenir. Take one for yourself. Drop them off next Friday at 10 o'clock. I think you know what will happen if you don't," he gestured toward the dark room.

My mind reeled as we walked to the front door, his hand on my shoulder the entire time. I was exhausted from the spikes of adrenaline. He stopped me and lifted my chin. Our eyes met.

"You know the interesting thing about Halloween, Christopher? Some people wear costumes every day of the year."

Retrieving Rat King's souvenir was easier than I might have

guessed. I will not lie and suggest it was not thrilling in addition.

I snuck out of the house that Friday night, the tribute in a sandwich bag in the pocket of my jeans. I shivered against the chilly wind, the Indian summer a distant memory. As I approached Rat King's house I saw a familiar vehicle parked on the street. I hid behind the bushes of a neighboring house.

My father pulled an over-sized cooler from the trunk of his car. It was too heavy to carry so he dragged it behind him. He looked up and down the street but didn't see me.

Rat King opened the front door and my father entered the home lugging his tribute behind him.

LeCumbra

He drove toward the setting sun, adjusting his position in the seat so that the visor blocked most of the light. Behind him the sky was a purple so dark it was nearly black, like an eggplant left on the vine for too long.

Squinting, he watched the sun swell as it touched the horizon. For a moment he was truly blind and he removed his foot from the gas pedal. here was no real fear of impacting another car. The last one he'd seen had been thirty miles ago, its ass end jutting out from the ditch along the side of the road. Its windows were smashed and two of its tires missing.

Before him Oklahoma spread like an unending brown quilt. The sporadic trees were strange, solitary things, like scarecrows crafted by a child. Cows meandered in fields, all facing the same direction. This part of the country felt exhausted, as though no more life could be wrung from it. He was beginning to feel the same.

He turned on the headlights and fiddled the knobs of the radio. It automatically scanned for an FM station and found none, hesitating only a second to blast a bit of static. He flipped the radio to AM and half-listened to sporadic bursts of Tejano music, interrupted now and then by a religious call-in show occupying the same frequency.

The sun faded like the flame of a dwindling match and the man returned the visor to its former position. Before him was a four-way stop

101

and he typically would not have heeded the sign in such a desolate place. But he did, gently touching the brake pedal until the car lumbered to a crawl. He angled to the right so that the view from his window was of the crossroad and a gently sloping hill in the background.

Where the sun had been was now a wash of orange streaked with white. Stars pulsed at the fringes of the light. Perhaps it was the isolation that imbued the moment with any sort of meaning. It was only a sunset after all. But it *felt* like something more.

He grabbed the camera off of the passenger seat and aimed it at the intersection. The letters of the stop sign were just visible in the dimming light. He snapped a couple of pictures and did not review them. What he might see on that small screen would be inevitably disappointing.

He had no training as a photographer, just a good camera and too much time on his hands. He learned what he needed to know off of the Internet and told his boss he would need a month off of work. Or something like that. The man scratched his neck, trying and failing to remember if this spontaneous road trip was blessed. Had he quit? No. Of course not. This was a lifelong dream…he thought.

The idea sounded stupid when spoken out loud so he did not speak it. His dream was to photograph the wonders of America without ever leaving his car. He imagined a coffee table book with the image of a ghost town or smoke-ringed mountain on its cover. *America Through My Window…*

He did not plan a route but drove wherever he was guided. This led him to drive in circles or to dead ends on many occasions. Twice he'd slept in his car on the side of the road. In New Mexico he dozed while coyotes spoke their names to the night and each other. He wished he could capture that feeling in a photograph. A part of him lamented the fact that there was not much wild left in the country. He wanted to travel north, possibly to Canada and its unrivaled impressive fauna. Plus it was cooler there.

The engine rumbled as he accidentally tapped the accelerator while leaning out the window to look at the stars. The car drifted to the right. He had not intended to turn here, but saw no harm in it. Most likely it would take him to some farm road that would end at a white wooden house.

The night air cooled slowly here, the earth holding onto much of the sun's heat long after it departed. Lately, heat corresponded to headaches that intensified his urge to travel north. He held his arm out the window and his fingers danced in the wind. Rocks and pebbles crunched beneath the tires. He inhaled the scent of sunbaked hay until his lungs felt close to bursting. On these forgotten highways it was easy to believe he was the only man alive.

The music relented to the raspy voice of a pastor who stretched *God* into two syllables.

"You are all sons of the light and sons of the day. We do not belong to the night or to the darkness."

The pastor's tangent was coming to an end and his voice, gravelly and tired, was just above a whisper. For the space of a few seconds there was no sound and he inched his hand toward the dial.

A woman's voice spoke, "There is no course but to run. You cannot burn them fast enough. There is no escape but in light places. Stay off of the main roads and trust no strangers."

The air went dead.

That was odd. He scanned the AM stations again, but there was nothing. No Tejano, no chorus of garbled voices accompanied by organ music.

The car coasted to a stop. He had taken his foot off the gas pedal without having realized it. The road and surrounding terrain sloped gently, almost imperceptibly upwards. But, it was enough to stop his momentum. He placed the car in park, opened the door and exited the vehicle, stretching so that bones popped in succession from the base of his skull to his hips.

He did not take the camera with him as he was truly committed to photographing only through the window. Light bled from the sky to the west and to the east it was full dark. He jolted as a falcon shrieked from some perch nearby. In the past twelve or so hours he had seen far more falcons than people, and more coyote carcasses than anything else.

Bands of mist formed in pockets in the fields to his right. He found the Oklahoma heat nearly unbearable at times. His skin seemed to shrivel during the day, like a grape left in the sun.

He trudged up the small hill to take in the view, the seed of a headache sprouting in his brain. *You have to go north.* Rocks and dirt shifted beneath his boots and he held out his arms for balance.

Other than the newly formed clouds snaking through the pasture there was little to see in the east. The naked sky and stars were beautiful, but it was the same beautiful he'd been viewing for how long now? Ten days? His eyes narrowed, headache blooming, wrapping wire-thin vines around his gray matter. There was…*something.* A gap in the barbwire fence and depressions in the grass indicating vehicles of some sort traveled through it. He scurried off the road into grass that brushed his knees as he walked.

The tire trails were lost in the darkness, but he was no longer concerned with them. In that same general direction there was light, a phosphorescent haze reminiscent of the sunset fifteen minutes prior.

It was a town. But, that could not be. It made no sense. The town would have to be in the direction from which he had come and he would have passed it, or at least a sign indicating its presence. Perhaps his mind had been somewhere else. Time was funny out here. Still, it made even less sense that it would be in the middle of a farmer's field.

More than likely it was some fracking operation, but with the right lighting that could be picture-worthy. It was impossible to guess how far off it was, so he skipped back to his car and guided it through the gap in the fence.

He kept the speed under ten miles an hour, unable to see if there might be holes or divots hidden by the tall grass. The aroma of dry earth tickled his nostrils. He nearly sneezed but held it in. A cow lowed, upsetting the silence and a light thunder of hooves followed.

He licked his lips and wondered when he'd last eaten. He couldn't recall the meal. The dives and fast food joints blended together in his mind. There was not even a hamburger wrapper in his cup holder to serve as a reminder. The smell of earth, even the manure that surely polluted the tread of his tires made him hungry. Perhaps it was that it smelled of anything when for hours he had smelled nothing but asphalt.

What *had* he eaten?

He truly could not remember. He could barely recall the name of the last town he passed through an hour or so before. His forehead touched the steering wheel as a thrumming headache pulsed in his temples.

What was he really doing out here, driving at night through a field in Oklahoma?

He scratched his eyelid, the orb beneath having become itchy as the car kicked up grass and debris. As he questioned himself there was a vague response in his mind about the coffee table book. But, he was not a photographer. He had no contacts in the publishing world. It was a passing fancy, a hobby from college and he had plenty of those. *Why am I doing this?* He wondered this but the shape of the words in his mind were tipped with blades. The question made him sick.

He was driving again, his headlights stabbing the darkness but illuminating nothing. The glow loomed larger ahead and that was his goal. He scratched his eye furiously and rolled up the window to shut out the allergens.

The car rattled as it passed over a hole jolting the man as he inspected his fingernail and grimaced. There was something gray and wet collected there, as if he had been digging into the body of a slug. It smelled nutty.

He drove with one eye closed, his fingers flexing as he fought the urge to claw at his eye to stop the itching.

The silhouettes of buildings appeared but the distance to them was impossible to guess. And, he had little time to do so as the lights extinguished, not one by one but all at once. Ahead was only darkness save for the twin beams of his headlights. The car rolled to a stop again.

To the west the sky was nearly black. There were no clouds, but the stars offered little light and the moon was but a sickle. As his eyes adjusted to the darkness he saw forms ahead, slight discolorations on a black canopy. That was the town, he surmised. And it seemed either his presence was known or there had been a coincidental power failure. He returned to the car and turned the lights off, driving with his chin hovering above the steering wheel as he squinted through the windshield.

At times he lost track of the shapes he pursued. When this

happened he took his foot off of the accelerator and crawled forward by inches. He closed his left eye and pressed his knuckles into it. The pressure felt good.

He arrived within ten minutes and parked the car. There were perhaps thirty or forty buildings that may or may not have been houses, mostly pre-fab structures. There were a few trucks parked along what appeared to be the main strip. Oddly, there were no roads. Grass, stunted and spiky, grew everywhere, as if the buildings had been airlifted into the middle of a farmer's field and dropped there.

What is this place?

It had the feel of a movie set that had been abandoned and left to the elements. But the buildings were not facades. They were real. And the cars and trucks were just as real.

His ears strained to hear anything above the sound of his own heartbeat. There were people here. There had to be.

He sat on the hood of his car. There was a two-story, white wooden house to his right, similar to what he had anticipated finding when he had accidentally turned right half an hour previous. A boy stood in the window above him. His face was small and pale, his eyes unblinking. The man waved and the boy stared. For a second the idea of a movie set made sense as the boy was as still as a mannequin.

Suddenly, the boy vanished and a woman appeared just long enough to close the curtains.

"Hello?" the man said, but his voice had gone unused for so long. He coughed into his hand and tried again.

"Hello?"

Again, he mustered only a whisper.

He walked toward the center of the lane. Grass crunched beneath his boots, the sound like chewing corn flakes.

He cupped his hands around his mouth, cleared his throat, and shouted.

"Hello!"

The effort sent him into a fit of coughs.

Deadbolts locked in the buildings that surrounded him. In the desolate night the sound was like gunshots. Curtains fluttered to his left and a door slammed somewhere he could not see. There were eyes on him, peering between blinds and through peepholes. He had a feeling as well that he was being watched through the scopes of rifles.

He held up his hands as if in surrender. He had no idea what he might have stumbled upon, but it would certainly make more sense in the morning.

He trudged over the crisp earth to his car. One more night of sleep in the passenger seat wouldn't do any harm. Though he was not especially sleepy he was tired.

He cracked the windows and a breeze passed through, chilling his sweaty skin. He wiped his forehead with the back of his hand and inspected it.

How strange. Maybe it was just a trick of the moonlight, but his sweat was as white as milk.

It rained during the night and he roused from his slumber. The wind had died so the rain fell straight down, yet a couple of stray drops landed on his arm. He sat up in the seat and wiped his eyes. The left eye was still itchy and he burrowed his knuckle into it.

The air smelled wonderful, of minerals and loam. It was still dark, the stars and moon hidden behind clouds. He rolled up his window and would have been content to just lie there, listening to the rain and smelling the air, but his stomach seized suddenly and violently.

He was ravenous. He had never been so hungry. His fingers fumbled with the car's lock and soon he was out the door on his knees. There were puddles on the ground, which had been as hard as stone, not prepared to receive the offering from the clouds.

He clawed at the ground without a thought in his mind, only the need to put something into his stomach and as much of it as possible. He scooped soil into the palm of one hand and stared at it. The rain washed some of it away and so he rebuilt his hillock with trembling fingers.

He had never tasted anything as good. It was the consistency of melted chocolate mixed with sand. He licked the soil free from his teeth and rolled it into a clump with his tongue. Before he swallowed his hands plunged into the wet earth again.

He feasted until his belly bulged, never chewing. The filling of his stomach had a reverse effect. He grew more ravenous and less satisfied. The weight in his stomach was like an animal itself. In the dark, with the cold rain running down his face, with dirt lining his teeth and throat, he had never felt better.

The man jolted in his seat, confused by the sudden light. He smacked his lips and recalled fragments of a dream about eating dirt…or something. Saliva deluged the vestibules beneath his tongue.

A face appeared in the windshield and the man screamed.

"Sorry, bud, been tapping on the window for a minute now," the stranger said.

The man was older, probably in his early sixties. His hair was billowy and white but yellow near the roots. He smiled adding tributaries to the meandering lines carved into his skin.

"John," the man said, though he did not offer his hand to shake through the partially open window.

The man in the car, still tasting phantom earth on his tongue, opened his mouth to reply. No words came out.

He swallowed and repeated the old man's name, "John, as well."

"What are the odds? Say, can I ask what brings you to our fair village?"

Why was it so hard to hold onto a thought? He knew his name was not John, but he couldn't stand the weight of the old man's gaze. He had to say something.

"I'm uh-a photographer," the man answered, his voice like dry leaves scattering in a wind.

John gripped the cone of his goatee and nodded, allowing the silence to speak for him.

Sitting up in his seat, the man inspected his fingernails and was relieved to find that they were relatively clean. He picked up his camera and showed it to John.

"I'm working on a book, a photography book. I think," he said.

John nodded, "You think?"

"I'm taking pictures through my car window."

John cleared his throat and rested his hands on his hips. He surveyed the town as if he'd never seen it before, considering each building for a handful of seconds. He lifted one hand and casually flipped it in the direction of a house across the road. A door opened and a man appeared. He stood in the doorway, his arms crossed over his chest. The man returned John's wave.

"Say friend, you look like you could use a bite. Care to join me?"

110

John said.

The man nodded and said, "What is this place?"

John turned and began to walk away.

"Let's go see about that bite."

There was very little furniture in John's home, a hodgepodge of weathered items that probably would have been rejected by Goodwill. There was also little in the way of personal touch, no pictures on the wall or collection of miniature cacti sitting in the window. It looked hastily assembled. Nothing matched and there appeared to be a yard sale quality to the living room.

John removed a kettle from the stove and poured its steaming contents into a mug that recommended a visit to *Colorful Colorado*. He sat at the small, circular dining table and waited for his guest to do the same.

The man who called himself John but knew this was not his name nodded and sat on a pockmarked stool. This was all becoming so strange. He wished at once that he was back in his car with the air conditioning blasting headed north.

"Are you hungry?" John asked.

The man considered the question. He *was* hungry, but knew nothing in John's pantry or refrigerator would satisfy his hunger. He recalled the dream of eating soil in the rain and his mouth flooded with saliva. He smiled and hoped it felt authentic.

"A cup of coffee?"

"Not a coffee drinker myself. I've got tea if you'd like."

"Sounds wonderful."

John returned to the stove and emptied the kettle into a smaller mug that bore a military rank the man did not know.

"Air Force?" the man asked.

"Twenty of the best-worst years of my life," John said and placed the mug on the table.

John sipped his tea, the steam dwindling to a ghostly trickle.

"So, forgive me for asking again, but how did you come to our fair village?" John said.

The man blew the steam away from his face, but had no intention of drinking. His stomach was balled into a knot and more than anything he wanted to leave. As well, his eye had begun to itch again and it took all of his will power not to touch it.

"Like I said, I am a photographer. I mean, I'm interested in it. I think. I-I just had a thought one day to hit the road and take pictures along the way. I did a few-ten-I think days ago and…I saw the light of your town from the road and decided to check it out."

John's Adam's Apple bobbed as he swallowed his tea. He placed the mug on the table and pushed it away as if suddenly disinterested in it.

"Ah, the lights. We'll have to see about that. So, where do you come from?" John asked.

The man did not know how to respond. Of course he had come from somewhere, but the effort to recall left him feeling ill. Without having realized it, he began massaging his throbbing eye with the knuckle of a thumb. As well as confused he felt anger at this man and his questions. He did not want to be here.

"New Mexico," he said as an image of a sign bidding him farewell from the state flashed in his mind.

John nodded and twirled his goatee around his finger.

"Did some time there. Whereabouts?"

The man grasped the mug and held it to his lips. He drank to buy himself time, and discovered that much of the tea missed its target and puddled in his lap.

John held up a hand, "Don't worry about it. So, you're from New Mexico, you're a photographer, and you're planning on going north?"

The man looked up from the wet spot on his jeans.

"How did you know that?" he asked.

"A lucky guess," John said, his conspiratorial smile indicating this was a lie.

The man placed the mug on the table and said, "I should probably get going."

John dismissed the idea by flicking his hand.

"Don't be silly. Look, if you'll humor me for a few more questions I'll tell you how I knew you were headed north."

The man hovered a few inches above the stool. He eyed the front door.

John sighed, his age-spotted hands resting upon the paunch of his belly.

"When was the last time you spoke with someone? Anyone. Anyone other than me."

"What kind of question is that?" the man asked, sitting once again.

"It's not any *kind* of question. It's just a question, a simple one at that, wouldn't you agree?"

The man shook his head, his thoughts a jumble.

"You know, I must apologize. I never did get you that bite, and I have the perfect thing. Give me a moment."

John pressed his hand to the small of his back as he trotted into the kitchen. The man found it difficult to grasp a single thought for more than a second. And that itch was back in his eye again.

"Here we are," John said, and placed the bowl on the table.

The man cocked his head, not understanding. At the same time his stomach seized as if it might burst from his torso and devour the bowl of its own accord.

"It's soil," the man said, mouth flooding with saliva.

"Is it? Kind of looks like chocolate cake to me, just like mama used to make," John winked.

The man was so hungry.

"Oh, go on. There's no judgement here. You can have a bit of cake if you want. All I ask is that you listen as I tell you a story. Eat up, and listen."

The man reached for the plastic spoon, hands unsteady. He had never seen a meal more appetizing. He scooped a small, tentative clump.

"Go on now, it's the only thing that'll satisfy the hunger."

The man slid the spoon into his mouth. His eyes rolled back into his head.

"Like I said, just like mama's. Keep eating while I spin you a little yarn. When you're done we can have a little chat and talk about the next thing."

By the third bite the man lost any reservations he previously held.

"From New Mexico, right? That's interesting because that's where my story begins. You see, there was this super-secret laboratory out in the desert, even more secret than White Sands. Oh, they did all kinds of naughty things out there. Experiments. Live test subjects. Real grimy stuff."

The man nodded, eyes still rolled.

"Even now we don't know the name of the agency, not even *three* letters. This agency was working on something kind of nutty. You see, there's this fungus in the Amazon that has specialized in just about the craziest manner of reproduction possible. The fungus infects carpenter ants, existing as a few cells at first."

John unfolded a worn piece of paper, an Internet article describing the fungus and its effects.

"Well, the cells begin to communicate over time, and to connect. Then they work into the muscles. They save the brain for last, and the ant becomes a prisoner in its own body. End result, the ant is forced to clamp onto a leaf and a stalk with a bulb of spores grows through its head. How's that *cake?*"

The man moaned. His teeth were black, lips coated with grit.

"Good, keep eating. So, this secret squirrel lab decides this would be an effective battlefield tool. Imagine not only stopping the enemy from advancing, but compelling them to kill their own. Practical application would be years away if at all possible, but the experiments had begun."

The man abandoned the spoon and buried his face in the soil.

"No idea how far along they were in the experiment, but spores are tiny things and awfully difficult to contain. Wouldn't that have been crazy if one *did* get out? Think how quickly that could overtake the population. Only, what if the experimental version was different? What if the spores corrupted the brain first?"

His stomach hurt, but he continued to eat.

"And these spores, in this hypothetical situation, crave dark, cool climates. So now you have a population, who knows how many, walking around infected with no idea. All they know is they want to travel north."

The man burped, "Just kill them then."

115

"A logical idea, but in this completely hypothetical situation the fungus has a defense mechanism. It's receiving information from the brain, you see. And if something seems screwy…"

John put a hand to either side of his head and mimed an explosion.

"Spores everywhere."

The man licked the bowl, eyes closed, moaning in the grip of pure pleasure.

"Oh, but people are smart. We can figure things out, can't we? Might take us some time, but we can figure things out. How are you feeling, John?"

The man blinked as if viewing the room for the first time, "Dennis."

John nodded.

"That suits you. How do you feel, Dennis?"

Dennis licked grit from his teeth and wiped his mouth with the back of his arm.

"I'm not sure. I don't know how I got here, to be honest."

John nodded, "Did you enjoy the story?"

Dennis rubbed his eye, "I guess."

"It seems like you might be out in front of this, but it doesn't last long. I need you to see something. After that we're going to have a chat. Your spores are juvenile, Dennis. I'd guess a week old. That means they aren't active yet. Haven't made all the connections. Not the ones I'd worry about."

"My spores?" Dennis mumbled.

116

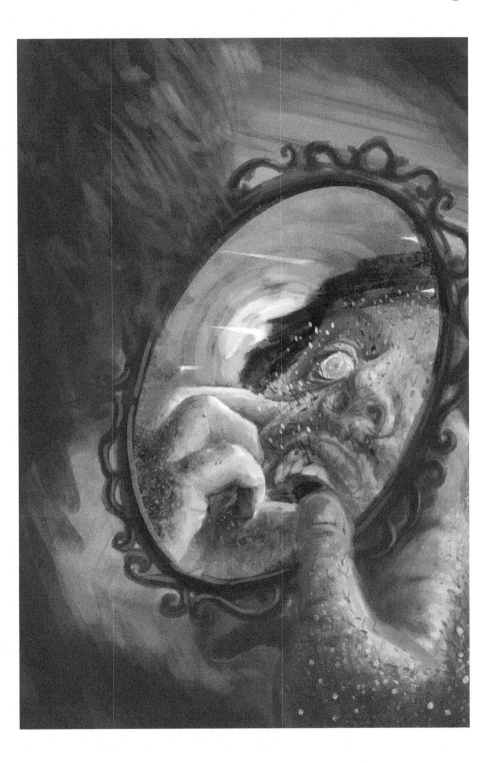

John offered a hand mirror. Dennis blinked a few times, trying to understand. The man in the mirror appeared as though he'd been peppered with birdshot. There were holes in his cheeks, pea-sized in the fattier parts. Where the skin was thinner, on the bridge of his nose and forehead, the holes were smaller, like flecks of pepper.

From each hole a narrow stalk protruded. The stalks concluded in a little bulb shaped like a kidney bean. There were hundreds of holes. Dennis brought his hand to his face and paused, seeing the holes in his palms, the fine down growing there, the stalks thinner and black in color.

He rolled his tongue and sensed the holes there, the resistance of the blunt pods against the roof of his mouth. He shook his head, grabbing the mirror.

There were no stalks in the holes in his eyes, but yellow liquid, like the yolk of a duck egg, leaked from the pits.

"I don't..." he began, fumbling through the words with his wounded tongue.

Soil trapped within the spongy orifices in his mouth broke free and he gagged as if tasting it for the first time.

"It's not your fault, Dennis. But you're not welcome in this town. Let's go," John said, demeanor darkening.

He seized Dennis by the arm and shoved him in the direction of the door.

"Sorry to be so abrupt with you, but we don't have much time. If I misjudged the age of your spores then the whole town is at risk."

"Where..."

"Away from here. Keep going north if you like. I'm going to take you away from town and drop you off. Sorry, I can't return your car to you. Can't have your fungus taking over and leading you back here."

They drove in John's old Ford Bronco. Dennis wiped his eye to clear his vision and grimaced at the strands of yellow between his fingers.

"Awfully sorry, buddy. We must endure, though."

Dennis said nothing. His stomach rumbled again.

After five minutes of driving through waist-high grass John coasted the Bronco to a stop and placed it in park.

"You see those buildings? That's all that's left of LeCumbra. It was a town of a couple dozen people prior to the Dust Bowl. Everybody up and went to California, just like in that book."

Dennis smacked his lips.

"You can hole up in there tonight. Move on tomorrow. Just don't come back."

The man opened the passenger door and hopped out. The sun overhead was unrelenting. He glanced about, peering through the milky yellow film over his eyes. The only shade he saw was the porch of an old house in the distance. He began to walk in that direction.

North. North.

His boots crunched over brittle grass.

North. North.

There was an awful smell out here.

North. North.

What was that in front of the house?

North. North.

The man stopped and surveyed the mound of ash and bones. Sweat trickled from the uncounted holes in his body. The stalks of various sizes growing out of them recoiled from the brutal afternoon heat. One hundred yards away, John exhaled.

"Nothing personal," he said, and pulled the trigger.

The head exploded in a burst of gray and red. The mostly decapitated body pirouetted in place, muscles firing at random. John took out the left and then right knees with two quick shots. Once, a headless body made it back to town somehow, the fungus activating the muscles without much coordination. John did not make that mistake again. The body crumpled backwards on the pile of ash, arms flailing, pods erupting prematurely.

The Bronco roared to life and John watched the body of the man who had once been Dennis twitch in place, the reality of the sun sending the fungus into a panic.

Let the sun do the work and he would be back to burn the rest, to add a few more cinders to the broken grass streets of LeCumbra, Oklahoma.

Down the Bunny Trail

Easter in Washington meant plans changed in an instant, plastic eggs culled from lawns hastily hidden indoors as the sky let loose. The forecast did not matter much. Rain was possible any day. Parents eyed the surrounding Cascade Mountains looming over everything like stone sentinels, clouds like dragon smoke always threatening. I remember everything was green. Always. My childhood felt like magic, and It did rain a lot, which only made me appreciate sunshine more.

The sky was a brilliant baby blue that day in April, no dragon smoke to eye through parted blinds. Although the community hunt was an annual occurrence it was subject to the same whims of Mother Nature. The previous year, the clouds ripped open just as the hunt began, sending children and parents sprinting through soggy fields to reach their cars. The plastic eggs floated in swelling puddles and went uncollected until the storm passed the following day.

Today was only sun. My brother leaned forward as some town official clenched a whistle between his teeth, drawing out the anticipation. I did the same and my macaroni noodle necklace, a *good* luck gift from Jake, slipped out of my blouse. I tucked it away and dug my heels in. This was the first year Jake was eligible for the big kid hunt. Mom said we were to hunt together. I grumbled at the decision publicly, but was secretly excited to witness him experience this life event for the first time.

I seem him as clearly now as I did that day, his overalls with the narrow blue-and-white stripes. He smiles that Cheshire Cat grin, looking both mischievous and wholly innocent at the same time. I have trapped him there in my waking memories. He is forever five years old. Forever smiling at the sight of all those plastic eggs. I trapped him there because I cannot cope with what happens next. When the whistle blows and Jake runs, lungs filled with pine-scented air, each step a countdown to the inevitable.

The children are restless, chattering like little rodents. Parents stand a few paces behind with folded arms, perhaps recalling Easter egg hunts of their youth. It is a sea of vibrating pastel, the cloudless sky guaranteeing no church clothes would be ruined this year.

The whistle blows and Jake takes off, wicker basket bouncing off his knee. He plucks a plastic egg from the grass but misses in his attempt to deposit into the basket.

"Jake! You dropped your egg!" I called, but he did not hear over the squeals and laughter surrounding him.

I turned my attention to my own collecting. Some of the eggs had candy inside, usually donated by local grocery stores. Others had coupons for ice-cream cones or movie tickets. That's what I was after that morning. I tested the weight of each egg before adding it to my collection. The lighter the better. Jake was less discriminating. He pursued his favorite colors and any egg surrounding them.

I hated my dress, a flavor of yellow I typically associated with ducklings. It flowed out from my body like an umbrella, forcing me to blindly pat the earth where I spotted the egg. Mom picked it out and I smiled with gritted teeth as I posed for her the week before. I hated it more that day as I saw children, including Jake, pulling further away.

I veered to the left where there were few children. Within ten minutes my basket was half-filled. I was ecstatic. Jake and I would have enough coupons to watch every kid's movie that summer. I stood and surveyed my surroundings. There were dozens, perhaps a hundred or more kids in the hunt, some wearing their cumbersome Sunday best as I was. Others were dressed for action. The park was a wide expanse of ankle-high green grass, still a bit wet with morning dew, and I was quite alone at its edges. Along the backside of the park was a thicket of forest that led mostly uninterrupted to the mountains.

Sweat dappled my forehead despite the cool air. I dabbed at my eyes with my thumb, and searched for the familiar pattern of my brother's overalls amid the bobbing sea of pastels. The terrain was rumpled, distant echoes of the looming mountains. Pigtails and towheads peeked up above emerald waves before dipping beneath. Plastic eggs held aloft in doll hands, jellybeans tucked in wicker baskets.

No overalls. No Jake.

"Jake!" I yelled, no panic at that time.

The hunt was abandoned for the moment, which was okay. Most of the eggs left were miniature in size and did not have the coupons I sought. Over my shoulder parents meandered where the hunt began, the cold gravity of class grouping them into clusters of comfort.

"Jake!" I yelled again, and almost heard the echo of his small voice responding.

I considered racing back to my parents, both likely avoiding the clusters as Dad was an introvert and Mom was his perpetual buffer to the outside world. But it was my responsibility. I was the big sister. I was supposed to be watching him.

There. By the line of trees. Jake was all alone. No children around for one hundred yards or more. My heartbeat settled and I jogged toward him with no particular urgency. I did not want to risk spilling my treasure. The summer depended on it.

Though difficult to make out, it appeared as if Jake was still picking up Easter eggs. He walked, bent for a moment, then walked forward again about five paces. He was getting very close to the forest.

I sprinted, spilling eggs onto the grass as a cold tongue unfurled in my gut, an echo of childhood indoctrination that the woods were the domain of villains and nightmare creatures.

"Hey Jake! Wait for me!"

He turned and spotted me then waved and pointed at something in the trees.

The ferns near the forest's edge were taller than him and when he breached the border, they swallowed him whole. I dropped the basket, the eggs and my summer plans secreted within momentarily sacrificed. I recalled bedtime tales of witches, of rogue wolves with a unique, cultivated taste. Dad's favorite urban legend, about a spider the size of a house that lived in the mountains was permanently tattooed on my psyche. Jake was small, in general and for his age. Despite momentary bursts of bravery, to touch a caterpillar or try a new food, he was a reserved, delicate soul. No match for a wolf or a giant spider. No match for an irritated squirrel.

I sprinted and arrived, breathless, ten seconds later. The visible forest was a mixture of pine trees and old growth, ferns here and there aiming their feathers at chaotic bursts of sun. Jake was nowhere to be seen amid the dancing shadows, the narrow shafts of light terminating in little glowing lemon drops.

"Jake! Where are you?"

The silhouettes of trees were gray and vague, a stark contrast to the children far behind me, skittering over the grass in search of the final eggs. Air burst from my lungs as if an anvil had been dropped on my chest. The Easter Bunny was in the forest, white fur glowing softly between two medium-sized pine trees. The bunny raised one gloved hand and waved at me slowly. I raised my hand and returned the gesture, confused but less frightened than I had been moments prior. It was part of the hunt. Of course! The Easter Bunny hid away from the sharp eyes of foraging children to make a grand entrance at the conclusion of the event.

I parted the ferns and stepped into shadows, shivering as the cool air draped over my skin. Jake was halfway between me and the Easter Bunny, bent to retrieve another egg. I jogged over the pillowed earth, spongy with discarded pine needles.

The Easter Bunny beckoned with both hands, kneeling in a shaft of sunlight. Jake darted past the trail of plastic eggs, eager to accept the embrace.

Goosebumps rippled down my arms. It was so quiet, no birds twittering, barely a breath of wind. I no longer heard the chattering of children, just Jake's footfalls. A muted whistle sounded, signaling the end of the hunt. Mom and Dad would be looking for us.

The Easter Bunny wrapped its arms around Jake, patting him on the back as it did so. Jake was lost in the fur, a hand and shoe visible, as well as the top of his head. A thought blossomed, that the costume was consuming Jake, inhaling his little body through an opening I had not seen. I bit my lip, unsure of what to do with the thought.

126

The bunny stood and held up a finger, almost as if it heard me, as if it knew just what I should do with the thought.

The Easter Bunny wore a silk vest, purple with yellow polka dots. Its bowtie was likely yellow as well, though it was difficult to discern in the murky light. This was not the same Easter Bunny we took pictures with prior to the start of the hunt. The fur was dirty in patches and the costume was ill-fitting. The sleeves hung so that the forearms were visible, coarse, dark hair contrasted against pale skin.

At that age I understood there was more to the stories about mythical beings than my parents told me. I was able to distinguish subtle differences between the Santa at the mall and the one who visited my school. One had a brilliant, cloud-like beard and the other was streaked with gray like dirty snow. I did not know what it meant, only that these were not the same person. I was undecided about the Easter Bunny, as he only mattered for an hour or so one day a year. Otherwise I did not give him much consideration. But, I did not like this version.

"Jake, it's time to go," I said in a watery voice.

The Easter Bunny held a finger up again, and stepped aside. In the small pool of sunlight was a collection of golden eggs. They glittered and glinted. Jake dropped his basket, a rainbow of plastic spilling onto the earth. I followed behind, the Easter Bunny stepping a respectful distance away as I passed.

"Woooow," Jake whispered, smiling as I frowned.

They were not magical, not special. They were eggs wrapped in gold foil with plastic peeking through upon closer inspection.

Jake reached for the eggs and I reached for him.

I sensed the Easter Bunny behind me just before the impact. It stank, like wet clothes at the bottom of a laundry hamper. There was a rush of air, and then I was asleep. I do not know what struck me, a fist or a stone, but I did not even have the chance to gasp.

The next minutes or hours passed in a daze. Intermittently, I was aware of the sound of an engine rumbling, the jostling of my body as the tires of what I later learned was a cargo van crossed over rough terrain. I did not fully emerge from the black hole of unconsciousness until later, though I lingered just below the surface. I sensed much of what happened to me without feeling it directly.

I had dreams. Terrible nightmares. That is what I tell myself today. They were only dreams.

That the action within dreams was inspired by external stimuli I do not doubt, but I try not to think about it. In every iteration, Jake was screaming. Amid the cries for help, the five-year-old pleas for mercy, one word, one name was repeated over and over and over.

My name.

"Alison! Help me!" he cried in my dream.

We were swimming in the pool and Jake drifted to the deep end. His tired little legs gave out and his arms slapped the water uselessly. I paddled as fast as I could, shouting that I was coming for him even as my own mouth filled with water. But, the pool grew and grew and became an ocean. Jake was a dot on the horizon, a single arm flailing as his body submitted to waves.

There were other sounds in my dreams, a man laughing, as if he was in a boat beyond Jake, amused by the panic. The screams and laughter often happened in succession. The hidden man sang nursery rhymes off-key, punctuating them with grunts preceding more screams. The sound of pounding conjured an image of a man assembling furniture but using his fists instead of a hammer. There were other noises, a whirring noise that made me think of Dad in the garage, but it did not make sense then and I dedicated little time to thinking about it after. I do not know how long I was unconscious, but the world I returned to was mostly quiet, the symphony of terror relenting to a jaunty whistle.

The back of my neck throbbed at the juncture of the skull and spine. My brain was clouded by fog, thoughts and senses delayed. I reached for the lump of pain only to recognize my arms were bound. That, and the silence cut through the fog. My first coherent thought was of Jake, the sight of him lost within the synthetic fur of the Easter Bunny's ragged costume, of him reaching for the golden eggs. The knowledge that my nightmare was actually half-awareness of his reality hit me so forcefully it felt as if the marrow was drained from my bones.

For a minute, maybe more, I begged God to kill me. I could not bear a world without Jake. I could not live with the knowledge of his suffering. God did not answer my prayers that day and I have not forgiven Him.

In that Godless silence I began to take in my surroundings. The room was sparsely furnished. In addition to the chair I was sitting on there was a relic of a couch that might have been plucked from the sidewalk on garbage day. It was something a grandmother would have, patterns of ivy and flowers in blurred velvet. Atop the couch was an open cardboard box, the word *Easter* scrawled on the side in marker. There were a few other boxes to the left of the couch, one of which was labeled *Santa*.

You're going to be next.

The thought came from outside of me, a ghost whispering in my ear, slipping down my ear canal like snowmelt, filling my spine with icy needles. Whistling from another room. No cries from Jake, no expressions of pain or pleas for mercy.

My breath caught in my throat and I strained to hear.

The tune was *Peter Cottontail.* I bit my lip to stop from screaming.

Jake is not here!

Where is Jake?

Where am I?

New questions battled for space in my head as my sense of smell returned. Pine dominated the room, but beneath was the wet, mildew stench of the Easter Bunny's costume. I imagine it only came out of the box once a year.

The whistling grew louder, accompanied by the thuds of someone walking up stairs. On instinct, I closed my eyes and drooped my head to the side.

Hinges squealed and, though my ears perked, I refused to peak.

"...hopping down the bunny trail. Hippity, hoppity..." he sang, voice transitioning back into a whistle. He had the voice of a lifelong smoker with a perpetual pocket of gray phlegm lodged in his throat.

He stopped. His eyes crawled over my body, lingering on my exposed flesh. I felt it. I felt the tickle of his gaze on my skin. The footsteps neared, gunshots in an empty tomb. I bit my cheek to fight the urge to flinch. The air shifted around him as he rocked back and forth, a tendril of nicotine breath snaking inside my nostril. His finger grazed my cheek, lifting a lock of hair that had fallen over my mouth.

"If you don't wake up it won't be any fun," he said.

How could he not see my heart thudding in my chest? I was practically vibrating. If his fingers, lingering on my cheek at that moment, strayed a few inches lower to my throat he would feel my pulse, fluttering like the wings of a hummingbird. He would know I was feigning unconsciousness.

I centered myself on Jake. After school we practiced handwriting. Over the course of months, the unsteady lines of his names began to straighten. Two days ago, he'd brought me a sheet of paper with his name written in crayon, each letter a different color. He was smiling that Cheshire Cat grin. We taped it to the door of his bedroom.

"What kind of fun do you like I wonder…" he said.

Whistling resumed and he plodded past the boxes on the floor. My right eye creaked open a hair and I saw his back was turned. I opened my eye fully then but did not turn my head. He was no longer in the costume, having swapped it for jeans and a plaid shirt with the sleeves rolled up. He rummaged through a few drawers of the rudimentary kitchen and, not finding what he was looking for, propped his hands on his hips.

He wore a white apron similar to the butchers at the meat market. I always found it odd, a bit distasteful, that the butcher wore the blood-stained apron in the supermarket as he restocked the meat. The apron the man in the kitchen wore had similar stains, but darker.

Alison…

I flinched, but it was not Jake's voice. It was the memory of a dream. The man in the kitchen looked in my direction. Had he seen?

There was blood in my mouth. I unclenched my jaw but concentrated on the pain in my cheek.

"Here comes Peter Cottontail…" he whisper-sang again, and walked out of the kitchen.

He approached a square opening in the floor leading to what I guessed was the basement, hands still on his hips. He hesitated, glanced at the kitchen and then shook his head before descending. He did not close the door behind him this time, meaning he planned to return shortly.

"Hopping down the bunny trail..." he sang.

Silver tape glued my wrists to the arms of the chair. I strained but had little strength in my arms and there were too many layers. I jerked my right arm and found there was some give, but not enough. Beneath the tape my skin began to sweat. If I had the rest of the day, hours maybe, I could have wiggled my way free. But I didn't. I had minutes, maybe seconds. Only the man in the basement knew.

There were metal clanging noises coming from the basement and other sounds of movement. *Peter Cottontail* was replaced by *Father Abraham.* He married the impact of his efforts with the gaps between the lines.

Father Abraham had many sons WHACK

And many sons had Father Abraham WHACK

How long was the song? How many more WHACKS before he finished his task? My head drooped, chin touching my sternum.

I knew men like the one in the basement existed. Not from any direct, or even indirect knowledge, but from the delicate way my mother discussed precautions I was to take while navigating life. She didn't give Jake the same advice, but maybe he was too young. It was the unspoken idea around which discussions of screening babysitters and summer camps orbited. It was the way my father looked at me with a mixture of pride and apprehension, slipping towards the latter with each passing year.

Right arm!

WHACK

132

WHACK

My stomach revolted at the idea of what was happening twenty feet from me. I would have swapped places if it meant saving him. I had only a handful of extra years of life, but I would have done it.

"It's for good luck," Jake said, draping the crude macaroni accoutrement around my neck.

I was embarrassed of it, thinking passersby would believe it to be my handiwork. Each time it slipped loose from my blouse I tucked it back in.

The song in the basement stopped and I pitched to the side, head resting on my right shoulder. Feather-light steps graced the steps, intended to be quiet, intended for me not to hear. One step. Two steps. Silence.

Was this how he saw me last? I opened one eye a millimeter, the slightest fraction. I could not see him, not clearly. Just a smudge of peach topped with a strip of darkness looming halfway out of the basement door. He was watching me, waiting for me to flinch, to give myself up. Because it wouldn't be fun if I was unconscious. Whatever he had planned for me.

I left my eye half-lidded, unfocused, and fixated on the smudge scrutinizing the rise and fall of my chest. Seconds dripped by like sap from a winter maple. If he could see my heartbeat from where he stood he would have known, would have guessed the ruse.

Father Abraham…

WHACK!

I opened my eyes to a raw macaroni noodle resting on the silver tape binding me to the chair. I lassoed it with my tongue, not aware of a plan at the moment. I was a passenger in my body, and as I fractured the

133

noodle between my molars I did not understand the reason for it. I was not hungry. The noodle in its raw state was not edible. I held a sharp splinter of broken noodle between by front teeth.

I understood then.

Left arm!

WHACK!

WHACK!

I pressed my nose to my wrist, noodle like a tiny dagger, and dragged it across the tape. Once, twice, three times. Not enough. More. Once, twice, three times. More. Again and again until I felt the sting of the tiny dagger on my bare skin. Right arm free, I went to work on the left.

Father Abraham had many sons…

Left arm free, I stood and took a step forward. The chair accompanied me, scraping over the floorboards.

"Shit," I whispered. I think it was the first curse word I ever said on purpose.

I was bound to the chair, but could not see the constraints around my billowy Easter dress. The basement was silent again. Surely, he had heard. He was not a large man, but I was sixty-five pounds and built like a scarecrow. I could barely keep our Dachshund on the sidewalk during walks around the neighborhood.

I hovered over the chair, ready to play possum again at the sound of the first footfall. Instead, the cabin filled with the sound of a power tool whirring to life. I pressed the dress into my body, but there were too many layers to see around. I probed blindly, just like searching for plastic eggs, and felt only confusing configurations of fabric. It was not tape around my ankle, I learned that much.

The saw blade contacted something that slowed its momentum. The engine chugged and the man in the basement hooted as if it was the replay of a game-winning touchdown. I conjured the image in my mind and spat a nugget of vomit on the floor. I couldn't do this. I couldn't plot my own escape while Jake was…

I sat in the chair and leaned back, lifting my legs as I did. The restraints, a white, nylon rope, slid free beneath the chair legs. It was either an oversight or lack of imagination, and I did not linger to consider the possibilities.

Ankles connected by rope but free of the chair, I waddled toward the front door, my stupid dressing filling half the room, and the noise from the power tool died at the same time.

The square opening was like the mouth to hell. I saw nothing, thankfully, to fill in the blank spaces in my nightmares. No blood splatter. No limbs draped over a nail. Was he down there, ear cocked to the side, waiting for me to move again? Had he heard the chair legs scrape over the floor?

My fingers rested on the deadbolt. The space between heartbeats stretched into minutes. He was singing again, and his voice was getting louder. If he checked on me then, or returned to the kitchen to find whatever he was unable to moments ago…I was done. I would be privy to whatever lay beyond the square of light. I would see what caused the saw to hesitate. I would see what he had done to Jake.

I am one of them, and so are you…

His voice was nearer now, aimed in my direction as he approached the steps. I slid the deadbolt as his boot slapped the first step and darted outside onto the porch, closing the door quietly behind me.

I had ten seconds at most.

I bolted, no time to orient myself or devise a plan. My only hope was that a grown, lanky man could not catch a girl in an Easter dress. There were no bushes, no ferns, nothing to provide cover, just thin pines free of branches around the trunk. Five of those trees bundled together would not be wide enough to hide me. I ran rabbit-fast, only a foot of rope between my legs.

The forest was a death trap. Whatever cruelty inside of that thing I struggle to label a *man* would be unleashed on my small body with the added outrage of having escaped his clutches, if only for a minute. I course-corrected, angling for his van, the same that brought Jake and I to the cabin. It was the second to last place I wanted to be in the world at that moment. The last was in the trees, my dress like a beacon for the murderer behind me.

It was a work van, roofing services advertised in chipped and faded paint. I grabbed the handle to the sliding door just as he exploded onto the front porch. He stomped on the floorboards, moving side to side not knowing which direction to follow. The crashing of his boots masked the sound of the van door opening. I hoped. I wormed inside and peered over the driver's headrest. He stared out into the forest, running grimy fingers through wiry, steel wool hair. I fixed my gaze on the crimson blotch over his belly.

Jake...

His eyes darted to the van as if he heard the thought in my head, and I remained still, certain any movement would attract his attention. My muscles were tired, toxic from the panic coursing through my body. He shook his head, patted his pockets, then stomped back inside.

Run.

Once chance.

136

I opened the door and a rush of buttery spring air, peppered with pollen from wildflowers in distant meadows, filled my lungs. I took two steps and realized I would not get far waddling in the woods like a penguin. I might as well march into the open maw of a leopard seal. I lifted my legs above the spread of my dress and saw the restraints were loose from the effort of my escape. After a bit of blind fumbling and tugging my left leg was free. That was good enough.

I closed the sliding door until it clicked, just enough that it would not pop back open and then ran into the trees with the devil licking my heels. The rope whipped my knees as I sprinted and the knot on the back of my head hammered with pain, but I kept running.

There was enough space between the trees that I barely had to change course to avoid colliding with them. Blackberry vines lashed my shins and tore chunks from my dress. I imagined Jake was beside me, that we were racing. I never let him win, not even when Mom told me to. I didn't have it in me to quit and I knew he would eventually be faster than me. The forest air was chilly. It burned inside my lungs. With Jake beside me I could run forever.

Though it felt like forever it was probably only a minute before I looked over my shoulder. The van, a thumb-sized swatch of white, was driving away. I stopped, bracing myself against a pine tree, sweat like frost across my forehead. I was alone. The sound of the van's engine cascaded over the trunks of trees like thunder issuing from a long-departed storm.

I fell to my knees. It was as if the terror and sadness had been restrained by a dam. In that moment, it cracked and then crumbled. I vomited a mixture of blood and chocolate onto my Easter dress as tears sprinkled onto my cheeks. Jake kept running though. I never let him win before, but this was his race, not mine.

I stayed within sight of the road, but far enough away that the man would not see me from his van, even in the tattered remains of my garish outfit. As I walked I called to Jake in my head, but he did not answer. I would never wake up to his smiling face again. I would never see wonder in his eyes again. From that day on I would only speak of my little brother, the boy I was supposed to protect, in past tense.

The forest was as silent as the moon, the only noise the sound of my shoes crunching over fallen pine needles. Mom and Dad still had hope. They did not know their son was already dead. I sagged beneath the weight of that knowledge. I had no watch and the sun was somewhere beyond the canopy. I don't know how long I walked or how much distance I covered. Hours and miles most likely.

Faintly, I heard the drone of a lawnmower, and I stumbled toward it on spongy legs with tears and snot sparkling on my face. My calves were bloody with kitten-claw scratches and my Easter dress was in tatters.

"It's you! You're the lost girl from the news! Where's your brother?" the old lady shouted over the lawnmower's noise.

I jumped, not realizing I had emerged from the forest. She wore gardening gloves and an over-sized hat to keep the sun off her exposed shoulders. She held a flower in one hand and a spade in the other. Her husband navigated the lawnmower around the side of the house and cut the engine at the sight of me.

The woman dropped her tool and the flower. I sobbed and sprinted into her open arms.

The thing about losing someone is, you get to experience the loss over and over. There is the immediate mourning. Then there are all the firsts. The first missed birthday. The first Halloween without him. One less stocking over the fireplace at Christmas.

Dad was the strong one for our family. He kept our heads above water with his love and strategic humor. But, he also drank. I found his empty gin bottles hidden in a box in the garage. By Christmas there were half a dozen boxes.

I believe our family would have survived. Mom and Dad began to talk about getting pregnant again. But the Easter Bunny had other plans.

They did not catch him. The little cabin was a pile of smoldering ashes by the time the police arrived. There was evidence of previous crimes in the rubble, but not of Jake. The property records led to various dead ends.

As a family, we decided not to acknowledge Easter the year after Jake was murdered. I was surprised, then, to find a single, golden egg on the welcome mat outside our front door Easter morning. The sick feeling of loss, like pond water in my stomach, swelled within me. The image of Jake plucking eggs from the forest floor, the sound of his voice in my dream.

It was light, seemingly empty, but it rattled when I gave it a shake. The street was quiet, stagnant rain clouds threatening to ruin another hunt. A man across the street popped his head out, looked at the sky and retreated within his house.

"Dad?" I called over my shoulder.

He did not answer, and so I peeled the gold foil from the egg with trembling fingers. I popped it open, my heartrate beginning to rise. I thought it was a small piece of candy. Odd, but not sinister. I shook it onto my hand and turned it over, then screamed as Jake's tooth slid off my palm.

This began a pattern that continued for many years. It wasn't always on Easter. He was too smart for that. But, somehow, a golden egg, precious treasure hidden within, was placed in my path. One time it was mailed to us. Another time I found it in the front pouch of my backpack during Algebra. Our family survived the tragedy of Jake's death, but it could not endure the insistent reminders of it. I lived with my father. Though life was never normal, it became good over time.

I moved across the country to attend college, and the eggs finally stopped, either because he could not find me or Jake had run out of teeth. Dad sounded better on the phone, hopeful. Detectives assumed the man who hid within a bunny costume died or was imprisoned for other crimes. Maybe that was just what they told themselves to sleep better at night.

My husband, Tom, understands why I don't celebrate Easter. Jacob turned five and it is getting more difficult each year to distract him from the reality of the holiday.

Tom makes breakfast Easter Sunday. It's a tradition between us. I'm typically a loathsome person to be around that day anyway. If he did not take it upon himself to cook the family would not eat.

Jacob is chattering downstairs. He smiles just like his uncle.

"Can you make my pancake special?" Jacob asks.

I inhale the scent of bacon and pancake batter, tucked safely within my blankets.

"What kind of special, buddy?" Tom replies.

"I want 'em to have ears!" Jacob chirps.

"Mickey Mouse ears?"

"No, like the Easter Bunny!" Jacob says.

Tom clears his throat before he responds, "The Easter Bunny?"

"Yeah! I saw him last night!"

I sit up in bed.

"Had a dream about him, huh?" Tom asks, his voice hesitant.

"No, Daddy. He was outside my window! He left me a special egg, too! Can I go get it?"

To Grandmother's
House We Go

The house was perched on flattened land halfway up a hill, like a tumbling boulder that stopped for a rest and never got around to tumbling again. Its white paint had not been refreshed in at least a decade, the grayed wood beneath peeking through in irregular strips here and there, only slightly darker than the deteriorating paint. It withstood more than one tornado, the odd blizzard, and the staggering heat of countless mid-south summers. Yet it looked brittle, as if one should take care not to slam a door lest the entire structure collapse.

This land was the echo of the Smoky Mountains to the east, undulating waves of pasture populated by meandering cattle destined for the slaughterhouse. In the field, though, they seemed happy. Trees grew where people allowed them to grow. Where they did not there was grass and corn.

The minivan kicked gravel as it made its ascent to the house, engine whining from the severity of the incline.

"Mom, I can't even get a signal out here," Darcy moaned, holding her cell phone over her head.

"I don't know how you'll get by."

The anticipated mockery from her younger brother, Joe, did not come. Darcy glanced in the rearview mirror and saw the boy's head nestled into the crook of his elbow, shirt sleeve darkened with drool. Had they not reached the end of their six-hour road trip Darcy would have introduced some foreign object to his open mouth. He once covered one hundred miles of Mississippi with two Chili Cheese Fritos between his lips. When she fell asleep first he was equally vindictive.

"Look, it's two weeks. You still have the whole summer to look forward to. Plus, Grandma's going to spoil you with her cooking like she always does. Homemade apple pies. Fresh eggs every morning."

Darcy rolled her eyes and angled her body away from her mother.

"Where are the cows?" she asked, eyes searching the pasture on the other side of the wooden fence.

"Oh, Grandma got a bit old for that. After Dad died a few years ago she sold most of them off to neighbors. It's just the chickens now, I think."

"And the cats," Darcy corrected.

"Actually no. Most of them have passed on as well. She doesn't replace them now when they do. I think it's just old man Leonard left."

"Are you sure she knows we're coming? It's been like a month since you talked to her," Darcy said.

The van slowed, nearing the spread of crushed rocks that hosted Grandpa's truck and Grandma's old Toyota Camry that might have been green once.

"Dad was the one who handled the money. I don't know if she's figured out how bills work. I'll get the information about the phone bill and just start paying it myself. Also, let me know if you don't have electricity or hot water," Darla said with a wink.

144

She parked next to her father's old Dodge Ram, surprised that the sight of it caused the pain of his loss to bloom in her chest. The truck was such a part of him, patched and re-patched like a favorite pair of jeans. It might as well have been his tombstone.

"Wake up sleepyhead!" Darla said, reaching behind to tap Joe's shin.

The boy roused with a groan, cheek wet with slaver.

"Are we there?" he gurgled.

"We're there!" Darcy said with feigned enthusiasm.

Darla approached the house as her children unloaded their belongings.

"Mom! Mom! We're here!" Darla called.

The kids dragged their luggage, rubber wheels bouncing over gravel. Between the two of them Joe was more enthusiastic about the visit. Grandma had two-hundred acres of mixed pasture and woods to explore, as well as the cemetery barely a stone's throw from the house. The people buried beneath the old oak tree were not relatives, but the presence of their crumbling grave markers, dates and names smoothed by time, was a source of endless fascination.

"Mom?" Darla called again, approaching the steps to the porch.

The unsteady tenor of her voice betrayed her fear. Grandma was dead. She fell down the stairs, bones splintering like rotted wood. She died in agony, a pile of grayed flesh, mouth sucking air like a catfish out of water.

Darla scaled the steps leading to the screened-in porch two at a time. She cupped her hands around her face and peered through a window.

Then she screamed.

145

"Jesus, Mom!"

The old woman appeared on the opposite side of the window. Darla was frightened both by the sudden emergence of her mother's face from within the darkened room, and the effect time waged upon it. Once proud, if not vain, the woman appeared to have surrendered to gravity. There was not a trace of makeup applied to her countenance. In Darla's memories of her mother, the woman always wore bright red lipstick, blush on her cheeks, and eyeshadow that typically reflected the previous decade's fashion.

The kids on the gravel shared a look. Joe shrugged his shoulders and nodded in the direction of the porch. Darcy rolled her eyes again, expressing a sort of aimless contempt Joe mocked once her back was turned.

The door to the house opened and Darlene's puffs of white hair were at once visible. When Darla last saw her mother the hair was that awful blue-tinged color that was seemingly a rite of passage for many elderly women.

Darla hugged her mother in the doorway, shocked at how diminished she felt within her arms. She was slightly plump in her old age, farm-hardened muscles turned to jelly. The smell from within the house hit Darla then and she broke the embrace to place a forearm to her nose.

"Mom, what is that?" she said, retreating a step.

Leonard, the old black cat with the crooked tail, passed between Darlene's legs to greet the new arrivals. It was less of a greeting and more of an acknowledgment. The cat must have been close to twenty years old, give or take a year.

"Oh, that's just Leonard's lunch. He prefers tuna over the wet cat

146

food," Darlene said.

Darla nodded, leaning to pet the cat, who accepted the affection for a moment before darting back into the house.

"Where are my grandkids?" Darlene asked.

She stepped out onto the porch, wiping her hands on her apron. Joe hauled his luggage up the stairs and set it down. Darcy followed behind.

"You're both so tall!" Darlene observed.

Neither were particularly tall, but it had been two years since she last saw them. The previous summer's visit was canceled when Darlene took a spill and had a live-in nurse for a time.

"Hi Grandma," Joe said.

He hugged the woman and stepped to the side to allow space for his sister to do the same.

"Hi Grandma," Darcy said.

She used her luggage as a barrier of sorts to avoid the full embrace, instead hugging Darlene's shoulders. Darcy became aware of several things at once. The house reeked of fish. The apron was soiled and likely carried the same odor. And, Grandma looked different than she remembered. The makeup she used to wear sometimes defined wrinkles rather than obscuring them, but it was more than just her bare palate. Her face looked like old dough hastily shaped to resemble an elderly woman's. Somewhere in those folds and creases Darcy might see a glimpse of the future, so she avoided looking directly.

"Come on in, then," Darlene said.

Darla remained on the porch as the children entered the house. No. Not children. Darcy was officially a teenager and Joe was a year-and-a-half behind her. Adolescents. That was the right word.

"Same room as always?" Joe asked over his shoulder.

"Of course," Darlene answered.

She smiled, pushing the dough of her cheeks up to her eyes.

"I miss Grandpa," Joe whispered once safely inside their room.

"Me too. I love Grandma, but it's so quiet without him. No tractor sounds. No races on the TV. Cows are all gone. What are we gonna do?" Darcy asked.

"Oh, darn. Forgot about that," Joe said, nodding toward the single bed.

In addition to being roommates they would also be bedmates for the next two weeks. They had not shared a bed since they visited two summers ago, both children then with puberty peeking over the horizon.

"I'll sleep under the sheets. You sleep on top?" Darcy suggested.

"Sounds good. Don't tell any of my friends, though, okay?" he pleaded.

The concern in his brown eyes, a shade darker than her own, was very real. Darcy would be equally mortified if any among her friends learned she shared a bed with her stinky little brother.

"That goes both ways," Darcy said.

She hoisted her suitcase onto the bed as Joe popped his open on the floor. Darcy migrated shirts and underwear into the oak dressers. As with all of the furniture in the house, the dressers were more like a growth, an extension of the house as opposed to something outside of it brought within. Very little changed in the house. The decorative paintings of cows and pasture scenes were the same, hung in the same places. The bedding was the same, roses and ivy upon a cream background. It was as if time stopped between visits.

"Kids!" Darla called.

Darcy sucked in a breath, "Here we go."

They left the unpacking to say goodbye to their mother, the smell of fish growing acutely pungent with each step toward the kitchen. It mixed with the smell of cleaning solution. Joe peeked into the living room and saw the bucket of sudsy water and mop at the base of the stairs leading to the second floor. Had Grandma's phone been operational Darla would have implored her mother to not exhaust herself cleaning in preparation for the visit.

They bypassed Leonard, who sat on the entryway mat flicking his crooked tail.

"Mom said the storm last week took out a lot of phone lines and power in the county. I'll put a call in to make sure Mom's on their radar, but it might be a few days. If you absolutely need to get in touch you can ride into town. Should get a cell signal there."

Darcy withheld her sarcastic response, which had become an automatic function of late.

"They'll be fine," Darlene said.

"Love you, Mom. See you in two weeks," Joe said, offering the briefest of hugs. He was eager to see the family plot again.

"Love you, Mom," Darcy seconded.

Darla patted her father's truck on the way to the van, waved a final time, then drove away trailing a cloud of Tennessee dust behind her. Darcy and Joe stood on the porch and watched the van shrink to the size of a toy at the base of the hill, the dust in the air hovering in place for a moment before settling upon the earth again.

"Well, who's hungry? Tuna fish sandwiches okay?" Darlene asked.

It was about the last meal either of them wanted, but both nodded. The old woman turned back inside.

"Grandma, what's that on your head?" Joe asked.

Darlene touched the hair at the back of her head and examined her fingers as she shuffled forward.

"Oh, I was, uh, trying to dye it myself. Thought I would save some money. That's embarrassing," Darlene said, changing course for the dining room, which led into the living room.

Darlene waddled toward the stairs, holding her hand to the back of her head.

"You kids make yourselves some tuna sandwiches, okay? I'll be back down in a bit."

Darlene, escorted by the cat, stepped around the mop and bucket, grasped the banister and hoisted herself up one step at a time.

"I'd rather eat Leonard's litter than a tuna sandwich," Joe said upon hearing the door to his grandmother's bedroom close.

Darcy nodded, "Not feeling so hungry. This house reeks."

Joe spoke the truth that hung in the air between them, "She looks so old. And her hair dye was red, too. Can you believe that? An eighty-year-old woman with red hair?"

"Yeah. I'm surprised Mom let us stay. Grandma seems a little off."

Joe tilted his head, listening for movement upstairs.

"I don't think she would have, but she needs time to work on her thesis and Dad's out of the country. You sure you don't have a signal? We won't be able to stream or listen to music," Joe said.

Darcy pulled her cell phone from her pocket, unlocked it, and shook her head.

"Going to have to make our own fun," she sighed.

"Cemetery?" Joe asked, eyes brightening.

"Ugh, maybe later."

150

The salty stench of tuna prompted her stomach to churn, the road food within sprouting legs and climbing the walls. Darcy sat at the table.

"Why is it up here?" she asked, indicating the plate of tuna that had been Leonard's lunch.

"I don't know. Might be too hard for her to bend over," Joe said.

Darcy's eyes fell to the salt-and-pepper shakers.

"I thought Mom talked to her about those years ago," she said.

The Aunt Jemima and Uncle Moses salt-and-pepper shakers resided on either side of an empty napkin dispenser. The features were cartoonish in their exaggeration, lips over-large and blood red, skin ink black. Darcy looked at the dark brown skin of her own hand, absentmindedly touched her compact curls.

"I think she just hides them when we come. Probably forgot this time. She thinks they're cute. Doesn't see anything wrong with them," Joe said, fingers tracing over his miniature afro.

Within the first five minutes of Darlene's first meeting with Darla's future husband she reported having only previously seen three real black men in her life. Two out of the three were on a chain-gang and the other was putting gas in his truck. But, his license plate was from Alabama, Darlene clarified, as if to suggest he did not count.

Darcy attributed her poor manners to ignorance, but always wondered if her grandmother noticed the looks when they drove to town together. There were a few black people in the area by then, but mixed children were as rare as *Coexist* bumper stickers in that part of the country.

The wooden floorboards above their heads squealed as Darlene navigated from her bedroom to the bathroom. The shower turned on, which meant water was, in fact, running in the house.

151

"Hey, let's check out Grandpa's book collection!" Joe said.

"You think it's still there?"

"I don't think a thing of his has been touched since he died. I'd be surprised if the truck still works."

He left the kitchen, Darcy following behind. They passed through the dining room, the site of many Christmas and Thanksgiving dinners. The table was set for a dinner it would never host, the porcelain dinnerware furry with dust. The candles in the center of the table sagged to the left, slowly melting in the sunlight that filtered through a window.

The living room was unchanged from their last visit. Grandpa's recliner bore the impression of his shape, as if he just got up to grab a snack during the commercials of a football game. It was a sad reminder of the loss of a man they both loved. It was also creepy.

"Don't think I'll be sitting there," Joe observed.

Grandpa's office was a little cove beneath the stairs leading to the second floor. The desk was topped by a bookshelf, the lower shelves housing thin Western novels with well-worn spines. There were legal pads with notes scribbled in Grandpa's compact, nearly illegible script. Joe would attempt to decode it later. His intentions were on the upper shelves, the books with red and black spines, titles unreadable.

The water from the shower pitter-pattered above them, a steady thrum, the sound of a departing storm. Darcy asked her mother about the books years ago and was told not to worry about them. It was a hobby. That was all. Although her mother said it with a smile on her face there was tension there as well, as if the smile held back a different emotion.

"Which one?" Joe asked.

"I don't know. Any I guess."

Joe rolled the chair back.

"Can you hold it?"

"Sure."

He stood on the chair held in place by his sister.

"Read some of the titles," Darcy said.

"Um, let's see…"

He leaned forward, "The Lesser Key of Solomon, The Red King, The Benighted Path, The Book of Thoth."

The sound of the falling water ceased.

"Just pick one," Darcy said.

"They all kind of look the same."

Grandpa died in Vietnam, officially for about three minutes. It was not enemy guns or a plane crash. It was, of all things, the result of bad dental work. His wisdom teeth had given him pain for months and he was finally able to see a dentist. Teeth removed, he was sent back to his tent with an escort, who left him there to enjoy a drug-induced nap. The wounds didn't clot, however, and blood pooled in his throat during his sleep.

He was found on his back with blue lips and blood leaking from the corner of his mouth. For three minutes he was not alive. He was not dead either, because he lived another forty-five years after he was revived. At night, after the farm work was done and the children were put to bed, Grandpa sought to understand what he had seen when he was not alive. Darcy was told the story after he passed, which prompted the obvious question her mother pretended to not hear.

What did Grandpa see?

The chair retreated a few inches as Joe's weight shifted. He gripped the sides of the bookshelf, shaking a few of the paperbacks loose.

"There's one on the desk, Joe. Let's just look at that one."

Darcy grabbed Joe's hand and helped him off the chair. The bathroom door opened on the second floor followed by frantic, muffled movement. The siblings froze in place, hands caught in the cookie jar.

"Jesus, it's just Leonard," Darcy said, letting out a breath.

The cat padded across the floor and sat a few feet away, tale sweeping dust bunnies.

Joe landed on the floor with a thud. He grabbed the book, green with gold script.

"Queen of Hell..." he read.

Leonard meowed, eyes fixed on Joe.

The floorboards squealed and he returned the book to its former place on the desk.

"We can come back for it when she's asleep," he said.

The kids left Grandpa's cove and began a search for the remote control under the watchful, yellow eyes of the old cat.

"Does this TV even have a remote?" Joe asked.

"Yeah, Mom bought a universal remote for Grandpa a few years ago. I think it works, but the TV only picks up local channels. Maybe Maury's on," Darcy said.

Leonard pressed his body against Darcy's leg, caressing the calf with his tail. More popping and squealing of wood from the second story.

"There it is," Joe said.

The remote was between two couch cushions. He pressed the power button but the old RCA did not respond.

"Need new batteries," Darcy said.

Darlene turned the corner at the base of the stairs, taking care to avoid the bucket of sudsy water. Joe glanced at her and then stared, jaw going slack. Darcy followed his gaze.

"Oh, Grandma…" she said, hand covering her mouth.

Darlene smiled as she stepped into the living room. She wore a silk negligee, red as a ripe apple. Waterlogged hair draped over her shoulders like bleached seaweed. One pendulous breast fell free and swayed with the movement of her legs. The skin was the color of old cottage cheese, the texture a tomato left to shrivel on the vine beneath an unforgiving sun. She shuffled on unsteady feet. Had the breast remained secreted within the thin material it would still have been inappropriate. There was no practical purpose to the outfit. It caressed every ripple of her form, barely covering her backside.

"Grandma?" Joe said.

Darcy rushed to her, spinning the old woman around and pressing a hand to the small of her back. She guided her back to the stairs.

"What is it, dear?" Darlene asked.

"It's nothing, Grandma. Let's just find something different to wear, okay?"

The kids settled into their agreed upon arrangement. Darcy slid beneath the sheets while Joe rested on top. The ceiling fan above them creaked with each rotation, an artificial chirp to accompany the serenading crickets outside. There was still light in the room, a dusky orange like fire obscured by smoke. They stared, wide-eyed, as the light bled from the room.

"She wasn't wearing underwear either," Darcy whispered.

"Weird…" Joe whispered back.

Darcy pulled the comforter up to her chin.

"Let's hope weird is all it is. We're stuck here, remember? I don't think Grandma could drive us to town to get a signal. It's like a five-mile walk. So…"

"Well, thirteen days left, then," Joe said.

The house popped and screeched as it, too, settled for the night. Grandma had fallen asleep on the couch, Leonard perched on her soft belly, and they left her there, bathed in the light of the television.

Darcy listened to Joe's breath slow into its familiar pattern of snorts and whispers. The fan blades glowed white against the backdrop of dark wooden beams. Little thoughts came to her, guiding her away from reality toward sleep. How much of the house was original? Who built it? Was it one of the men buried less than seventy feet from her?

The people buried in the pasture knew an entirely different world. There was no electricity. No escape from the cruel summer sun, not even a creaking ceiling fan. In that world there were still mountains to be conquered, rivers to be mapped. Men grew anxious counting the days between storms, the absence of rain God's silent judgment of their character.

Yet, there were connections. The language was the same, though employed differently. They might have even read some of the same books. Darcy read *Great Expectations* during school, which predated the construction of the house.

Her eyelids fluttered on the border of sleep. Moonlight spilled across the comforter, fractured by lace curtains. Darcy edged over the precipice, but was pulled back, the moonlight interrupted. Eyes dewy with sleep, she looked to the window without turning her head, and screamed.

The person in the window was the color of a stone gargoyle. Hands cupped around the eyes peering through the window, nose nearly touching the glass. The hair was white and missing in patches, the gray skin beneath peeking through. The face was hidden by shadows cast by the hands. The person did not react to the scream or the flurry of movement within the room.

"What?" Joe said, sitting up in bed.

"There's someone in the window!" Darcy said, pointing at the place where the figure had been seconds before.

She threw the comforter aside and bolted out of bed, socks slipping over the floorboards. Darcy raced to the window and parted the curtains. There was no one in the yard. There was only moonlight and one ghostly white sheet hung from the clothesline, dancing to the rhythm of the night breeze.

"Where?" Joe said.

They pressed their faces to the window and scanned the shadows. The untended grass in the pasture shivered in the wind. The branches of the oak tree swayed, leaves trembling like butterfly wings. The headstones beneath were still, as was all else. Darcy's breath fogged the glass, coming in rapid bursts.

"What's on the fence?" Joe said, pointing.

It took a moment for their eyes to make sense of the shape.

"It's a cat. It's Leonard, I think," Darcy said.

The cat flipped its crooked tail, stood and arched its back. It was not unusual for the old feline to be outside, though his days of hunting mice were over.

"Are you sure—" Joe began.

He retreated from the window.

"I-I think so. I was dreaming. I think I was dreaming. I was dreaming about the people in the cemetery, what life was like for them," Darcy said.

She pulled the curtains closed. They padded back to bed, but Darcy did not linger there. A moment after her head hit the pillow she was back up.

"What if it was Grandma?" she said.

"Did it look like her?"

Darcy stood, eyes bouncing from the window to her brother to the door. Hardly a minute passed and the face in the window had already lost its clarity. If she had been asked to draw it the rendering would have been very rudimentary. Shrouded in shadows, the hair, backlit by the moon, was memorable. Everything else was a guess, or a dream her mind held onto a little too long.

"I don't know. I don't think so. By the height and the hair it was probably a man. If it wasn't a dream," she said.

Darcy grabbed the doorknob.

"I'm gonna check on her just in case."

The stench of tuna was stronger in the hallway. She scrunched her nose and fought the urge to sneeze. The kitchen was dark save for the green glow of the microwave clock and flickering light from the TV in the living room. As Darcy crossed into the dining room she convinced herself the apparition was imagined. For a neighbor to have walked to the house would not have been impossible, but it was unlikely. Most folks who lived off the battered county road were around Grandma's age. To scale the hill on foot was a challenge even for Joe and Darcy and she would have heard a car's approach up the noisy gravel driveway.

Thin fingers grasped her shoulder from behind. The strength in Darcy's legs gave out and she held a chair to stop from falling. Another hand gripped her elbow as she teetered.

"It's just me," Joe whispered.

Darcy whipped around, "I just saw a freaking face in the window and you're gonna grab me in the dark?"

"I said I was sorry," Joe said, unsure whether to smile or look away.

"You didn't!"

"Well, I am," he said, eyes on his feet.

Darcy scanned the living room but saw no sign of her grandma. The remote was on the coffee table, TV playing an informercial for a life-changing, extra-absorbent towel.

"Probably went to bed," Joe said, yawning.

Darcy nodded, grabbed the remote, and turned the television off. She straightened the blanket draped across the couch and fluffed a pillow, then paused to inspect her fingers.

"What is it?" Joe asked.

Darcy looked from her fingers to the pillow and grabbed the latter. She turned it to catch the light of the floor lamp behind Grandpa's chair. It was still damp from Grandma's wet hair. It was also discolored.

Darcy held it out for Joe.

"I think it's blood," she said.

There was something different about Grandma. Each moment in her presence solidified that fact. She slept for most of the day, always with Leonard on her belly or between her legs. The old cat had lost a step as well, it seemed.

Grandma didn't match her clothes. Fashion, at least a country version of it, was previously an aspect of her vanity. No longer. The next morning she served breakfast wearing a backwards oversized t-shirt, and nothing else. Darcy once again helped her find more suitable clothes.

"Her room is a mess," Darcy confided.

Grandma prided herself on maintaining a tidy house, washing linens weekly for beds that had not been used for years, dusting unseen, hidden corners. No more. Her laundry sat at the foot of her bed, a small mountain of smelly clothes. There were brown streaks in the toilet. The plants on the windowsills were dead or dying, soil as hard as bricks.

"I think she's losing it," Joe said.

They opened every window on the first floor and left the front door ajar in an effort to purge the fish market odor. Grandma napped on the couch, Leonard curled into a black and silver-streaked ball in the crook of her arm. The boy's curiosity demanded action.

Joe hopped the fence into the pasture. It was different without the cattle, quieter. Without a few dozen herbivores to maintain the grass it grew to chest height.

"At least there aren't any cow patties," Joe observed.

"Don't miss those," Darcy said, joining her brother in the small cemetery.

The oldest headstone was from 1832. Only the date was legible. The most recent was from 1892. In the sixty years between the two deaths nine additional family members died. Despite the advances in technology in those sixty years life would have been essentially the same, the combustion engine likely not having made it to this out-of-the-way part of Tennessee by the late 1800s. No electricity in the house. Skies free of all flying things save for birds, bugs, and bats.

"This one says 1863. Do you think he died in the war?" Joe asked.

Darcy traced the date with her finger.

"Maybe. If so, I doubt there's actually anything buried. We learned

160

in History that a lot of soldiers didn't make it to burial. Imagine trying to keep a body from rotting in the South in 1863."

"What do you think you would find if you dug?" Joe asked, indicating the graves to either side.

"After more than one-hundred years? Nearly two-hundred for the oldest? Who knows? I doubt they had the best materials to work with back then. No airtight coffins. Probably bones and rotten wood."

Joe's eyes locked onto something hidden in the tall grass. He scooted between headstones to retrieve it.

"Maybe Grandpa wondered the same thing," he said, plucking the shovel from the weeds.

None of the graves appeared to have been disturbed. But, Grandpa had been dead for a few years. If he *had* succumbed to a strange curiosity nature would have covered any trace of it by then. Darcy turned her focus back to the house.

Joe eyed a small wooden grave marker off to the side, and realized it was new. Before he could investigate, his sister directed his attention toward movement in the attic window.

"There!" Darcy said, pointing.

"What is it?"

Joe dropped the shovel and skipped to the fence. This time he did see. A shape beneath the reflection of a cloud passing overhead. In the instant his mind attempted to process it the vision was gone.

"We should check on her," Joe said.

"Do you think she's coordinated enough to climb the ladder to the attic? She can barely walk a straight line for ten feet."

"If it's not her..." Joe trailed off.

Darcy hopped over the fence and her little brother followed

behind.

"Was probably just the clouds," Joe muttered as if to reassure himself.

The air was fresher with the ventilation, the stench of tuna localized to the area around Leonard's bowl. It didn't *feel* right, though. It didn't feel like the house of their youths. It felt like a house of ghosts, a sterile place inching toward ruin.

It seemed they were destined to navigate through the house on tiptoe for the duration of their stay. Neither wanted to interact with their grandma if it could be helped. The old woman had not moved from the couch, though Leonard was now stretched across her midsection. Darcy frowned at the sight of her. Despite her ignorant upbringing Grandma was a good person. How lonely the house must feel for her. Husband dead. Children moved away. Cows sold off and slaughtered. In Darcy's brief foray into the barn earlier that morning they found a few stray chicken feathers. No chickens. It was only Leonard now, the old black cat who used to catch mice and arrange them in a line on the front porch, a tribute to the family who took him in.

The mop and bucket were in the same place at the bottom of the stairs. Darcy made a mental note to address it before her grandmother stumbled over it in the night.

"It's like she can't hold more than one thought in her head. Take a nap and feed Leonard. That's it," Darcy said, sliding the bucket to the corner.

If it was a house of ghosts even they had abandoned the second level. There were four bedrooms and only one in use. The others hid behind sturdy doors, artifacts of old lives growing pelts of dust, leather shoes turning to brittle bark in closets quietly morphing into mausoleums.

"Darcy?"

"Yeah?"

"Look," Joe said, pointing.

The hall was still and quiet. The air conditioner was not running. The pull cord to the attic swayed.

As if touched by an invisible hand.

Back and forth.

Back and forth.

Dinner was served at three in the afternoon. They ate around the small table in the kitchen, with Leonard at the head. He looked up after each bite of tuna, seemingly curious as to why the other plates of food went undisturbed. Darcy nudged the noodles around the plate, slathered in pasta sauce the same color as the water she dumped out of the mop bucket. Joe held two fingers to his mouth. If he'd eaten more than toast for lunch he would have vomited it then.

Darcy prepared the noodles because the old woman, milky eyes wet with sleep, appeared to be incapable of it. She scanned the directions on the back of the box and stood with her hands on her hips, gaze alternating between the stove and the faucet. Darcy took over and asked her grandmother to tend the sauce. Whatever she added to it when Darcy was not paying attention did not benefit its appearance or smell.

"You gonna eat, Grandma?" Joe asked.

The old woman smiled. She admired the tines of the fork, plunging them into the noodles. But she did not eat.

"What *is* this?" Joe whispered.

The pair learned the woman could not hear them if they spoke at a low level.

Darcy absently twirled the noodles. She had discovered her grandmother dumping a ladle of water into the sauce. Judging by its consistency it was not the first.

"We need to call Mom," Darcy whispered back.

Leonard finished his meal, licked his left paw, and wiped the wet debris around his mouth. He surveyed the table.

"Darla, aren't you hungry?" Darlene asked.

"It's Darcy, Grandma."

The old woman smiled wider. As she did a narrow stream of blood leaked from her nostril.

"Grandma, you're bleeding," Joe said.

"Hmm?" she said.

Joe touched the space above his own lip, "You're bleeding."

She lifted a shaking hand but stopped before the fingers reached her face. Her eyes were wide and unfocused, staring at something beyond her fingers. She shook her head, white hair like the moving flame of a lit match.

She belched, a wet expulsion from deep within her belly. The putrescence overwhelmed the stench of the fish and strange pasta sauce. She coughed, making no attempt to stifle or restrain it. All gathered, even Leonard, watched as something black and wet rolled across the table. It glistened beneath the overhead light then unfurled and began to crawl over the wooden surface. It passed the children, Joe's hand now pasted to his mouth. Darcy pushed herself away from the table, chair legs screeching.

Leonard considered the beetle for a moment. He raised a paw and held it in the air until the insect was close enough. He batted it, knocking it to the floor. The cat met eyes with Darcy, then pounced on the bug, lancing it with its claws.

"Excuse me," Grandma said.

"I'll go tomorrow. You stay here with Grandma," Darcy said.

"Why do I have to stay with *her*?" Joe whined.

The window was cracked and through it passed a pollen-scented breeze. With each gust of wind, the crickets quieted momentarily, the rustling of thousands of leaves taking their place.

"If you got hurt and Mom found out I sent you I would be in deep shit. Like, can't come back from it deep shit."

Joe blinked in disbelief, silenced by the use of the swear. The last expletive he recalled her using came after she stubbed her toe on the coffee table. A week passed before she learned it was broken.

"Okay, fine," he muttered.

There was more to say, but neither could summon the words. They played the scene, only a few hours old then, on a loop. The beetle, glistening with Grandma's saliva, unfolding on the table. The cat sweeping the bug onto the floor before jumping on it and ripping its body apart. When no one spoke, Grandma smiled again and resumed playing with her food.

Darcy thought of a different way to sell it, painting her little brother as the hero of the odd tale. Before she spoke she heard the rumble of distant thunder. There were no flashes of preceding lightning. The storm was too far away. Darcy did not like the idea of walking ten miles through stormy weather. She did not like it at all.

When she woke there were too many things happening to focus on a single one. There was the engine noise from outside. There was the slight difficulty breathing. And there was the nearly imperceptible sound close to her, wet like a baby nibbling its pacifier.

She tried to turn in the direction of the noise but could not. Darcy only had control over her eyes. She returned her attention to the warm weight on her chest. It was difficult to focus as the object was so close, and the room was dark. It was a shadow, a smudge of black rising and falling with each breath.

Darcy recognized the engine sound. It was a riding lawn mower. At night?

Lightning flashed but the thunder was lost in the drone of the mower. Was Grandma mowing the lawn at night and in a storm?

The weight on her chest shifted, blowing a puff of fish-scented air at Darcy. It was Leonard. He was a little furnace, the skin beneath him slick with sweat. Though it was not uncommon for the cat to use a person as a pillow, he had never previously done so with Darcy.

She opened her mouth to speak her brother's name, but succeeded only in mouthing it silently. Darcy strained her eyes, looking in his direction. Another shape in the darkness, this one lighter. Her vision limited, Darcy did not understand what she saw in that moment. The wet, suckling sound corresponded with the slight movements of the pale shape.

Grandma squatted beside the bed, neck and upper chest bare, hair a mess of wispy knots. The old woman enveloped the flesh of her grandson's arm, her soft, slippery gums massaging the skin. She sucked his knuckles like a calf at the teat, eyes rolling back in her head to expose the whites. Her delight was mirrored in the gentle vibration of the black cat, purring and kneading Darcy's chest with his paws

166

Why can't I move? And, what is Grandma doing? Darcy thought.

She sucked in a breath and blew it through her nostrils in a steady stream then focused inward, connecting her intention to the index finger of her left hand. She imagined the digit twitching, and then it did twitch. She envisioned the finger lifting from the bed, and it did that as well. She saw the hand collapse into a fist and then spread like a starfish.

Darcy repeated a single phrase in her mind as she tapped her liberated index finger on the bed.

Joe, wake up! Joe, wake up! Joe, wake up!

She tapped thirty times on the bed as she repeated the mantra in her mind. Then she redirected her energy to forming the words with her mouth.

"Joe wake up! Joe wak-"

The utterance, barely a whisper, was halted. Leonard stood on her chest. His paws covered her mouth. The cat's eyes were like moons reflected in a dark puddle. She slept.

It was raining outside, alternating between a downpour and a shower. Darcy stood on the porch and listened to the drumbeat of drops on the roof. There were small pools in the yard. It had been raining for some time. The cat dragged its body across the girl's bare leg. She was not startled. Darcy bent to scratch the cat behind the ears.

It purred and snaked its crooked tail around her calf. She folded her arms, looking behind to the open door leading into the kitchen. Joe was not there and she could not hear him elsewhere in the house.

"Joe?" she called, facing the yard again.

Leonard sat on her feet and together they watched the rain fall. There was movement within the curtains of water, a brief glimpse of color.

"Joe?" Darcy yelled.

Must be playing in the rain. She stood at the head of the stairs, rain falling inches from her face.

"Joe, come here!" she yelled, searching for the flash of color.

The rain was a downpour again, steam rising from the grass. She saw him down the hill fifty or so feet distant, but there was more movement to the left a bit further away. Joe came closer, but there was something off about his gait. He hobbled, bent over at the waist, knuckles on the grass.

Voice now tentative, she spoke his name again but knew he would not be able to hear over the white noise of falling rain. Leonard meowed at her feet, though his gaze was fixed on the approaching figure. It was not Joe. Darcy retreated a step, a steadying hand over her heart.

"Grandpa?" she whispered.

He was nude, scrambling through the wet grass like an ape. His hair, a mixture of cotton-white and silver, was plastered to his forehead. Before she could process this development, the other shape revealed itself. Grandma, also nude, crab-walking a few paces behind her husband, who died more than three years ago.

Darcy mirrored their movement, taking one step backward for each step forward her grandparents took. Leonard remained at the head of the steps, flicking his tail.

Grandpa was first. He spat the mice he held between his teeth onto the step, bowed, and slinked away. Grandma scurried forward. The mouse in her mouth wriggled, threatening to escape, her gums too slippery to secure the animal in place. It fell to the step, and began to drag its body over the concrete, the rear legs limp.

Leonard stepped forward, flinching as the rain contacted his fur. He punctured the mouse with his claws and sank his last tooth into its neck.

It rained throughout the day. Occasional rumbles of thunder were loud enough to hear over the constant din, but the wind never picked up. The plan to walk to town was abandoned as soon as Darcy peered through the blinds and saw the white sheet hung from the clothesline saturated and limp. There were strange patterns in the grass, strips of it mowed but haphazardly. The nightmare still had its hooks in her, the vision of her grandparents presenting mice to the black cat, their gray, sagging bodies slick with rain. Joe was not in bed, but there was television chatter from elsewhere in the house.

Darcy gathered fresh clothes. She felt dirty from the dream and needed a shower. She peeked into the kitchen and saw it was empty. Darcy would need to talk to Joe about Grandma, but she needed the shower first. Let him decompress with some TV.

She was well into her shower before she realized there was no soap available. She hopped onto the bathmat and retrieved the hand soap from the bathroom sink. If it got the smell of tuna off of her she did not mind.

Dried and clothed, Darcy stepped into the kitchen as if it was the middle of the night, half expecting to see her naked grandmother with a writhing mouse between her lips. It was no longer a matter of the old woman being *off* or *weird*. It was beyond that. She sensed her subconscious making connections she was not prepared to acknowledge.

"She's upstairs I think," Joe said.

He sat on the couch, a bag of Doritos on the coffee table.

Darcy nodded at the chips.

"Expired two months ago, but they're okay. I haven't seen Grandma today, but I heard her go to the bathroom. It's almost lunchtime you know," he said.

Darcy sat beside him, leaving his preferred amount of space between them, enough so that their bodies would not accidentally touch.

"Joe, did you have any dreams last night?" she asked.

His left hand immediately stroked his right forearm.

"It wasn't a dream, Darcy. I couldn't move either."

"You saw Grandma…"

He shuddered, "She was a foot from my face. Yes, I saw her. I couldn't stop it. I couldn't move."

His voice was becoming agitated. Darcy reclined into the couch cushion. There was a news report on one of the local stations about a disease outbreak in New Mexico. Joe flipped through two channels, both broadcasting the same story. He found a game show and tossed the remote onto the stack of magazines on the coffee table.

Darcy noticed the legal pad on the table and grabbed it.

"I can't read his writing. Some of it I can read, but the words don't make sense. flipped through the book on the desk as well. It's over my head."

The handwriting was compact, frenzied at times. She recognized words here and there, but not enough to impart any sort of meaning. There were numbers as well, formulas with various measurements attached.

"Do you want to go outside?" Joe asked.

"It's raining," Darcy said.

"I know. I just can't stay in the house. It stinks. It's creepy. I don't want to have these memories of her."

His voice cracked, the boyish tone she knew so well breaking through. They met eyes. When she reached across the couch to touch his hand he did not recoil. He looked away, but held her hand as he did.

"Sure. Let's play in the rain. Maybe there's still toys in the shed."

Neither bothered to search for an umbrella or raincoat. The rain was warm and their mother was not around to suggest they could still catch a cold if they weren't careful. The shed was secured with a lock that was not fastened and their childhood toys *were* inside, along with spiders minding barren webs. Joe emerged with pool noodles and a deflated soccer ball. Darcy carried a Frisbee that once glowed in the dark but seemed to have lost that capability.

"Which one do you-"

Her question was interrupted by the smack of a pool noodle to the back of the head. Joe sprinted toward the barn, splashing through puddles that swallowed his feet. Darcy gave chase, paused and hurled the Frisbee at him. It missed by several feet and came to a stop in the grass. Joe seized the opportunity to change direction, slapping his sister on the head as she bent to retrieve the disc.

When they exhausted the possibilities with the toys they selected Joe found more. He emerged from the shed on a tricycle crafted for a toddler. He pedaled it to the front yard and parked right before the hill sloped downward.

"Think I can make it?" he asked.

"Yeah, but you might be dead at the bottom."

"I'll make a handsome corpse."

"Don't make jokes like that. Also, you'd make an ugly corpse."

Joe nodded. Darcy saw, beneath his cherubic countenance, the man he would soon become. He looked like Dad, skin a few shades lighter, nose a bit narrower, but otherwise a spitting image.

"Well, have fun dragging my body back up the hill," he said, then inched over the precipice.

The pedals whirred as the brittle, rubber tires bounded over the uneven terrain. Joe squealed, alternating between delight and terror. It went faster than he would have guessed, the soggy earth doing little to slow the tricycle in its descent.

Darcy folded her arms, biting her cheek as she watched his form diminish. He abandoned the bike and rolled a dozen or more feet. Darcy held her breath, the words she would speak to her mother already forming in her mind. Joe stood and waved, the joy in his barely audible bellow obvious. She muttered and turned away, looking for a puddle to disturb.

Near the porch steps she found a puddle. Floating in it, facedown, was a single, bloated field mouse.

Grandma's sleep pattern mirrored Leonard's. The persistent deluge had a somnolent effect on the cat. The only evidence of her having been awake at any point in the day was the open tuna can on the kitchen counter, the mound of canned fish on Leonard's plate recently refreshed. The kids retired from their activities after Joe fetched the tricycle from the ravine and walked it to the yard.

Darcy made peanut butter and jelly sandwiches with stale bread, pairing it with the Doritos Joe found in the pantry. They ate on the couch, avoiding the kitchen table and the memory of the beetle.

It was the first time since their mother left things felt normal. Perhaps in a subconscious effort to preserve the normalcy, they did not speak about the night visit. Joe, on occasion, rubbed his arm where his grandma nursed on his flesh. The skin had a slightly bruised appearance.

Darkness came early, the sun still hidden by clouds fat with rain. Grandma walked to the bathroom twice during the day, alleviating their fears about her having died in bed. They ate sandwiches for dinner as well, finding no better option in the refrigerator or pantry.

Darcy cleaned in the living room, dusting picture frames and sweeping cat hair into little piles. The family portraits needed a refresh. In the most recent picture Joe stood below Darcy's waist, probably between his third and fourth birthday. The décor throughout the living room was similarly outdated. A porcelain bell with a red ribbon bow tied to its handle celebrated Christmas of 1998. There was a hand-drawn birthday card Darcy made for her grandmother when she only knew how to write in capital letters.

With no cable, no lightning bugs to catch outside, there was little appeal in staying up late. Joe dozed on the couch until his sister's sharp elbow found the soft spot between his ribs. He whined but climbed into bed without changing out of his jeans. Darcy lay beside him, comforted by the sound of his breath and the silence in the rooms above her.

The rain eased outside and she considered whether or not she should make the journey to town tomorrow. It would be a messy walk, the first two miles on unpaved roads. She did not have boots, only flip-flops and sneakers. She recounted the events of the past couple days, crafting a reasonable explanation for each odd occurrence. Except the beetle. She could not think of a good reason for that. Everything else could be explained away, even if the cause was painful, like the possibility that Grandma was losing grasp on reality.

The dark wood above groaned as the woman moved around

upstairs. To her knowledge, Grandma had not eaten that day. Might be time for a late snack. Leonard would also be hungry.

Darcy lost track of her movements through the house as she sank deeper into her own thoughts. At the center of everything was the beetle. Her thoughts danced around the insect like coyotes around carrion claimed by a much larger predator. It unfolded its black body, legs slicing air, tearing holes into the reasoning she employed to dismiss everything else.

At about 10 o'clock she roused, realizing the house was still again. There was no face in the window, no cat on her chest, no ghostly pale Grandma gnawing her grandson's arm. Leonard did that, she realized. Leonard lost all but one of his teeth over the years and had taken to nibbling on toes, a strange but not unpleasant sensation for the person whose foot he selected. She wondered if Leonard or Grandma would pass first, imagining it would likely not be long for either.

Darcy watched her brother sleep for a moment. Satisfied he would not be disturbed by her departure, she padded out of the room. If the sun was out in the morning she would make the trip into town. She did not know how to explain the events to her mother without sounding insane. She did not know which combination of words would inspire Darla to come for her children without doing so in a panic. But there were still a few stones unturned.

Once again, she stepped into the glow of the microwave's clock. Her spine went rigid at the memory of Joe's hands on her shoulders in the dark. She dashed into the living room, sliding over the floorboards on her socks.

There was a little lamp on Grandpa's desk. Darcy fumbled in the dark and found its cord. It offered the only light in the room, immediately attracting the attention of a moth, which had been dormant until that moment. It slipped beneath the lamp shade, casting exaggerated shadows on the wall. While maintaining the idea all was well, or at least explainable, Darcy still wanted to understand Grandpa's unusual obsession.

She traced the gold lettering on the book, speaking the title out loud. The paper was thick with rough, uneven edges. She searched for the publisher's information but found nothing, no author or table of contents. Scanning through pages at random, very little of what she read made sense to her. Grandpa circled and underlined passages, jotting notes to himself in his compact script.

Darcy's heartrate accelerated as she read the chapter titles.

Rites of Possession

Gates of the Abyss

The chapter most heavily perused was titled *Familiar Companions*. The notes were frenzied, many underlined and accompanied by exclamation points. When Darcy heard the voice she felt, for a moment, as if her soul stepped out of her body. The voice was like papyrus rubbed together, like a snake discarding its skin through dried leaves.

"Don't look over here, darling. You don't wanna see what I've become."

Darcy said nothing in reply. She gripped the desk, readying herself to sprint.

"It didn't work like I thought it would. I'm very sorry. I'm sorry you had to see your grandma like that."

Silence for a moment, then Darcy spoke, "Grandpa?"

"Promise you won't look over? You don't want this memory, darling."

"I-I won't look."

There was little to see amid the shadows, just a few additional lumps on his recliner.

"Grandpa, are you dead?" she asked.

"I died. Now I am here. But, I shouldn't be. I need your help to move on. *We* need your help."

"W-what do I do?"

"It's in the margins, Darcy. You'll find it in the margins."

The recliner squeaked as its occupant pulled the lever. The floorboards accepted the weight with little protest. Darcy wanted to see her grandpa again. But, the figure shuffling to the stairs was not her grandpa.

"I love you. I love your mother and your brother, too. Even your dad. You don't have to tell 'em. Just know it in your heart."

"Grandpa?"

"Yes?"

"What did you see when you died?"

The sound of movement halted.

"I didn't understand it the first time. Didn't understand it the second time. Decided I wasn't meant to. I just need to rest, now. Maybe we'll see you again...when the time is right."

"I love you, too, Grandpa."

The moth walked along the inside of the lampshade, its shadow creeping over the wall in concert. Darcy watched it for a time.

She turned her attention to the book, her grandpa's words repeating in her mind. She searched the margins of the pages, eyes squinting at the miniscule letters. Only about one out of three words was recognizable and those were mostly inconsequential. Except for the chapter titled *Familiar Companions.*

There was one word she recognized. It was scrawled with a heavy hand, circled multiple times. One name.

Leonard.

Darcy dozed but did not fall into a restful sleep. There was movement in the night, doors opening and closing, soft footsteps. She stirred early in the morning, and was greeted by the somber light of a cloudy dawn. Rain streaked the window again.

"Joe, are you awake?" she asked, knowing he was not.

The boy blinked his eyes a few times.

"Yeah. I am now."

"I think I figured it out."

"Figured what out?" he said, sitting up in bed, rubbing his eyes.

"What's been going on. I got out of bed last night and read through one of Grandpa's books. I think I know what he was trying to do."

"What?"

"I think Leonard died and Grandpa brought him back. Like as an experiment. But, it wasn't just Leonard that came back. It was something else, something powerful."

"Like what?"

"I don't know."

Joe yawned and stretched, frowning as he noticed the rain falling outside.

"Joe!"

"Yeah?"

"Grandma's dead and Leonard is controlling her."

178

The boy rubbed a knuckle in his ear as if he feared he had not heard her correctly.

"What?"

"Grandpa died in Vietnam and saw something. I don't know what. But, he spent the rest of his life trying to figure it out. Leonard died and Grandpa brought him back. I don't know how. But, it wasn't just the cat that came back. And now *it* brought Grandma back and is controlling her."

"But, Grandma's not dead."

Darcy sighed and nodded. She had not processed the idea herself. Not just that the woman was being controlled by Leonard but that she was dead. Their grandmother was dead.

"I think I know how it happened."

Joe left space for her to talk.

"I think she fell down the stairs again, only this time she didn't survive. The red on the back of her head? Blood. Like I found on the pillow. The mop bucket and water at the base of the stairs. She started to clean up the evidence, but got distracted. The beetle. The clothes. Leonard really only cares about one thing, his food. And naps I guess."

"She hasn't eaten in days."

Darcy nodded, "Doesn't need to."

"So, what do we do?"

Darcy squeezed the back of his neck.

"Help her move on."

There were many things Darcy did not say, many truths she believed but did not speak. She did not mention Grandpa at all, fearing it would be too much for Joe. She believed Leonard struggled to control both grandparents and Grandpa regained a bit of independence because of it. It was likely his face in the window, him mowing the grass as he had done for decades. Perhaps this was the desired result of his experiments. He escaped death, but did not find life in the process.

Grandma's room reeked. Mildewed clothes were piled to chest height. The smell of decay, of pooled blood trapped within a motionless body hung in the air like a fog. The woman was face down on the floor, a fact that would have been startling to Darcy had she believed her grandma to be alive. Leonard was on the bed, a compact ball on Grandpa's old pillow.

There was a noise in the room as well, and Darcy soon discovered the source. A collection of flies congregated on the back of Grandma's head. The snow-white hair was stained the color of rust there. They disappeared within the wound like divers jumping into a pool, emerging gray and slick. They buzzed their fat little bodies, flinging flecks of brain tissue.

"Grandma?"

No response.

"Grandma it's breakfast time!" Darcy shouted.

Leonard roused first, then the woman. She peeled her body off the floor and swayed as the cat stretched and arched its back. Darcy left the door open and scampered down the stairs, wiping a tear from her cheek.

The flies came with her, buzzing about her head, dipping in and out of the fracture. Neither child could look at her. One eye was sealed shut, yellow pulp leaking from it, little black dots like strawberry seeds dotted the eyelid. The other eye was the color of the clouds outside and focused on nothing.

Leonard's breakfast was prepared. He took his place at the head of the table and buried his face in the fish. Darcy stirred the eggs on her plate as Joe stared out the window, his breakfast untouched. There was no plate in front of Grandma, just a card.

The old woman picked it up as Leonard ate, her one good eye scanning the letters.

HAPPY BIRTHDAY TO THE BEST GRANDMA EVER!

She smiled and it felt genuine, familiar.

Leonard stopped eating. He looked from the food to the children. Joe cried silently, still staring out the window. Darcy held her grandmother's cold, stiff hand. The cat shoved the plate of tuna away and hopped onto the floor. It began to cough, sputtering like an engine that would not turn over. It spat fish onto the floor, but the poison was already inside of him. Leonard spasmed and hobbled through the pet door to the front porch.

"It's okay, Grandma. You can go now," Darcy said.

The Magician

The clouds came not to relieve our misery but to deepen it, walls of dust that blotted the sun, erasin' our will, erodin' the very enamel of our teeth. Wind peeled away the topsoil, dislodged seeds yet to sprout roots. The season was over before it began. There were no breadlines here. The banks had no money left to loan. And, you can't eat money anyway.

Folks packed battered Fords until the windows threatened to burst from within. They disappeared in the white-hot glow of the settin' sun. There were jobs in California. The wind there brought not dust but the salty tang of the sea. *Opportunity*, a mantra repeated among the departin' as if it was the name of the destination, itself.

Those left behind fashioned a life for themselves, scraped the dust from their eyes to try again. Each season brought that terrible hope, that it would be different than last year, that they coax life from dead earth. The rain would come. If they formed the right words God would remedy His mistake. The rain would come.

Dad was up north a couple hours. There was oil out there, and it was about the only dependable labor a man could get. He did slaughterhouse work for a while, but the herds dwindled until most days were spent snapping at flies with a hand towel. Eventually, there was nothing left to slaughter. We felt fortunate he found any sort of work. Others weren't so lucky.

One county over, a man put a bullet between the eyes of his two children, waited for their mother to run to the commotion and then ended her, too. Walked out into his field, the stalks of petrified crops snapping like old bones beneath his boots, and sprayed his brains onto the soil that once provided his livelihood. The worst part, I think, wasn't the crime but that no one was surprised by it. Whenever I saw a man stare into space I wondered if he was workin' out the logistics in his head, justifyin' murder yet to come.

It was an unusual time and place for a carnival, but it was about all I had to look forward to then. School was out, which typically meant field work, but the only thing to do in a field at that time was walk through it kickin' up dust. I would have gone up north with my dad, but it was too dangerous, he said. A man lost an arm on his shift and bled out before they finished arguin' about which hospital was closest.

It was called *King's Carnival,* and it came through every year right at the beginnin' of summer. That was a good time for it. Kids were out of school, and it was hot but not enough to kill you.

King Henry took his name from the tall tale about John Henry, the powerful freed slave who could drive a railroad spike into the earth with his bare hands. But, it was a joke. King Henry was a dwarf, you see. At fourteen years old I had not seen many people outside my county. That King Henry was black and a real, live dwarf made him extra special.

I saved everythin' I could for those three days and nights in June. Every wheat penny. Every dime. By the time the carnival trucks puttered down Main Street, destined for a parcel of land just outside of town, I

184

had enough money for three rides, one show, and popcorn and cola each night. Mom insisted I go. I offered her the money first, but it was nothing that would make or break us. If we needed that $1.65 to survive we was already broken.

Since last year's carnival I really only thought of one thing, the magician. Called himself Dr. Vanesco, but I think that was just a stage name. Dad said he'd been part of the carnival as long as he could remember, even when Dad was a boy. After all those years, his hair was as black and slick as a water moccasin, though he showed is age in other ways. Make-up hid some of it.

He did *real* magic, see. Not the rabbit out of a hat stuff. *Real* magic. Turned a cat into a toad and then back into a cat again. He swallowed a live rattlesnake at the beginning of his act, kept it inside of him during the hour-long performance, then vomited it up, angry but alive. My favorite trick was the vanishin' act. He picked a volunteer from the audience, put 'em in a glorified outhouse. No ceremony. No stage. Just right there on the grass inside a tent the size of a classroom. Then Dr. Vanesco entered a similar compartment fifteen feet away.

From inside, he shouted words in a language I didn't understand. The doors opened and POOF, both gone. The doors closed and opened again to reveal the magician and the volunteer switched places! I sat right up front last year, lookin' for the gimmick. But there was no gimmick. It was *real* magic, see.

It never went over as well as it deserved. A smatterin' of applause. My guess is most people didn't realize the magician and the volunteer switched places. No fire. No smoke. It was just magic.

The pennies were hot in my hand and slick with sweat, like I was tryin' to keep egg yolks from slippin' 'tween my fingers. Though the sun was settin' in the west its heat was trapped in the desert-dry earth. I could nearly smell the leather of my shoes cookin'.

The carnival touched each of my senses. I first smelled the popcorn. At home we ate food that tasted like the packaging it came in, and so the of aroma of hot, buttered popcorn turned my walk into a sprint. As I neared I saw the lights of the Ferris wheel, little fireflies forever tracin' the same path. Then came the calliope music interspersed with the screams of children. I believe the tune was *The Lincolnshire Poacher,* which I associated with the carnival and what happened that night for the rest of my life.

The town was a blur to my right. I joined the throng of folks eager to part with a bit of pocket change to forget about the dust for a night. We were covered in it even then. The dust was our second skin.

"Step right up! Step right up!" King Henry bellowed with an East Texas twang that changed his *right* into *rot.*

He stood on a wooden crate, tappin' it with a cane and doffin' his boater hat as ladies passed. In addition, he wore a full tuxedo, the fancy kind with the tailcoat.

"See the Bearded Lady! See the Wolf Boy! Ride the rides and see the sights!" he barked.

Black folks weren't allowed to go to the carnival until Sunday. That was *their* day. Weren't many of 'em in the county, but they came from towns nearby. Small as the town was, it was the biggest thing goin' 'til you reached to Abilene. I stared at King Henry longer than I should have, tryin' to understand the logic of his stunted legs and child's hands. He

186

smiled and winked at me, teeth like alabaster in the dark.

I joined a line of kids, shirts stiff with dried sweat. They likely stank, but so did I, and I was accustomed to my own odor. I'd have been content to just walk around for the night, eatin' popcorn and sippin' cola. The people were so different from how I usually saw 'em, smilin' and laughin' even as the world went to ashes. The popcorn and cola were double last year's price.

"Are you sure?" I asked the boy in the booth.

He was the same age as me or younger, a spray of acne on his cheeks the same red as his hair. He pointed to the sign listin' the prices rather than answer.

I did the math in my head but worried the prices for rides and the magic show might have gone up, too. One night of indulgence was better than a few half-assed ones, I decided, and dumped my greasy coins into his palm.

I took my treasure on a walk through the crowd. Each time a kernel shook loose from the bag or failed to make it into my mouth I blew the dirt off and ate it. I might not have another snack until next year's carnival.

There were friends from school out that night, but my closest friends were in California, with 'bout half the county it seemed. Gracie, a girl in the grade ahead of me was out in her best Sunday dress. She was a bit of a pixie, arms as thin as a broom handle, hair the color of straw after a heavy rain, but pretty in her own way.

"Do you want the rest?" I asked her, gesturin' with the popcorn.

She had been watchin' couples on the Ferris wheel, perhaps wishin' she had someone to take her.

"Excuse me?" she said, smilin' once she remembered who I was.

The dress had no pockets and she wore no purse. If she had cash or coins she was storing them in a place I was not allowed to see. My guess was she didn't, that she was just out there to be around people, the smells, the lights, and the music.

"Stomach's achin', don't think I can finish," I held the bag out.

She looked to the left and right, eyes gray like the river rocks you wouldn't go out of your way to pick up. The exchange was complete before I had time to process it. She skipped away with half a bag of popcorn and I rubbed the damp place on my cheek where her lips had touched.

I moved on. The Bearded Lady was outside of her trailer smokin' a cigarette. It wasn't much of a beard, but the hair was long, touchin' the top of the pale melons spillin' outta her dress. I waved but she flicked the cigarette butt in my direction and went back inside.

There were games of skill, the prizes of poor quality. Used to be you could win a baseball bat. A nice wood one. That night's top prize was a wallet, something most men in town had no use for at the time. I enjoyed watchin', sharin' the excitement while holding onto my precious dimes.

Dr. Vanesco's tent was tucked away at the rear of the carnival, the squawkin' of children a bit quieter there. Compared to the lights and competin' music from other attractions, it was forgettable. Patches in the fabric of various colors, just like the knees in the denim of most boy's overalls. The sign in front read *Magic Show* and didn't even bother with an exclamation point. The performance was not for another hour, but I made my way to the tent anyway. It was my whole reason for goin' that night.

I rocked on my heels, massagin' the coins in my hand and wishin' there were more of them. I thought of my mother, wonderin' if she really needed the money. She was probably in bed by then. No reason for her to be doin' anything else. If she was not in bed she'd be sweepin'. The dust found a way in. On a day when neither of us opened a window or door the dust found a way in. Could she ever have imagined such a life? Alone amid a brown sea of barren earth, cursed to sweep into small piles the source of her misery?

"Would you like to see something you've never seen before?"

I yipped in surprise, the slick coins spillin' onto the dirt. I kneeled to retrieve them.

Dr. Vanesco stood beside me clad in full magician regalia except for the top hat. We were about the same height, which surprised me. He was such a large presence I expected him to tower over me.

"W-what?" I said.

"That's why you've come. Isn't it?"

"To s-see somethin' I've never seen before?"

He had one of those mustaches that curls at the ends. His face was long and hawkish, the angles castin' shadows. His voice was a bit higher-pitched then I remembered. No need for the thunderous performance bellow at such close quarters.

"You want to know the secret. Is that it? You want to know how it works? Not the kid stuff. No. Not you. You want to know how I disappear."

He said this as if he was readin' my memories, almost more to himself than me.

"Yes. I've thought about it all year. Can't figure it out. There's no trap door. Don't make sense," I said.

I wedged my hands into the pockets of my trousers, felt a jolt of panic as my finger poked through the hole there. Then I remembered the money was in my other hand.

"Oh, my boy, if only you knew how little sense it makes! It's preposterous, isn't it? A man can't disappear! And to take another poor soul with him! Preposterous!"

I wiped my arm across my forehead, smearin' the sweat into a slurry from the dust.

"So, it's not real magic?" I asked, confused.

He straightened his lapels. There was a little, red carnation there, which he adjusted though it looked no different once he returned his attention to me.

"My boy, that is a matter of opinion. I did not say it was not magic. The word means nothing to me."

He followed my gaze as I looked at the sign.

Magic Show

"For the rubes," he said, wavin' a gloved hand as if shooin' a fly.

"What I said was, it does not make sense. What happens when I disappear. But, there's only one way you'll know for sure. You have to experience it yourself."

In that moment, he and I were alone. The laughter and music faded until I heard only the sound of my breath and my heart beating in my ears.

"W-what do you mean?"

He placed a hand on my shoulder, my dust corruptin' the pristine whiteness of his glove.

"If you want to see something you've never seen before, you just have to ask."

I heard little of the show. When the audience clapped I joined in, often delayed and then for several seconds after the applause ended. Dr. Vanesco was a blur on the scorched patch of grass that served as his stage. I was to be his volunteer, the local boy selected to vanish and then reappear.

As my excitement marinated I chewed on the few words he provided. I expected he would share the secret of the trick. He assured me there was no secret.

"What do I do?" I asked.

"All you have to do is wait," he said.

A few restless souls peeled away, disappointed there was no rattlesnake to begin the show. Others responded with the anticipated level of wonder, gasps followed by whispers as Dr. Vanesco ran through his repertoire.

"Is there anyone among you who would be so kind as to volunteer for my final...*trick?*"

He placed an odd emphasis on the last word, as if to confuse the likelihood of it being a trick.

I lifted my arm along with a dozen or so others, mostly boys around my age. Dr. Vanesco made a show of selecting me, his gloved finger aiming at various members of the audience, some of whom squirmed out of the way as if the finger alone had magical properties.

"You!" he shouted.

I lowered my hand as the boys whined in disappointment.

"We do not know each other, correct?" he said, lightly holding my fingers.

"We don't."

"And you are from this town?" he asked.

I saw familiar faces in the audience, dirt streaked and haggard.

"He goes to my school!" a boy named Arthur yelled.

"Fantastic. If you will take your place over there, I will navigate to the opposite side. After our journey through time and space we shall return, our positions reversed."

He placed his hand on my spine in between my shoulder blades and nudged. I stumbled into the compartment. As I turned to face the audience the door closed. It smelled of pine and earth. I inhaled through flared nostrils. Had there been no audience I would have burst free and run. I decided, chest rising and falling, that I did not want to experience *real* magic firsthand. I wanted to be at home, a wind-weathered, dust-filled shack on the precipice of hell.

He spoke the words, the unfamiliar language, soundin' as if there was pebbles in his throat.

Then my world expired.

I must take a moment to describe the darkness, as only a blind person could ever truly understand it. It was not dark. It was nothin'. I have been in a dark room in a dark house. I have hidden under my pillow and under the blankets. Even then I could see the faint glow of the pillowcase. There was nothin'. If you traveled to the remotest corner of the Universe and saw the glint of light from a single, rogue star ejected from its galaxy it would have been brighter.

I was aware my feet were wet, as if I had the misfortune of steppin' into two separate puddles. I reached out my arms, unable to see them, then fell into the ankle-deep water.

"Hello?"

Strong hands snaked behind my arms, liftin' me up until I stood again.

"Do not worry, my boy. You still have your eyes. Go ahead and feel them if you like."

"Dr. Vanesco?"

"The very same. Now, to the matter of seeing something you have never seen before…"

"Wh-where are we?"

He patted my back and I could tell he was smilin' by the shape of his words as he formed them.

"I told you the trick did not make sense. Is it magic? Not for me to say. But, here we are, as others have been before you."

"*Where* are we!" I demanded.

He cleared his throat, "We are nowhere. We are in the *never was*. We are outside of time, outside of reason, outside of sanity. On the edge of possibility, yet we are nowhere."

"H-how do we get back?"

"In good time, my boy. But for now, a choice."

He released his grip on me and sloshed away a few paces.

"I will grant what you wanted. I will show you something you have never before seen. Tell me where. Tell me when. Your only limitation is your knowledge of the Universe. There is no restriction, but there is a stipulation. The first one is free. The next one will cost you."

I had never before seen a mountain, only black and white pictures and a few paintings in a book. I had never seen a body of water bigger than a pond. My teenaged mind reminded me of tales in adventure books, of jungles where the native girls wore banana leaf skirts and nothin' else. But, in that moment, I only wanted the magic to end.

"Home."

"Home?"

"Yes," I whispered.

We were not transported. I mean, there was no rush of wind. Not a single greasy hair on my head twitched. I was in my house again. It was evenin', almost night. Compared to the absolute nothingness I came from it was blindin', the sickle moon and glow from beneath my mother's bedroom door the only sources of light. I sprinted to the door and watched my hand pass through the knob.

"You aren't really home, my boy," Dr. Vanesco whispered in my ear.

"Mama!" I yelled, breaching the door like a specter.

The blankets moved and shadows danced on the walls and ceiling. The lantern on her bedside table flickered, the flame weak.

"Mama?"

"She cannot hear you. You are not really here," Dr. Vanesco said as if speaking to a toddler.

The blankets were cast onto the floor and I saw a man's back as he rose to his knees. My mother's pale legs gripped his hips.

"Dad?"

Her hands spread into claws, the nails digging into the meat of his shoulders. The name she moaned was not my father's name. Dr. Vanesco jumped in front of me and waved his arms.

"A fluke! A fluke!" he said, then snapped his fingers.

Back in the void. I was sightless again and reachin' for purchase.

"Mama..." I whispered.

The man sighed and patted my arm.

"She does get lonely. Do not judge her too harshly, my boy. Tell you what, I'll give you the next one for free. But everything after that, if you're interested, will cost double."

I barely heard him, but must have muttered in the affirmative.

"What would you like to see? A planet where dinosaurs still roam? There is such a place. Dragons? None that breathe fire, but impressive nonetheless. The future. The past. They're all in play."

I should have been more interested. But what did it matter if it was but a fleeting glimpse? I would walk home that night to face my mother and pretend to know nothing of her betrayal. We would wither in that house, and I would hate her every minute of it.

"Listen closely, my boy. The next trip through reality is free. If you wish to see more you must tell me so in explicit terms. Every additional minute you spend in the vision, seeing whatever it is you wish to see, you forfeit a year of your life to me. Two years, actually, per the terms of our bargain."

The words did not echo in the space we occupied, but they repeated in my mind.

"What do you mean?"

"This opportunity comes with a price. But, you do not have to worry, my boy. Just tell me you are done while it is still free and you will walk out onto the Texas grass to the cheers of your friends. If not, well, just know that life is long, and you won't miss a year or two of it. Not really."

Dinosaurs. Dragons. Topless native women. They would all be memories. They would fade with time until, as a grown man, I questioned whether or not the experience actually happened. I needed something practical. Something I could hold onto.

"Show me my greatest mistake in life," I said.

Dr. Vanesco, smilin' again said, "My boy, you could not have chosen better than that."

"Is this a joke?" I spat.

The calliope music served as a backdrop, peppered with outbursts of delight from children who were usually in bed by then. I watched myself retrieve the pocket change as Dr. Vanesco stood over me. Was I really so thin and filthy?

"It is interesting, isn't it?" he answered.

There was a tightness to his voice, like a guitar string stretched to its limit.

"I don't find it interestin'. This happened an hour ago. How can this be my life's greatest mistake?"

"Well, that would be a *new* question now, wouldn't it? I can show you the answer, but at the cost I discussed."

"One minute for one year?"

"Two years, as *this* vision was free of charge. My apologies for having to see your mother like that previously."

I had no real hands to ball into fists. He had no real body for me to strike. I imagined even a glancing blow would reduce his thin beak of a nose to mush. But he was in control, not me. Despite the hatred brewin' in my belly I did not think him a liar.

"What if I want to see ten things in one minute? Six seconds per trip? Would that work?"

"It would…" he said, the octave of the final word rising as if he was unsure.

What was a year? What was two years? It would be the difference between living to seventy-eight and living to eighty. I did not imagine I would die as a healthy and robust man at eighty. It might even relieve

197

some of the burden of aging.

"Let's do it."

"As you wish."

We were back in the darkness, my hands pawin' at the air again.

"Time is strange here, my boy. More of a concept, a possibility. I cannot claim to understand the science. My guess is that science doesn't really apply. It is possible ten years have passed at the fair, that the audience in that tent got up and left when they realized you and I were not coming back. I wager a few would have inspected the compartments, looked for a hidden panel. Yet, I know this is not what has happened. I am tethered to that place."

"Tethered?"

"You cannot see me, but I am tapping my head. I can feel it there. Our reality. It doesn't really matter to the journey you are about to take, but I wanted you to know."

"So, what question do I ask?"

"The simpler the better. If you begin to introduce variables it can make the journey…less certain."

I skimmed my shoe over the water I could not see.

"What happens in my future that I would look back and think of this experience as my greatest mistake? What's the first thing?"

"A fine question. Simply tell me to stop and we will return to this place. Let us see what the Universe has in store."

I did not have to sprint through a door to get to my mother's room. I was already there. The man on the bed was smaller of frame. A new man I imagined. The shadows on the wall flailed in concert with the movement of his limbs, the flame of my mother's lamp having dwindled to barely a flicker. As I watched I attempted to work the math. How many days did I sacrifice for each second?

She was not moanin' as before, but she was thrashing at the small man atop her...

"What's goin' on?"

The shirt was familiar, the sweat rings around the collar. The hair, hidden within shadows, was likely the same dirt brown as mine. I could have stood next to this man at the carnival, never knowin'.

"What is this? When does this happen?"

She did not moan because she could not. The man's hands were wrapped around her throat, the veins of his forearms like little garden snakes. She lifted an arm to defend herself but it fell uselessly back to the bed. My arm was just as useless as I attempted to push the man off of my mother. Her eyes swelled, filling with blood.

"I can provide no insight. You may watch the scene play out if you wish," Dr. Vanesco said.

"Is this happening now?"

"You may watch-"

"Show me the next one! Show me why tonight was a mistake! Next!"

"Very well."

I lost track of the time. It was three minutes. Five minutes at the most. It felt like seconds. At the end, when I'd seen enough, Dr. Vanesco returned us to the darkness.

"Well, *that* was interesting, was it not?" he said.

I shook my head because I could do nothing else. There was vomit on my chin, but I did not remember throwing up. I was powerless, in the dark, unable to comprehend what I witnessed.

"Now, as for our arrangement…"

The water sloshed as he paced around me.

"You owe me eight years, give or take a week."

"Eight…"

"Give or take a week. Also, I might not have explained the process fully, but well enough. For example, I will take my eight years now. You might have thought you would simply die eight years earlier in life. Some sort of alchemy or spell, right? Most people think that. Not true, unfortunately for you. The Universe functions on balance. We cannot leave here, you with a debt of eight years and I with a surplus of the same amount. I will take your years from you and you will simply *be*. Here, in the dark."

His fingers coiled around my arms and he pressed his dry lips to mine. I do not know what happened in that moment, but it felt as if everything within me shriveled as he inhaled, as if my body was a cigarette and what he left behind was ash. He stole more than the breath from my lungs. I collapsed into the water.

"Thank you, my boy. I feel *renewed*. Do remember what I told you about time in this place? Eight years can feel like a lifetime. And now, for my final trick, just for *you*, I will stop time."

He snapped his fingers, and then I was alone.

"Hello?"

I spoke the word with hope, though my voice was but a whisper. I spoke the word a thousand times after that with nearly the same level of it. There was no response then. No response thereafter, not even an echo of my voice.

I was alone in a place outside of reality, a place of darkness without walls or limits, without a ceiling and with no texture other than the unseen liquid sloshin' 'round my ankles. After I spoke the word a thousand times I spoke it a thousand more. I walked with my fingers outstretched, searchin', searchin' for anything. I probed beneath the water and felt nothin', no surface. I was surrounded by nothing, and it extended to forever.

Even without a clock it's possible to notice the passage of time. Light and darkness. Using a longer scale, the changin' of seasons. The migration of birds fleein' a northern winter for warmer climes. There are many points of reference. Hunger. Hair growth. Sowin' and harvestin'.

I had none of 'em. It was only ever dark. I was never hungry, and nothing' 'bout my body changed. No hair growth or stubble. I couldn't sleep even if I managed to find a comfortable position in the shallow water. I did try. I stripped off my clothes and balled 'em into a pillow, but it sank until the water pooled in my ears, trickled into the canal. Though I tried I felt no need for sleep.

There are no words in any language to describe the feeling of that place. *Isolated* was how I felt on the farm sometimes, Dad gone off to make a nickel doin' dime's work. Mama followed a broom around the house as if it was leadin' her to salvation. A fella marooned on an island had at least grains of sand to pass from one hand to the other, the constellations to look forward to each night.

Scared? A person lost in a cave knew there was an entrance. Even if he couldn't reach it his search wasn't hopeless. Stranded on a deserted island? You can still see the sky. I had no sand, just the dirt beneath my nails. Even my money was gone, havin' slipped through the hole in my pants when I accidentally placed it in the wrong pocket. I had only the memory of stars. And, for me, the search for an entrance or an exit was only ever hopeless. There was no beginnin' and no end to that place. It just *was*.

Madness? Yes, I was quite mad. With no reality to grip my mind created its own. I saw and heard things in the dark. Never pleasant. I did not see loved ones or my dog, Rusty. I saw pale shapes, far, far away, like glowing worms. Of course, distance was just a word. It meant nothin'. They might have been very close and very small. No matter. They were not real.

I heard the rush of blood through my veins and arteries, a constant whir. And sometimes, clear as a church bell, I heard the carnival music.

Eight years.

If it had only been eight years.

The magician said time was strange in that place. That is too soft a word for it. Time was not strange. There was no time. From the moment we vanished inside of our pine boxes to the moment he abandoned me in the dark twenty minutes might have passed. But, I had seen the trick performed before. In the tent it was only about thirty seconds. *Maybe* thirty seconds. Just enough for people to start squirmin' in their seats. Then Dr. Vanesco burst through the door and the volunteer opposite him emerged.

Dennis. That was the boy last year. He was in my grade and I desperately wanted to know the secret of the trick. I looked for him after the performance, but never saw him again after that night. He and his family joined the caravan of exiles headed for Bakersfield. I recalled his eyes, how he shielded them from the subdued light of the tent, open mouth as if to scream. As the tepid applause began he pressed his hands to his ears. He was afraid. Terrified. Haunted.

For me, twenty minutes passed here before Dr. Vanesco vanished. I had eight years. Eight years in a place where time did not exist. Eight years that might equal thousands of years. How many years did he steal from Dennis? What I could not figure out, despite all the time to think about it, was where Dr. Vanesco went.

Over the time the years, the decades, my memories of home, of my life before the *never was* lost form and color. I attempted to recall my mother's face but only saw a smudge with hair the tint of an old penny. My father was a ghost in denim overalls. I forgot their faces, forgot the names of things. My whole world, the one inside my head, began the night of the carnival. I could have written a book about Gracie's straw-colored hair. I froze her in place and counted the strands, recalled the dimples of her cheeks so deep they could have held acorns with room to spare. But, I forgot her too, in time.

I didn't forget the sound of my mother's last, choked breath. I didn't forget the way her arm collapsed, like the branch of a sapling heavy with snow. I didn't forget the hands that crushed her neck or where I was taken to next. The screams. Each time I shouted *next* I was taken to a new horror, seconds and then fractions of a second between each journey.

I did not forget what I saw last.

No new information came to me. No new words. Ideas that might have felt new drew from the same, shallow well. But, I did leave with new knowledge. I had years, hundreds of years in the dark, and only the contents of my mind. I forgot the trivial things, the taste of salt, the scent of rain upon the parched earth, faces of people I loved. I did not forget what mattered, in the end.

I didn't understand the light when I first saw it. Just a sliver, a band of yellow in the distance. I saw many things in the dark, many false hopes. The face of Jesus until I could no longer recall the painting from church, Gracie with a bucket of popcorn until I couldn't shape her ghostly form into anythin' recognizable as human. It had been years, decades since my hope manifested as one of these mirages.

It didn't disappear but grew larger as I neared. The light seared my eyes. I closed them and touched the wood of the door with my fingertips. I heard the nervous chatter, library quiet but deafening to me. I nudged the door open and stepped through it.

"There he is!" Arthur yelled.

I fell to my knees but was quickly hoisted to my feet.

"Welcome back, my boy. Been a long time, hasn't it?" Dr. Vanesco said.

I was a different person. I was hardly a person. I was hate wrapped in human skin.

I lumbered out of the tent as Dr. Vanesco thanked the collection of filthy, decrepit townsfolk for being such a good audience. I walked home without thinking about it. My mind forgot the route but my feet had not.

My mother was asleep in the room, her lover recently departed and the air reekin' of her treachery. The flame of the bedside lamp was low, barely a flicker. She was the first person my hands touched in hundreds of years. The veins in my forearms popped as I squeezed her neck, like little garden snakes. Her arm drew a lazy circle in the air, then fell to the bed as I knew it would. I squeezed after her body stilled. I squeezed until the muscles in my arms spasmed, the strength finally leavin' my fingers.

I sat on the bed as her body cooled beside me. I was glad to have done it. Had she only been asleep when I first followed Dr. Vanesco through time and space my life would have continued along its normal path. Had she been sweepin' her useless piles of dirt I would not have been granted an opportunity for a second journey.

I wished only that I could experience it again. Her eyes, the same color as mine, brimmin' with tears turnin' red as capillaries burst, understandin' it was me who did it but not knowin' why. Not knowin' I was trapped in purgatory for longer than she could imagine. Couldn't experience it with her again, but there'd be others.

There were others. Women who, when they disappeared no one really noticed. I knew their faces when I 'em, because I saw those faces in the *never was* hundreds of years ago for me but just a blip in the real world, the visions of what was to come. It was never as satisfyin' as with Mom.

The fault was not entirely hers. No, her crime was one of many teeth of a gear already set into motion, turned by another man's hand. Dr. Vanesco vanished, not in the fanciful way he'd done in that tent. He was simply gone.

The carnival meandered through broken cities, squeezed the final few pennies from calloused hands of men desperate to wring life from soil dry as brick. I meandered behind it, adjustin' to the feeling of the sun on my neck and the sound of trains thunderin' over tracks. If I gained anythin' from my time in the dark it was the peaceful acceptance that God, as the Bible described Him at least, did not exist. No God of the Bible could design such a Universe. I peered behind the curtain and there was no director.

Therefore, I felt no guilt at the lives that ended at my hands. So many last breaths blown through cracked lips into my face. So many eyes beggin' that same question of me. Carin' less about *what* was happenin' than *why. Why me?*

It was ages ago the magician guided me through time. I didn't believe or understand the offer then, and in my panic, I began to scream. *Next! Next! Next!* The last half-dozen victims were a blur, but not the final one. I don't believe Dr. Vanesco was in a position to see, to understand before I ended our time together and began my sentence in the dark.

I found him in Pueblo, Colorado. The carnival was on its last legs and purged attractions to save money. Dr. Vanesco's poorly attended magic show was the first to go. He was in a hotel on the outskirts of town.

I rapped my knuckles across the door, paint flakin' away in thin shards. It had been months, possibly years since the magic show. But, he knew me the moment he opened the door. His smile twitched beneath his ridiculous, curled mustache.

"My boy! You have grown, haven't you!"

He wore a white shirt, the collar browned from sweat. His underwear hung loose around thin, bone-white legs. His knee-length black dress socks completed the ensemble.

"Before you get any-"

His voice was watery. On the bedside table was a small hill of handkerchiefs, many spotted with brown and red. I raised a hand to cut

206

him off.

"Why don't you just take it? The time? The years? Why don't you just take them from people?"

He nodded but did not leave the door, likely wantin' to make a quick exit if needed.

"Belief, my boy. It doesn't work if you do not believe it will. The show is necessary. I need them to believe before…"

It was a possibility I considered during my time in the dark.

"Why not just take the years and send me on my way? Why did I have to stay there?"

My hands flexed inside the pockets of my trousers. I needed no other weapons.

"As I said, and you may have forgotten, it is because of balance. If I took your eight years and we both reappeared back in the tent it would put a great, big target on my back. The Universe knows. The Universe finds a way to correct itself. We had to come back the same as we departed. I did take your years and had a wonderful time with them."

"Where?"

"Where? Many places. When? Many times."

The room indicated the sad place to which the magician had come. His props were loaded into crates stacked against a wall. His once meticulously cared for suit was draped over the back of a chair, holes in the knees. The red carnation on his lapel was nearly black, the petals mostly stripped. And then there were the handkerchiefs.

As I absorbed these details I heard a click and looked toward the door. Dr. Vanesco stood in front of it hands behind his back.

"Come to finish me off, is that it?" he said, closin' the distance between us by a few paces.

"Yes, to put it simply."

"Saw it on your journey? Saw lots of nasty things, am I right?"

My heel struck the leg of the bed.

"Necessary things."

"And now it's my turn? Well, you could not have come at a better time."

I glanced at the handkerchiefs again. A bit of drool trickled from the corner of his mouth and coursed through the stubble of a three-day beard. I pulled my hands free from my pockets.

His eyes shone with not madness, but delight.

I lunged.

He snapped his fingers.

I fell and crashed into the water.

It was pitch black.

He laughed somewhere behind me.

"Thought you saw my end in your little vision? Thought it went by too quickly for me to notice?"

"Wait!"

"I told you the Universe has a way of creating balance. Well, I tried my hand again and lost. It's so difficult to convince people now. They've lost so much that was *real* it's tough to *imagine* other possibilities. I got careless," he said, coughing wetly.

"No, not-"

"When I die back there, which should be soon, you will be here. Forever."

"Please I-"

"All because you believed in magic."

He snapped his fingers again.

I see new things in the dark now. Faces. My mother's, usually, but many others. They speak to me. They whisper. They shout. I have tried to take my life, but this place will not let me. I have tried to drown in the water. I have attempted to bludgeon myself. Nothin' changes.

I'll walk for what might be a decade in your world, hoping to find a crease or a seam. A tear in the fabric of reality. If death was on the other side I would happily pass through it. Sometimes it feels like I am gettin' close to something, and I'll raise my arms to touch it. But the feelin' passes and I continue on.

The carnival was centuries ago, but I can still hear the music. I recreate the sound as best I can, because I have forgotten all other songs.

When I was a boy my mother sat me down at our kitchen table. She said if I ever got lost to find an adult and tell them either my house number or my grandpa's.

"What are the numbers again, so the adult can help you?"

"Um, 37415 or 66475."

"That's right, my boy. And, don't forget it!"

Funny what you remember and what you don't. Remember those numbers but forgot a lot of other things. Things that *felt* important, I think. Gets so that I don't know what's real and imagined. Been tellin' myself this story for a long time, longer than I care to guess. And I'll keep doin' it 'til another door opens or the Universe ends.

What if, a voice says in the back of my mind, *what if the Universe ends and you're still here?*

The Nightmare Room

The man strolled into The Nightmare Room on a Tuesday evening. By the look of him, he had come directly from the municipal airport, likely flying on a private jet. His rumpled suit was charcoal gray and a bit snug around his midsection. I draped a dishtowel over my shoulder as the door swung shut and the shaft of orange sunlight on the floor expired.

I squinted through the perpetual haze of cigarette smoke. There were no smokers in the bar at the time. The Nightmare Room is many things, but well-ventilated is not among them.

East coast I thought.

It was always one of the coasts.

The man sucked his teeth, watery green eyes dancing with acute disinterest over the artifacts on the wall. He wore his indifference like armor, a barrier between him and the less important people he might encounter during the day. He adjusted his tie, mostly for effect, then stepped fully into the room pulling his small, wheeled suitcase behind.

I smiled at the juxtaposition of this man in his expensive suit and his surroundings. The Nightmare Room was the definition of kitsch. Posters adorned nearly every square inch of the walls. Leatherface, victim half-hidden by his considerable bulk, butted up against a gore-splattered advertisement for Sleepaway Camp. Flat screen televisions occupied the remaining space, one playing Plan Nine from Outer Space on a loop and the others cycling through every sub-genre of horror imaginable.

The Nightmare Room was also a cultural touchstone for our small community in the shadow of the Rocky Mountains. It was the place many of the younger residents enjoyed their first sip of alcohol. Some nights the bar was overrun by gaggles of glittery bridesmaids, the bride-to-be draped in penis-themed plastic accoutrements. Other nights, a couple dozen Harleys sat out front and the smell of sun baked leather overpowered the stench of tobacco and spilled beer. The dance floor of alternating black and white tiles was about the size of a standard bedroom, small by most standards. For this town, though, it was perfect.

There were only two people in the bar on that day, a husband and wife munching deep-fried appetizers, their faces caressed by the white-glow of their cell phone screens. They were regulars and mistakenly thought it was trivia night. Neither looked up when the man approached the bar, his dismissive scrutiny of the establishment complete. His opinion manifested on his face in the form of a curled upper lip.

"This *is* The Nightmare Room, correct?" he spoke, voice drowned beneath the crunch of industrial rock music.

I turned my head so that the man could speak into my ear.

"This is The Nightmare Room?" his voice a bit less certain.

I cocked my head, one eyebrow lifted.

The man glanced at the fixtures on the wall, the various movies playing on TV screens, as if to reassure himself. Perhaps the stories had not been true. Perhaps he had been sent across the country for nothing.

I smiled, "I'm fucking with you. Yes, it is. John, owner-operator. What can I get you?"

I passed a laminated menu across the bar.

The man smiled and cleared his throat.

"I think I'm looking for something off the menu."

I nodded, "Reference?"

The man withdrew a slip of paper from the inner pocket of his jacket, folded it in half, then handed it to me.

"I'll need your identification as well," I said as I read the name on the paper "Hm. Wouldn't have guessed Gary would have any friends."

The man held the driver's license to his chest.

"This *is* anonymous, correct?"

"Anonymous? Yes. But *I* still need to know who you are."

The man shot a quick glance at the couple at the opposite end of the bar.

"It's just, my reputation…"

"Gary sent you, didn't he? Wouldn't you say he is in an important man?"

"Yes, it's just…"

"Aren't you here based on his recommendation?"

The man tugged at his collar. We operate by reservation except for Tuesdays, which are a first come first serve basis. My only requirement is a reference from an existing client in good standing.

I plucked the driver's license from the man's hand and read the name.

"Listen, Samuel Carpenter, of Samca Integrated Solutions, correct?"

The man nodded slowly, as if he thought he was being set up.

"Listen, Samuel, you're in the right place. You *are* early, however. Let me pour you a drink and cook up some food for you. We start at midnight on the nose. No sooner. Don't bother asking."

The power dynamic had shifted. Samuel nodded, unable to maintain eye contact with me. Samuel Carpenter, founder and CEO of Samca Integrated Solutions, was a self-made billionaire. He was among the youngest to ever cross that threshold. He retrieved the menu and scurried to the nearest booth.

I squinted at him. He seemed to have shrunk by half a foot since he first walked into the bar.

He'll order a burger and fries. He'll eat them separately.

Samuel removed his coat and glanced about, unsure of what to do with it. His white dress shirt bore half-moons of sweat beneath the armpits. He fidgeted with his tie and relieved the top button of his dress shirt, which restored some of the natural color to his face. He folded the coat in half and placed it on his lap. I let him wallow in his discomfort for a few minutes further. He retrieved his cell phone but soon returned it to his pocket, feigning interest in the movies playing on various screens.

"What'll you have?" I asked, my pad of paper ready.

"Oh," he picked up the menu again, "Just a burger and fries. Diet Coke to drink, please."

"Sure thing, Sam," I said.

I retreated to the kitchen to drop a patty on the griddle and toss some fries in oil. Our food is good, but that's not why men like Samuel Carpenter come to The Nightmare Room. hey certainly don't come for trivia night either. There is something different about this place, something special, just like the town itself.

I peeked my head back in the bar and saw that Sam was now alone. His eyes darted from screen to screen, and he glanced over his shoulder at the door every fifteen or so seconds. The couple at the bar left a crumpled twenty-dollar bill, which brought my tip to about $1.18 if my quick math was correct.

What is The Nightmare Room? To most it is a place to grab a cold beer after work, to watch a monster movie marathon, or to dance on a Friday or Saturday night. To someone like Sam, though, it was a place to become someone else, and not in the way a recently divorced dad on the dancefloor might after a few shots of Jack. I wondered what someone Sam wanted to be. I had my suspicions. He was not the first thirty-something self-made billionaire to sit in that very booth.

I flipped the patty and dropped a slice of American cheese on it. He had not specified which type of cheese he wanted, but I knew. I wiped my hands on the dishtowel, slung it over my shoulder, and returned to the bar. Sam smiled as I approached with his Diet Coke in hand.

"So, what kind of experience do you want tonight?" I asked, taking a seat across from him.

He sat a little taller.

"I don't really know," he confessed, glancing over his shoulder again.

"What were you told?"

He cleared his throat and leaned a few inches closer.

"That you could do *anything* here. Literally anything. And no consequences."

I nodded, "It's true. You can. Did Gary tell you how it works?"

"I'm not sure he understood it himself. He did tell me about his experience, though."

"Oh yes. Gary had fun. He's been back three times if memory serves. I enjoy watching his scenarios."

Sam frowned, "You watch?"

"I have to. Liability. Just because nothing has ever gone wrong doesn't mean nothing ever will. Would not be a good look for me to have a billionaire die in my place."

He reclined and heavy metal, blaring at a reasonable volume, occupied the space between us.

"You *have* to watch?"

I held my hands up.

"I've seen everything, Sam. You name it. There's nothing you could ask for that would surprise me. No recordings. No video. Just me. My lips are sealed. That's a good portion of what you're paying for."

I slid out of the booth.

"Be back in a second with your food," I said.

He nodded but his eyes were fixed at some point in the distance.

"So, how does it work?" he asked, a strand of melted cheese plastered to his chin.

They always ask that question and I have yet to develop a sufficient response. It is second nature to me, as effortless a process as digesting my food. I don't think about it. It just happens.

"Well, Sam, I can tell you that I don't think it *would* work anywhere other than here. A lot happens here that shouldn't," I said, prompting him to ask a question that would divert the conversation.

"Oh, yeah? Like what?" he asked.

His fries were untouched, ushered to the opposite side of the plate from his burger.

"I could tell you stories, but you're not paying me for that. A couple of things come to mind, however. Every May 23rd it rains from the ground up. It only lasts a minute or so, but it happens without fail. Last week I stepped into the walk-in freezer to grab some pizza dough and walked out of the freezer into a candy store three blocks away. Startled a man stealing candy straws by stuffing them into his underwear."

He nodded, cheeks fat with meat.

"Any reason you can think of?"

"I grew up here, so it's a pretty normal existence for me. By saying that I mean I don't really think about it that often. It's just the way things are and always have been. But, I think reality is thin here. Like when you were a kid and you slid your jeans in the grass so much that the fabric wears. Maybe it is human suffering that has worn the fabric of reality. I don't know."

The monster smacked the base of bottle of ketchup, painting his fries in the stuff. He didn't have the decency to dip.

There were no other customers that evening. A woman walked inside, scoffed at the décor, and about-faced out of the building. I closed out the cash register, which did not include the $50,000 Sam paid me for his experience, and washed the few dishes that remained. By eleven o'clock I was killing time, restocking items at random.

At eleven-thirty I rejoined Sam in his booth.

"So, regarding the experience, I have some standard options for first-timers."

Sam's face was flush and he licked his lips in increasingly brief intervals.

"Like what?" he asked.

"I think a horror movie scenario is a good introduction. It's a familiar setting but still gives you that adrenaline rush."

His eyes darted to Plan Nine and he frowned.

"No one ever chooses that one," I said.

"I'm just anxious to get started. I have some ideas, but I'll let you guide me. Can I be the bad guy, though?"

I chuckled, "No one ever chooses the victim, Sam. That would end the scenario too quickly. Which bad guy did you have in mind?"

His eyes darted from the screens to the posters.

"Him," he said, nodding toward Leatherface.

Texas Chainsaw was a popular request, though as an experience it was a bit lackluster. Fans of the movie know the violence was mostly implied. Clients always had the option to go off-script, however, which has led to some very entertaining alternate scenes.

"Sure thing, Sam."

At about five minutes before midnight I escorted Sam into the bowels of the building. The door to the *experience* room was nondescript, a mirror of the supply closet door on the opposite side of the hallway. The sensation flowed through me, like warm bath water filling my insides.

"Do I have to get changed?" he asked as I opened the door.

"No, Sam, everything is provided. Give me a second."

I closed my eyes and sucked in air until my lungs ached. The particles floating in the atmosphere coalesced as I imagined the world we would enter. The walls of the room dissipated and the warmth inside of me spiked momentarily, then cooled until it matched my body temperature. Light dazzled our eyes as the sizzling Texas sun roasted our necks. Sam's tailored suit was gone, replaced by a blood splattered apron over a short-sleeved buttoned shirt. It was an improvement in my eyes, as the suit made him seem like a child playing businessman. He hefted

218

the chainsaw up with a grunt of effort and inspected it. I doubt he had ever seen one outside of the movies.

"Amazing," he said.

I stood at the entrance to the room.

"This is your reality now, Sam. You can walk into those hills for forever if you want. It's up to you. The walls are gone. You can kill indiscriminately. You can go take a shit in the woods. You can make some fries and dump ketchup on them like a barbarian. The scenario starts in two minutes. You can act it out or you can explore. Think of it as an open-world video game. Nothing that happens to you is permanent, but don't be a moron and cut your own head off or something."

Sam stepped forward, the inertia of the chainsaw propelling him a few additional feet. I retreated and closed the door, which disappeared in his world, then stepped a few paces away to my booth. I sat on the plastic lawn chair, the brittle legs flexing beneath my weight. I can afford better but had once fallen asleep in a more comfortable chair during a client's experience and the entire apparatus depends on my mind. That client, a fading pop star with a suppressed sexual orientation, was trapped in an orgy imbued with the evolving textures of my nightmare. For three hours he was chased by a college wrestling team (his request) with canon-sized, carnivorous penises (my nightmare).

I watched Sam from four different perspectives on four screens. These are also powered by my mind, though I can't explain how. I think of it as a projection of my imagination. Instead of seeing something with my mind's eye it plays on the screens.

"You bitch," I whispered as the asshole knocked before he went inside the infamous Texas Chainsaw house.

219

I have been able to manipulate reality for as long as I can remember. Like many other children, I once had an imaginary friend. Only, my friend was not imaginary. I willed him into existence. At the age of three my favorite book was <u>Where the Wild Things Are</u>. When my mother discovered me in the bathtub soaping up a monster the size of a small buffalo she fainted almost instantly.

Over the years I evolved my talent and devised a way to monetize it. I have an idea of how it works but no manner in which to test the theory. Matter, in its most minute fragments, is essentially the same. A tree and the soil from which it grows are comprised of the same particles, just arranged differently. Reality, then is like a massive puzzle. Rearrange the pieces and you get a different picture. I rearrange reality. I was born knowing how to do it.

Try explaining *walking* as if your audience was unaware of it. Easy, one foot in front of the other, right? Well, how does that one foot get off the ground? Which muscles do you activate and in what order? How do you disperse the weight across the foot evenly? Sculpting reality is as easy as walking to me. I just can't explain it very well.

Sam strolled through the house as if he was in a museum. I mentally projected an extra couple of pounds of weight onto the chainsaw and he eventually left it on the floor.

I switched the display on one of the four screens so that it now showed Sam's vitals as well as a three-dimensional image of his brain. There was a knock at the door and his amygdala flared while his heartrate accelerated. I paused the entire scenario except for Sam.

"Sam," I projected my voice into his reality.

He looked up at the ceiling.

"Are you familiar with the movie? I can guide you through each

220

scene or you can do your own thing."

I restarted the scenario and the knock sounded again. Sam retrieved his unnaturally heavy chainsaw and pulled the chord. It sputtered to life noisily and issued a puff of smoke.

"I thought so," I muttered as he stomped toward the front door.

His first attempt at a kill was a miniature catastrophe. The chainsaw missed its target and bored into the woman's arm just below the shoulder. Blood and flecks of bone exploded from the wound as she screamed and fled, slowly, so that he could catch her. Sam tripped in his pursuit and the chainsaw plunged into the earth. He farted audibly as he regained his footing. I stopped the blonde with the ragged arm while he collected himself, but his attention was drawn to another target.

The young man in the wheelchair begged for mercy as Sam descended upon him.

"Give me the mask! I want the mask!" Sam yelled.

I conjured it for him, but imbued it with the slightest scent of shit, which he did not seem to notice.

"No, please!" the man in the wheelchair pleaded, shielding his face with his hands.

"Now I am become death," Sam gurgled through the mask.

I groaned in the booth.

Sam revved the chainsaw and buried it in the man's stomach. Blood and viscera splattered Sam's apron as his victim squealed and writhed. A vermillion river flowed from the dying man's mouth.

The chainsaw's engine stopped. The cutting chain was clogged with organ meat and chunks of rib. The victim returned from the brink of death to make awkward eye contact with his killer.

"Um," Sam said, squeezing the throttle again.

He looked up, "Little help?"

"Oh goddammit," I muttered and cleared the gore from the chain.

One hour and fifty-five minutes later Sam's universe evaporated and he stood in a featureless room, out of breath but otherwise unchanged from when he first stepped foot inside. I turned off the monitors, left the booth, and opened the door for him.

His eyes were as wide and bright as cymbals, "I want to do it again."

"I'll check the schedule, but I believe the next availability for regulars is a month from now."

We stepped into the hallway.

"I'll pay double. I'll pay triple."

I shook my head.

"Doesn't work that way, Sam. I have to be fair to my other clients. Some are wealthier than you, by the way."

"Fine. Fine. But what else can I do?"

"Well, now that you're a regular, so to speak, we can expand our options. I can create a world with you using your mind. If there is something you want to experience that I am not familiar with we can build it together. We can make you the most popular kid in your high school. You can score the winning touchdown for your football team."

We stepped into the main body of The Nightmare Room. He finally asked the question that had been burning the tip of his tongue.

"Can I have sex?"

"Yes, with anyone you could legally have sex with in real life as my only stipulation."

"Amazing."

He traced his bloated fingers over his face, searching for dried blood which was not there.

"Oh, one more thing," he said as he retrieved his luggage, "Can I have a to-go cup for my Diet Coke?"

That motherfucker.

Over the next few months Sam became my most persistent client, not my best client, just relentless. He booked every opening I allowed and somehow always knew when another client canceled. On more than one occasion, the wire transfer I received from him was my first indication that the scheduled client would not make it. He alternated between murdering and fucking, and once had himself elected President with Carmen Electra, of all people, as his First Lady.

Samca Integrated Solutions' stock soared as its founder distracted himself with his various alternate guises within The Nightmare Room. When he wasn't in the room he was thinking about it. The stock was up by twenty percent, which inflated his bank account by another billion or so dollars. I should not have been surprised when the check arrived along with his demand.

John,

I have a special request for my next experience. I know you have previously dismissed this entreaty from me, but ask again in the hope that you will allow me to find closure for a painful part of my childhood. My younger sister passed away when I was thirteen. She was a couple of weeks shy of her ninth birthday, and she was also my best friend.

The manner of her passing is a mystery to our family. No satisfactory investigation took place as her wounds were consistent with a fall down the stairs. I would like to visit with her again. For this scenario, however, I respectfully request privacy. If you are willing to not watch, just this once, the money is yours.

Your Faithful Client,

Sam

The check was for five-hundred million dollars. A big deal until you consider it was less than half of what he made doing nothing.

I agreed to his condition, and it was not the money that made me do so. I was rich by any standard and had no real use for the additional funds. It's never been about money for me. The reason I accepted the condition was because he unintentionally left a loophole and I was curious.

Sam arrived at two in the afternoon and was apparently emulating, in dress, his appearance from the era of his childhood he wished to revisit. The Ren and Stimpy t-shirt was two sizes too small for him, and his belly was intermittently visible if he lifted his arms above waist-height. He took a seat in a remote, dark corner of the bar and ordered his usual.

When I checked on him an hour later the cheeseburger and fries were untouched. The fries were betrayed in typical fashion, however, growing soggy beneath narrow bands of ketchup. His mood did not match the tenor of his letter. He was not somber or sullen. He vibrated with excitement.

It was karaoke night and Sam's agitation at having to share the space with so many people grew by the minute. He paced the room with his hands behind his back, often pausing by the bar to flash his wristwatch at me.

"It's fine," I mouthed.

He marched away with that robotic, ineloquent walk of his. The night's third rendition of "Africa" by Toto, this time sung by three young

225

ladies at once, washed over him with no effect. He did not even nod his head. Sam found his booth, retreated within it, and gulped from his fourth Diet Coke of the night.

The Nightmare Room cleared by eleven and Sam followed like a forlorn specter as I closed the bar, hovering so near I felt his breath on the back of my neck. None of my employees stay past eight. I need a buffer between the business as most understand it and the true Nightmare Room, which exists from midnight until two in the morning.

I cut the power to the stereo system, the final crunching guitar riff portending silence that pressed upon my ears.

"Jesus!" I whisper-shouted, unaware that Sam stood directly behind me as I closed out the cash register.

"Is it time?" he asked, pink tongue darting lizard-like between his lips.

"You've been showing me your watch every goddamn half hour. You tell me," I said,

He retreated, hands raised in submission.

"I'm sorry. It's just that this means a lot."

"Yeah, the check was a good indication. You know I can't just deposit that thing, right? Midnight as always."

Sam rubbed his hands together as if he was washing them beneath a stream of water.

"This will be like the football game scenario. I'll act as a conduit, but you will primarily be responsible for creating the world," I said.

"And you won't see anything?"

He leaned forward, his breath sweet with the scent of cola.

"No, and it's not because of the money. If you have a true need for privacy I will respect that. I will not watch just this once."

He nodded and faced the door, "Ready."

The process was fairly simple. Sam conjured memories of the house and the family members he wished to encounter, in this instance only his sister. I plucked these memories out of the ether and created a temporary reality, which we refined as he made minor corrections to the placement of a bush or the color of paint on the front door. Connected by an invisible umbilical cord, he used me to make the changes himself. A minute later Sam was inside his childhood bedroom and I closed the door behind me.

I sat in the hard, plastic chair again. The monitors were off except for the one which displayed Sam's vitals.

"Emily?" Sam called.

I sat a little taller in the seat. I had agreed to not watch the scenario, but there was no mention of listening to it. I felt him tugging at my power as he fabricated his environment, but I resisted the temptation to access his mind. Instead, I turned my attention to the monitor.

"Emily, it's Sam," he called again.

He said he just wanted to have a conversation with her, to do something simple in her company like watch her favorite movie, which was Fern Gully.

"In my room, Sam," Emily said in a small voice.

His heartrate nearly doubled. His heavy footfalls plodded over noisy floorboards.

"Sam, you know you're not allowed in my room when Mom and Dad aren't here," Emily said.

I watched the three-dimensional image of his brain. Lights flashing as his anticipation built.

"It can be our secret," he said, and a door closed behind him.

I was true to my word. I did not watch Sam's experience, but there was no need. I heard everything. I heard the screams stifled behind a clamped hand, the grunts of force and laughter, and the eventual sobbing. I watched the brain, bits of light flashing here and there as neurons fired. The patterns might have seemed random, but they were not.

I could have forgiven him for the incest. I could have forgiven him for the murder. A well-liked governor from a northeastern state requested a similar experience a few months prior, but it was his own wife he killed. Better for him to exorcise the urge in that fabricated reality than in real life.

Obviously, Sam was not interested in closure. He was not interested in having one last meaningful interaction with his little sister. In addition, he was not experiencing something new. Neurons flared, red and blue sparks drawn from deep within his memory.

He had done this before. This was a reenactment.

"I loved you Emily. I wish you could have understood how much I loved you," Sam whispered.

The alarm sounded and his world dissolved. Emily's blood vanished from his Ren and Stimpy shirt. I opened the door to find him standing with his hands on his hips, a jack-o-lantern smile splitting his face.

"Thank you. That was just what I needed."

I did not hear from Sam for two months. I knew he would come back. Men like Sam always come back.

"Hey, John, sorry I missed you. I know you said last time was a one-time thing, but it was very beneficial for my…spirit. I'd like to make you the same offer as before. Let's use our previously negotiated price as a starting point. Let me know. I can be in there in four hours from the moment you say okay."

Lucky for Sam I had an opening.

He looked terrible, as if he hadn't slept since the last time I saw him. Wisps of a beard that would never fill in twitched as he spoke. The bags beneath his eyes were like plums, smooth and shiny. He licked at the crusted remnants of his last meal in the corners of his mouth. He wore the same shirt as before, yellowed at the pits and brown around the collar. He'd been wearing that shirt a lot, it seemed.

"Same as last time, right?" he asked, not making eye contact.

"Of course, Sam. I'm so glad you were able to find closure," I said. My power connected to his mind and the walls of the room shimmered for an instant before melting away. Before I even closed the door, he was calling her name.

"Sam, you know you're not allowed in my room when Mom and Dad aren't here," Emily said a couple minutes later.

I sat in the booth, arms crossed and eyes closed. The monitors were dormant as I assured Sam they would be.

I recalled the creative authority from Sam but maintained the environment. I saw Emily on her bed, hidden beneath a collection of stuffed animals. Sam took a step forward and closed the bedroom door behind him.

"You fucking bitch," Sam said.

Emily gasped, "I'm telling Mom!"

Sam laughed, "No you won't. You'll be dead. But not before I play a little bit. You're the reason they hate me. You can't keep a fucking secret you stupid whore."

Sam unbuttoned his jeans and attempted to step forward.

"What the fuck?" he said.

His feet sprouted roots. He fought against them, gripping behind the knee and tugging with all of his strength.

"What is this?" he yelled, looking behind as if he expected to see me there.

"John? Can you hear me? Something's wrong. I can't control it anymore."

Emily jumped off the bed and stepped forward. The walls of the room withdrew and for a moment it was only the two of them.

"Yes, Sam, I can hear you," I said through Emily.

Empty black surrounded them, a void as wide and infinite as the space between galaxies.

"Wh-what are you doing? I paid you," he stuttered

"You're afraid of a lot of things, Sam. A lot. You have enough fears to last a lifetime."

Emily stood before her brother who shook his head, tears vibrating in his eyes.

"Like your fear of holes," Emily said and nodded at Sam's hands.

He screamed. The palms of his hands looked like a honeycomb. Hidden in the crimson wetness were trembling worms. The itch was maddening. He bored his finger into one of the holes but the worm evaded his touch. Sam withdrew his finger with a wet sucking sound.

"Or your fear of being humiliated," Emily said.

Together they stood at the fifty-yard line of a high school football field. The bleachers stretched skyward with laughing, leering faces. Sam attempted to shield his naked body from their gaze, but there was too much skin and not enough hands to cover it.

"Or your fear of being alone," Emily said.

Sam floated in an unbounded abyss, an insignificant stripe of peach on a backdrop of limitless black. He opened his mouth to scream, but there was no air, nothing to convey the sound waves. I developed an expansion to my power over the past few months. One unfortunate mouse and Samuel Carpenter were my test subjects. I never saw the mouse again and assumed the same would be true for Mr. Carpenter.

I imagined a pair of scissors hovering above my connection to him.

The scissors severed the link and Sam drifted away like a balloon into an endless sky.

I opened the door to the experience room and saw that it was empty.

"Good luck out there," I said, and closed the door.

Comancheria

When Boxcar Joe opened his eyes, he thought the world was on fire. The train thundered down the tracks, but it was slowing. The sky was an electric orange with stagnant clouds like the ripped sails of a pirate's ship. There were strange silhouettes, shapes his muddled brain did not understand. He thought he was in Texas, but it didn't look like Texas from where he sat.

He scooted to the edge of the boxcar, dangled his legs over the moving ground and squinted at the setting sun. It was late afternoon when he dozed heading south from Amarillo. That part of Texas was prairies and scrubland, with more oil derricks than trees. This was something different.

The train stopped and, though Boxcar Joe couldn't imagine why it would do so, he took advantage of the opportunity to inspect the strange world, which more closely resembled Arizona's most famous geographical landmark. He left behind his meager belongings, the treasures culled from rest stop trash bins and poorly supervised flea market stalls.

The grass crunched like glass beneath his boots as he ambled forward, shielding his eyes from the light of the sun with a bronzed hand. Above was twilight and behind was full dark. Ahead was the end of the world. At least, it looked that way to Boxcar Joe.

233

He didn't know the words for the formations he saw then, the steppes and outcrops, the earthen skyscrapers. Light and shadow confused his perception. He walked forward, hand still steady above his eyes in a perpetual salute, but seemed to come no closer to the precipice. Faintly, he recognized the sounds of cattle, the agitated grunting and muted drumbeat of hooves. That was the reason the train stopped, but Joe was no longer connected to it.

He did not hear the train churn back to life as the herd departed. He continued forward, squinting as the last of the sun's light leaked from the sky leaving behind a patch of crepuscular orange and bruised purple.

Joe strolled toward the canyon's edge, realizing at the last moment his next step would have been air. He backpedaled and stood with his hands on his hips and wondered if this was what Mars looked like. In the waning light there was little to see, just suggestions of shapes and formations, but it felt very meaningful, as if he was supposed to be there at that precise moment. The air smelled of earth and dust and other things he did not recognize.

Boxcar Joe whipped his head around, realizing his bindle, and all his worldly belongings within it, were speeding away along with the rest of the train. He sprinted half a dozen steps and skidded to a stop. The train was moving too fast. Though he could barely see it he knew by the sound it made. Perhaps it wasn't the worst thing to sleep beneath the stars at the edge of the world.

Boxcar Joe walked with his hands in his pockets, rubbing his last two pennies together, a wary eye on the precipice for fear he might fall in. What dwelled in the canyon, burrowing to escape the sun's heat, anxious to feed once the light went out? The tracks would lead him somewhere. Might take a day or a handful of hours, but the tracks would lead him somewhere. He didn't mind his situation. His treasures could be replenished, and he enjoyed the effort involved in that.

The evening air was perfectly balanced between warm and chill so that it felt as if it had no temperature at all. The coyotes initiated their nightly serenade and owls yawned in the thin branches of mesquite trees. It was not the desert and it was not the plains but somewhere in between.

Joe wiggled his toes. There was too much room in the boots. He thought about this and then he thought about the man who'd worn them only three days before. He was a lanky man. Joe thought he might have gone by Boxcar as well. Boxcar Bill maybe?

Boxcar Bill had a lot of stories. Said he fought in the Great War and that he'd helped Bonnie and Clyde escape from the law near Wichita Falls. He had big stories, and wore nicer clothes than most. For all his talk, though, Bill ate at the same beanery as the rest of the tramps. And more than once Joe saw him backdoor bumming looking for handouts, his coat collar pulled up to his eyes as if Joe wouldn't recognize that stupid top hat of his.

Boy, was Bill surprised when Joe interrupted one of his stories by pulling a razor across his throat from ear to ear. Didn't even lift an arm in self-defense. He just sat there and looked at his hands as if willing them to put up a fight. Joe really only had an eye for the boots, which were still wet with blood when Joe first tried them on. In Bill's coat pocket, though, Joe found a military medal. Maybe he wasn't lying about that.

Right about the time Boxcar Joe's stomach woke up from its daylong slumber he spotted the campfire. It looked to be in the canyon, itself, and Joe didn't know how he could navigate there in the dark. He walked carefully in his too-big boots, keeping respectful distance from the escarpment.

Joe was on a lucky streak, however, and after a quarter mile the ground sloped gently before him, creating an easy path to the campfire and whatever awaited him there. Rocks skidded beneath his boots and a minor avalanche followed. He patted his jeans.

"Shit!" he hissed.

If he had any plans of making a stealthy approach, perhaps claiming the campfire for himself, those plans were a wash. His razor was on its way to Lubbock, but that was not his only weapon. Joe found the pocketknife in a hidden compartment of his coat. Wouldn't be easy to kill a man with such a small blade, a dull blade in addition. But, there's a fair distance between easy and impossible.

He could not hear the crackle of the wood but smelled the burning mesquite and his mouth watered. Above was every star God created and a sickle moon the color of old milk. Joe inhaled all of it, more certain with each step his oversized boots were guiding him.

He'd made enough noise on his approach to alert the campfire's attendant, but still called out as a courtesy. It's never a good idea to surprise a man at night when you don't know what he's packing.

"Got the cover with the moon tonight?" Boxcar Joe called from some distance. It was hobo-speak, something Joe heard in Arkansas that might not have made its way west.

The silhouette shifted on its perch but did not respond audibly.

"Care if I share your fire?" Joe said as he walked forward, crushing bluebonnets beneath the heavy boots.

The wind picked up a little, just enough to tickle his ears and redirect the flames so that the man behind the campfire was left in shadow. The silhouette nodded, or so Boxcar Joe thought.

"If you plan on eatin' anything I'd be happy to finish your scraps," Joe said.

There was something to the right of the man, who sat on either a rock or a small mound of earth. Its contents reflected some of the fire's light. Joe squinted at it, and his hand instinctively found his knife again.

"Got a name, friend? I'm Boxcar Joe, or have been for the past couple of years. Used to call me Baby Joe on account of I can't grow a beard, but that name didn't stick. Still can't grow a beard, though. Anyway, got a name?"

The shadow shifted, boots carving divots in the dirt as the man adjusted his posture.

"Lots of names," the man said with a voice like a flutter of bat's wings.

"Ride the tracks or are you the walkin' sort?"

In the dark, somewhere near the man's face, an ember glowed. The man shifted his legs, pulling his boots away from the heat of the fire. Once again, Joe was distracted by the glinting objects to the man's left.

"Just…lots of names," he said as smoke curled around the brim of his hat.

Boxcar Joe rubbed the back of his neck and chuckled, "Any I can call you?"

The ember swelled again.

"Comancheria. That's what they call this place. The new people. These canyons and west to the desert. The people who lived here before them called it other things. Different names, all very beautiful. But, they're gone now."

There was no longer a breeze. Beyond the popping of wood in the fire the land was cemetery still, the silence punctured here and there by a coyote's yap. Despite the lack of wind, the flames still did not illuminate the stranger's face.

"You lived here long?" Boxcar Joe asked.

"Long? I suppose. Long can be half a minute if your face is on fire."

Joe smiled, a nervous reflex, and the rumble in his stomach felt like something other than hunger.

"Well, that's fine. I can be quiet if need be. Like I said, if you have any food, anything, just toss it at my boots. Just like throwin' a bone to dog."

The ember rose and fell one time.

"You're lucky, Boxcar, I'm actually planning to indulge a bit tonight. More than one man can eat alone, I assure you."

"That's good," Boxcar Joe said, his smile returning.

After a minute of silence, in which the only sounds were the campfire and the whisper of smoke exhaled by the man in shadows, Boxcar Joe cleared his throat and spoke again.

"Quite a collection you got. Is there a story behind it?"

Joe nodded to the mysterious vessel, pottery of some sort, and its glittering wares.

"Gifts from friends. As I said, long gone from this place."

"Like ranchers? Cattlemen?"

The man laughed once and tossed the ember into the fire.

"They drove their enemies into the canyons, my friends. It was perfect at night, the canyon walls reflecting their fear back to them. I watched. I followed. Small as a mouse or soaring above with a falcon's wings. They were brutal men, but small men. Small of mind. And when I finished there was nothing left of them, not even a puddle."

Boxcar Joe nodded but understood little of the strange man's words. His attention was focused on the treasures in the vase. He thought he saw a glint of silver. And though silver wasn't gold it was better than just about anything else. Joe reached inside the coat as if scratching his belly and withdrew the knife, palming it so the man did not see.

"So, you Indian or something? I got drunk with a couple Indians near Tulsa once."

A new ember appeared in the shadows. The man leaned forward and would have been exposed in the fire's light if not for the brim of his hat, which blocked his face from view. He blew a stream of smoke across the flames. Boxcar Joe coughed and waved his hand.

"Or something," the man said.

"Pardon?" Joe said and coughed again.

It certainly wasn't tobacco.

"Am I Indian or something was your question. Or something is my answer."

"Jesus, what's in that?" Boxcar Joe spat to get the taste out of his mouth.

"Magic. Careful you don't spit on your boots. You might wash the blood off."

Coughing and sputtering, Joe said, "How's that, friend?"

Over the flames, Joe glimpsed the basic form of the man's face, and something deep within the shadows, like the headlights of a car still many miles away.

"The blood on your boots. From the man you killed three days ago."

Joe's spine stiffened one vertebrae at a time. He looked to the east and longed to be on the train headed to Lubbock, but saw only the campfire's glow on the canyon wall. He should never have left the boxcar. But it was gone along with his razor and everything else he *procured* over the years.

"I didn't..."

"Still hungry, Boxcar? How about dinner and a story?"

"I guess," Boxcar Joe mumbled.

He couldn't hold a thought in his head.

"Got a knife? You see, I have all of this treasure, all of these gifts. But I don't have a knife."

It felt like there was cotton in his skull. The words made sense individually, but combined they might as well have been another language.

"Knife?" Boxcar Joe said and opened his hand.

"No? Try your pocket."

Joe fumbled with the pocket for a moment, his fingers numbed and disconnected from him. They collapsed around something. It wasn't a knife. Joe withdrew it and the snake sank its fangs into tender skin between his thumb and forefinger. He opened his mouth to scream, but forgot how, and instead issued a long, silent exhalation.

"That is going to be a problem for you. I hope you are comfortable where you are sitting. You'll be there for some time."

The snake was already gone, its path indicated by a shadowed, endless S.

"I am sad to leave this place, but the ghosts of my friends walk these canyons now and I can do nothing for them. Our time together is over. I wish I could have stopped it all, but I cannot be all places at all times."

"Places..." Boxcar Joe watched the wounds in his skin swell and shrink in size. He thought he saw bone peeking through, and then there was no wound at all.

"A story for you. And then food," the man in the shadows said.

"Food…"

"The little boy had skin like the petals of a dandelion. His hair was red like these embers, red like his father's. The man killed seven of ours and would have killed more if he'd been able. I found him standing at the canyon's edge, his belly fat with the meat from our bison. He had a predator's gaze but not a predator's instincts.

I could have nudged him over the edge and he would have reached the valley floor broken and battered, tatters of skin and pieces of bone trailing behind. I could have simply devoured him as I have done so many others. His father might still be wandering these valleys, an old man now, searching for the boy who never came home.

No. When his father found what I did he aimed that rifle, the one he used to slaughter my friends, and painted his brain across the wall of his house."

Boxcar Joe fluttered on the brink of understanding. The strange man's words formed a picture in his mind, but he was disconnected from the meaning.

"What did you do to him?" Boxcar slurred.

He was slumped on the ground, staring at the man in shadows around the side of the dwindling campfire. As he watched his vision focused on an ant scurrying towards him.

242

"I consumed him from the inside. I ate everything except for the skin. That I left for his father, a sack of flesh and that damned red hair. Everything is more than just his bones and organs. Much more. It's that little glowing pearl, the one inside of you right now, that makes you Boxcar Joe instead of anyone else. It's not hard to find if you know where to look. His was gray and tasted like the sea."

There were more ants now, a line of them marching towards Boxcar Joe's open mouth.

"It's still inside of me, the little pearl, his and many others. I wonder what yours tastes like?"

The figure stood and stepped around the fire. He wore a long, black coat, the kind gunslingers wore in the outlaw days.

"What do you think yours tastes like? Nasty I'd wager. Like those old pennies you've got in your pocket."

He lifted his hat and placed it on the ground. Then he eased onto the dirt and Joe saw him clearly for the first time.

"I haven't eaten so well lately, Boxcar. I'm so glad you came by my fire. I'm so glad those cattle wandered onto the tracks and your train stopped long enough for you to get off."

His face was made of ants, shifting and crawling all over each other, little red and black bodies forming the shape of a skull. The concavities where the eyes would have been were darker than night, with twin glints of starlight at their very centers. Joe's mouth opened wider. The light in those pits was just in front of him, close enough to touch if he'd been able to control his limbs. But it looked farther, much farther. It looked as far as the stars themselves.

The ants crawled onto his face and their pincers went to work, carving slices of flesh. Others entered his mouth and crawled up his nose.

243

Everywhere they went they sliced and gouged, tearing strips free and ferrying them back to the colony, the million ants in the shape of a man. Boxcar Joe felt all of it. He would have screamed but they were in his throat. Thousands of tiny legs, thousands of tiny pincers disassembling him.

"I hear that question inside of you. *Why? Why am* I doing this?"

The ant-skull was inches away from him then. As the ants bored into the stiff jelly of Joe's eyes he locked onto the twin points of starlight.

"You're staring into the infinite, into the abyss. And you only care to know why?"

Ants peeled the tissue from his pupils, tore through capillaries.

"I wondered the same, Boxcar. When your grandfathers set fire to sleeping villages and made a sport of slaughtering those who escaped. Yes, I will indulge tonight, and the meal is far more than one man eat alone. Fortunately, I am something else."

Boxcar Joe's vision darkened. His skin was on fire, and it did feel like forever.

When it was all over all that was left was a dead man's war medal and two pennies. The man with many names and none to share added these to his collection as the sun rose over Comancheria.

Daddy Longlegs

"There!" the boy said, smiling at the picture he created.

His mother leaned over him, placing a hand to the small of his back. He could not see her face then, so it freely displayed the confusion she felt, brows straining to unite above the bridge of her nose. he words she spoke did not match her bewilderment.

"It's wonderful! What is it?"

Joel was six, his passions as malleable as warm Play-Doh. What Hollie saw might have been a bug. Joel had been on a bug kick lately, but it could also have been a crab. The colors were random, a sun tucked in the corner of the page that began green and morphed into yellow. There was a single gray cloud, two teardrops of rain, the purple house with the triangle roof, and the crab-thing.

"It's the Daddy Longlegs, Mommy!"

"*A* daddy longlegs?" she corrected.

"No, not *a* daddy longlegs. *The* Daddy Longlegs, like from the stories at school," Joel said, returning to the paper to add grass.

She squinted. It sort of resembled a spider. If you didn't look directly at it but off to the side a bit.

"Why does it have a face?" she asked.

Joel giggled, "Of course it has a face! Daddy Longlegs has a face!"

"Is that what the kids at school say?" she asked.

She turned back toward the sound of bacon popping on the stove.

"No, it's what he looked like when I saw him," Joel said.

Hollie grasped the spatula, "What's that, dear?"

"Nothing," Joel said, tongue peeking from the corner of his mouth.

He added a big, wide grin to Daddy Longlegs' face. That was how he remembered him, smiling from ear to ear.

The picture was promoted to the refrigerator, usurping a pencil drawing of a dinosaur eating a car. Joel thought that was the funniest thing, dinosaurs eating cars. But, he crumbled the paper up and tossed it into the kitchen trash can before Hollie could protest. She placed the picture at Joel's eye-level, as requested, but used a magnet to cover the spider's face along with its uneven smile.

That evening, after books, Hollie lay next to Joel as his excitable chatter about school grew soft around the edges, the river of words filling with silt. This was her favorite time and place in the world, Joel's warm little body underneath the covers next to her, the cool breeze from the open window. A poster of dinosaurs engaged in combat flapped in the slight wind, a corner tearing free of the tape that secured it to the wall.

She had been drifting towards sleep, but was suddenly awake.

The window.

She never opened the window and Joel was forbidden to do so. She slipped out from under the covers and padded across the floor. The window shut with a brief screech, and she locked it with both latches. There was a smudge on the glass, as if Joel had pressed his face to it. Hollie wiped it away with the sleeve of her nightgown.

Joel stirred from the commotion.

"What is it, Mom?" he gurgled.

Hollie fluffed the pillow and snuggled next to him.

246

"Just closing the window, buddy," she whispered.

"Oh, sorry about that. I opened it for Daddy Longlegs," he said, turning on his side.

She wondered if the stories his friends told were the same shared in her youth. Until she saw the picture and heard the name she had not thought of the myth in years. Daddy Longlegs had a face like skull and the body of a spider. He was just as tall or small as he needed to be. He could grow his legs to the size of a house, or shrink to the size of a mouse. But, the face was always the same size.

The story developed in the 1960s after the disappearance of three children in the span of six months. With the expanse of alpine wilderness around them more children did tend to go missing. Hollie once heard this part of the country was a haven for serial killers, with its long stretches of seldom-traveled roads, remote cabins with no mailing addresses. Daddy Longlegs, it was said, took children to the underworld. He used secret tunnels hidden all around the mountains.

"Joel?"

"Hmm?" he said, dreamily.

"What does Daddy Longlegs look like?"

He smacked his lips, "He's a big spider. As big as our house. Reached all the way up to my window."

"Anything else?"

"His face is…like…the moon."

Hollie slept beside her son that night, but not out of fear of a house-sized spider. She drifted to sleep without realizing it, her thoughts bleeding into a dream. She roused with milky yellow light in her eyes, the sound of her cell phone alarm chiming in another room. Joel was not in bed next to her. Panic sprouted in her chest, growing tendrils that gave a rush of energy to her extremities.

She sat up in bed, heart steadied at the reassuring noises from downstairs, Joel humming and the tinkling of cereal being poured into a bowl. Hollie took the stairs two at a time, hoping to reach her son before he attempted to add milk to his breakfast.

"Hey, buddy, why don't you wake me up next time?"

Joel mopped up a small puddle of milk with a hand towel.

"I tried. You were too sleepy! I think it was because of Daddy Longlegs," he said.

"What do you mean, buddy?"

Joel carried the towel, dripping milk with every step, into the laundry room. Hollie turned the coffee maker on as she awaited his return. He plunged a spoon into the bowl and slurped a mouthful of cereal before answering.

"He came by last night. He didn't want to wake you so he gave you a special little kiss to keep you asleep. Right on your lips, too!"

Hollie touched her face, her smile tentative.

"Why did he want me to be asleep?" she asked.

Joel wiped his milk mustache with the back of his arm.

"He has a special job for me. And he was afraid you might get mad if you woke up and saw him there."

"A special job?"

Joel crunched another spoonful, attention alternating between his mother and the back of the cereal box.

"Yeah, but I don't know what it is yet."

Hollie mussed his hair, "You got some imagination on you, buddy."

It was too late to shower, but she could still splash some water on her face before work. She left Joel to his breakfast and jogged up the stairs. The conversation with her son supplanted by her work schedule for the day. She might have asked him more questions had she noticed the window in his bedroom was cracked open again, just a sliver.

That afternoon, after school, Joel closed the window. If Mom saw it she would be angry. He could not quite reach the latches, but didn't think she would notice it was unlocked as long as it wasn't open. He played in his room as his mother prepared dinner. It smelled like spaghetti and meatballs, which was one of his favorites.

Joel held a toy dinosaur in either hand. The triceratops was his favorite because it could beat a tyrannosaurus. That was what the library book from school said, anyway. He clashed the toys together, adding roars to the sound of plastic clattering. In his mind, the triceratops was actually Daddy Longlegs. The tyrannosaurus was still a tyrannosaurus.

He glanced at the window, but it was too early. He only ever came at night.

"Time for dinner, buddy!"

"Coming, Mom!" he said, clashing the dinosaurs together one final time.

The tyrannosaurus fell on its side, vanquished.

He skipped downstairs, the aroma of garlic awakening his salivary glands.

"How was school today?" Hollie asked.

Joel's face froze in concentration as he twirled the noodles with his fork. Until recently his mother chopped the spaghetti into manageable, inch-long segments. But he was a growing boy and growing boys did not

249

need their mothers to cut their spaghetti. The noodles slid off the fork as soon as he lifted it from the plate.

"Rats," he whispered.

"Do you want me to-" she began.

"No, I got it," he said, twirling the fork again.

Although his features generally resembled hers, he could sometimes contort them in such a way that they looked like his father.

"Do you want to try to talk to Daddy this weekend, buddy?" she asked.

Daddy was in an undisclosed location, but judging by his attire when they were able to video chat Hollie guessed it was somewhere hot and sandy.

He smiled at the three strands he managed to capture.

"Sure!"

Joel slurped the spaghetti, slapping pasta sauce on his cheeks.

"How was school today?" she attempted again.

"Oh, fine. I can spell good. It's just hard to make the letters look nice."

Hollie chuckled, "I struggled, too. My third grade teacher asked me if I was afraid to hurt the paper I wrote so lightly."

Joel scoffed, "What? You can't *hurt* paper. It doesn't feel!"

"I know. She was being silly I think. Books tonight?"

Twirling his fork again, Joel muttered, "Yeah, but don't fall asleep or Daddy Longlegs won't let me help him."

Hollie sat erect as if a spider walked the length of her spine.

"Help with what, buddy?"

"I don't know. He hasn't told me yet."

Hollie reached across the table and gently flicked the tip of his nose.

"Well, you tell him I don't want any more night visits. You need sleep. You can't be up all hours playing with giant spiders."

Joel chased a meatball around the plate, eventually securing it with one hand before lancing it with the tines of the fork.

"He's not *just* a giant spider. He's a person, too. And he can be small if he wants."

"Joel, buddy, did you open these latches?" Hollie whispered.

In response, Joel turned in his sleep.

Hollie stared out the window. Fog hugged the ground, still as a ghost. She had the odd feeling that it would only come nearer if she was not looking at it, like when she played red light green light as a child. The lights of the nearest house were distorted, bent into strange shapes in the distance. The mountain was like a black shark's tooth, its summit hidden by clouds.

Daddy Longlegs can be just as tall or small as he needs to be.

Maybe she would sleep next to Joel again, just for tonight.

Hollie locked the latches and tested the window. The fog encroached upon the house, probing with smoky tentacles. She drew the curtains closed and quietly padded out of the room, returning a minute later with her cell phone in hand.

Sleep came quickly, but it was polluted.

She dreamed about the spider. Imagined waking to see its moon-face glowing in the dark, a pitted, smiling disc peeking over the foot of the bed. In her terror at the sight of him she froze in place, a barnacle trapped in a sea of dinosaur sheets. It loomed over her, head nearly scraping the ceiling. Its legs stretched to all corners of the room, narrow body floating beneath the ceiling fan.

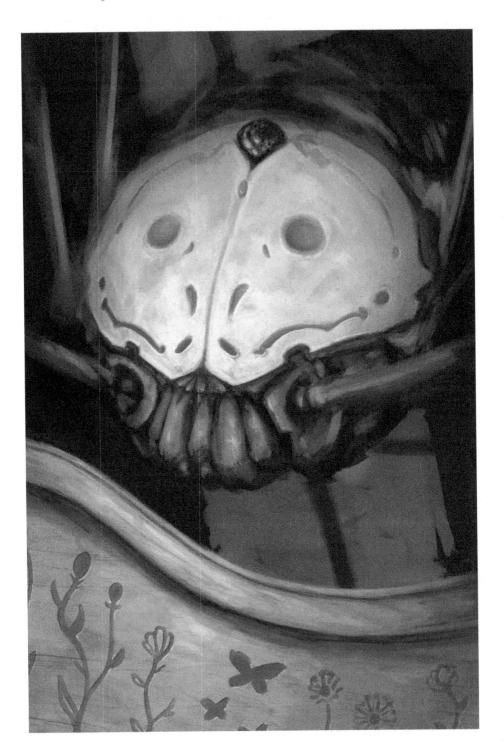

The face, unchanging, lowered to within an inch of her own. Joel's rendering, though unskilled, captured the simplicity of the creature's visage. There were no pupils, just empty, white space. The smile was carved from stone, a harsh, crooked line, fractured in the middle, that conveyed not joy but something else, barely contained.

The disc moved, not its features but the entire apparatus, and her already racing heart beat faster, a little hummingbird trapped in her chest. The face slid backwards and behind, like a garage door opening, and Hollie understood it was not a face at all. It was a decoration, camouflage, a mask to ward off predators…or entice prey. The real face behind was a horror. It looked like a log lined with black, glistening frog's eggs, but the eggs moved and she realized they were eyes. Its jaws unhinged laterally and a proboscis unfurled.

A little kiss to keep you asleep. Right on your lips, too!

She had no strength in her limbs. The appendage enveloped her mouth, filling her cheeks with a puff of sweet air. Its black face with its countless eyes became a strip of outer space dotted with starlight. It grew in her vision, an ocean of darkness with those strange stars all blinking at the same time. The creature and the room began to disintegrate. As sleep pulled her back into its embrace she watched the spider retreat from her and turn its attention to the little boy by her side.

Hollie heard the alarm, but it did not penetrate the layers of her unconsciousness to impart meaning. The chimes were church bells in the background of a dream. She went right on dreaming as sunlight spilled into the room, crawled across the floor, and settled on her skin. Joel roused to the music, hair a mess of golden tangles like corn silk. He nudged his mother, tapped her maroon head. As before, she did not respond to his efforts and so he left the room with a stretch and a yawn, pulling a dinosaur t-shirt over his head.

Hollie woke when the alarm began its fourth cycle. She slapped at the nightstand with her whole hand, knocking the phone to the floor. Her other arm searched the space beside her and did not feel the sleeping form of her son. The hummingbird in her chest fluttered its wings and she sat up, memories of the nightmare now at the forefront of her mind.

She finally responded to the phone's demands and the chime ended. Her mouth attempted to construct the syllables of her son's name, but the sound that emerged was more of a grunt. After her outburst she did not hear Joel's comforting sounds from downstairs. She stumbled out of the room as if the floor was in a different place with every step, arms searching the open air for purchase.

She grasped the bannister with both hands and took the steps in a flurry, lips and tongue working together to form the shape of her son's name. At the dining room table attached to the kitchen she found him hunched over not a bowl of cereal but a drawing.

"Hey, Mom, I tried to wake you again, but you were extra sleepy."

Hollie considered each letter as she spoke it, "What are you doing?"

Joel sighed, placing the pencil on the table. His mother stood over him.

"I had to change his face. He's not smiling now because he's sad."

"Why?"

Sighing again, Joel said, "Because he's dying. That's why he needed my help."

"Oh, well, I'm sorry then," she said.

It was likely her mind playing tricks on her. The nightmare was so vivid it seemed more like a movie she had watched than something she imagined. But, there was a bit of sweetness at the back of her mouth, an invisible peppermint she *almost* felt.

Joel replaced the drawing on the refrigerator and scrambled out of the kitchen saying, "My shirt's itchy. I'm gonna grab a new one before school."

Hollie crouched in front of the refrigerator. The drawing was identical to the previous version, save for the absence of a smile. The moon face of the new rendering frowned, with dewdrops of tears spilling from the craters of its eyes. But, she knew the beast really couldn't frown. Its false face was forever smiling. That meant the creature was *not* real. Because it could not frown. Whatever Joel saw during the night was fabricated, just like her nightmare.

"Shit!" Hollie said as she glanced at her cell phone.

If these late mornings continued she might have to switch to evening showers.

"Be ready in fifteen minutes!" she called.

"Okay, Mom!" Joel answered.

He stood at the window in his room, the immobile fog beyond, a suggestion of the mountain's shape at the limits of his vision. He pressed his face to the glass, his breath leaving a small cloud of condensation. He drew a circle in the moisture, two thumb-sized craters for eyes, and a great, big frown.

The talk of the spider with the face of a man ended as abruptly as it began. Joel did not mention his conjured friend that evening, but filled his mother's ears with information about the ankylosaur he absorbed from his newest library book.

"There's only been three skulls found, so we don't know a lot. Also, you know those bony things? In the fossils they're all out of order. So, they don't really know what they look like. They can guess 'cus of other dinosaurs they found, but they don't know," he said in one breath.

"That's fascinating, buddy," Hollie said.

The chatter continued as they settled into bed. Joel took a turn reading, pausing and sounding out the word an-ky-lo-saur each time he encountered it. By the end of the book his voice was just above a whisper, the words strung together, heavy with sleep. She took the book from him, closed it, and pulled the comforter up to his chin.

Mike had about a four-day beard going, which meant he lacked access to clean water for a while. The skin of his forehead peeled and Hollie bit her tongue to not scold him for neglecting to wear sunscreen. He had more immediate concerns, she believed.

It was a few days after her nightmare. Joel moved on from the giant spider, even removing its image from the refrigerator in favor of an ankylosaur smashing a car with its club of a tail. Her work as an emergency room nurse eradicated the memory of the legend. The day prior, a motorcycle rider was admitted and the hours she spent scrubbing the gravel out of his skin cleansed her psyche.

"Hey Joel-io, want to see something cool?" his dad said.

"Course, Dad!"

Mike disappeared from view for a moment and then held something up to the camera both Joel and Hollie did not, at first, understand.

"It's a camel spider! I guess they're not real spiders, but they're still pretty cool," Mike said.

The image was grainy, but appeared to show a sand-colored

arachnid about the size of Mike's palm, obviously dead with its head smashed and two legs broken.

"Whoa!" Joel said.

Hollie gritted her teeth, waiting for the stories to spill from her son's mouth, supposing the cycle of drawings and open windows would begin anew. But, they didn't. Joel quickly navigated the conversation back to the ankylosaur until the connection began to fizzle.

"Love ya, Joel-io!" Mike said, raising a gloved hand.

Joel returned the sentiment and blew a kiss as the screen went blank.

On Monday morning, Joel woke complaining of a tummy ache. Hollie placed her hand to his forehead and found that it was just warm enough to cause concern. He showed little interest in breakfast, but did his best to convince his mother he was okay to go to school.

"If you feel sick, like you're going to throw up, go to the nurse. Don't wait until you start throwing up, okay?"

"I won't," he said.

The call did not come, and Joel's appetite did not return that evening. He admired the macaroni and cheese, delighting in the sizzling sound it made when he stirred it with his fork. During previous meals he was too busy talking or chewing to notice such a small detail.

"Think you're up for school tomorrow?"

Joel lanced a macaroni noodle and held it up to the light.

"Yeah, I guess so. I'm just not hungry is all. I feel fine."

"Books tonight?"

"Yeah! Can I read the dinosaur book?"

"Sure thing, buddy."

Hollie twisted the doorknob and collided with the door in anticipation of it opening.

"Locked?" she whispered.

She heard the voice of her son, singing the theme song to a cartoon, muffled by the sound of the shower water pelting the tub. Hollie rapped her knuckles on the wood.

"Joel? You okay in there, buddy?"

"I'm fine, *Moooom,*" he answered, stretching the letter O to indicate his annoyance at the question.

"Why's the door locked, buddy?" she asked.

She almost heard the sigh.

"I just need privacy. I'm almost seven," he said.

"I don't like locked doors, buddy. How about next time just leave it shut and I won't come in?"

"Okay, *Moooom.*"

Showered and dried, Joel emerged from the bathroom in dinosaur pajamas with a spring in his step.

Joel never got ill enough to take him to the doctor. He just seemed a bit *off* over the next couple of weeks. He developed new quirks. The locked doors continued despite Hollie's protests. Each time he entered the room he wore a new shirt. It was strange but in a way that was difficult to quantify. His spirits were high at the prospect of his father's return. The quirks filtered into life until they became normal, expected, for a while.

Hollie woke with a start, unprepared to see her son's face hovering inches from her own in the middle of the night.

"We have to go now!" he said.

"Wha- Go where?" Hollie said, sitting up.

"We have to go!"

He bolted out of the room and thundered down the stairs. She had no time to gather her bearings. Drunk from sleep, Hollie stumbled from the bed in pursuit.

"Joel?" she yelled.

She reached the open front door and saw the shrinking form of her son, sprinting into the fog. Hollie raced behind, bare feet slipping over fresh dew. This felt like a nightmare, but the chill in the air and feel of wet grass was very real.

Deliberately or not, he ran in the direction of the mountain. Had he worn pajamas of a darker shade she likely would have lost sight of him.

She called his name, rousing a neighbor's dog, to no effect. All at once, he seemed to blip out of existence, disappearing over a small hill. She ran faster, legs recalling track days from decades ago. Her lungs ached with cold air.

Hollie nearly passed him without realizing it, but Joel moaned as she neared, and she screamed his name.

The boy sat up, fog chest high. He shook his head, eyes locked on his mother's.

"I don't feel so good," he said.

"Baby, what are you doing out here?"

"I don't..."

He was on his knees, back arched. The pajama top rippled from movement beneath.

"Joel?"

"I had to come, Mommy," he said, employing the moniker he had not used for a couple years.

He peeled the pajama top off and revealed, in the scant moonlight, the horror of his back. The skin boiled, little bubbles rising and falling. Resting on his forearms, Joel's labored breathing coalesced into a singular expression of pain.

The skin perforated in half a dozen places at once. A torrent of little bodies issued forth, the same color as the moon.

The moon.

Each spider, about the size of a sand dollar, wore the face of the man in the moon, with its permanent, false smile. The boy writhed, like a fish on land, as the spiders emerged, scuttling across his back. They disappeared in the gray grass, diaphanous legs a flurry, in the direction of the mountain, with its hidden dens, its endless, unexplored lairs.

"He wanted me to help, Mommy," Joel mumbled, voice slurred from pain.

Hollie knelt over her son, stomach turning at the sight of the glistening, colorless liquid leaking from his wounds. She draped her body over his, shielding him from the chill.

"Mommy?" he murmured, "Can you help me put my shirt back on?"

A Sundown Town

As a child, I loved the scent of Autumn, crackling fires and cinnamon-sweet brews bubbling on stovetops. I loved the snap in the air, the gray canopy of clouds that promised snow but only ever provided rain. In the South, snow is for postcards and movies. Once in a while, after whispering prayers to the skies, a stray flake would land on my cheek, but by the time I found Mama in the house it was just a tear exploring the depths of a dimple.

My love for Autumn ended on October 31st, 1991. I was eight years old, young enough to know Santa and his elves were in high gear, churning out toys for good girls and boys, of which I was surely one. But, I was also old enough to wonder and worry about the logistics of the journey, of his ability to eat so many cookies and travel so far. I was old enough to know my family looked different than almost any other, and it was a difference we almost did not survive.

"It's not picking up anything," Bernie said, twisting the knob of the car's radio as the speakers fizzed and popped.

It was a fourth generation, heavily modified Ford Thunderbird, my stepfather's retirement gift to himself, a creamy off-white with a convertible top a few shades lighter. *Retired* was a good way to describe the car in addition to its owner, as it almost never left the garage, though I often found Bernie sitting in it listening to his music.

"Come on Bernie," my sister, Amber, chided from the backseat.

"Just keep your eyes on the road, dear," Mama said as she took control of the radio.

The windshield wipers struggled to keep up with the rain, and Bernie could not find the right balance of heat relative to the temperature outside, so the windows were fogged. We would not be using the convertible for its intended purpose this evening, but that was okay because it was chilly out and we didn't have far to drive, anyway.

Bernie's chin hovered just above the steering wheel as he squinted at the road ahead. Our neighborhood was comprised of one to two acre plots of manicured lawns separated by patches of forest. The streets were named for trees or Native American tribes dispatched to Oklahoma during the previous century. Deer were as common as squirrels and they often appeared in the road as if by magic, which inspired my stepfather's attention. Our destination that stormy evening was the *trunk or treat* event in old downtown Prattville, the city's historic district. Mama tried to convince me it was better than trick or treating because we did not have to walk so far, and as rain pelted my window I began to believe her.

It was strange celebrating Halloween when it wasn't full dark, and I felt silly in my Peter Pan costume, mostly at the green hosiery I had to borrow from my sister. I willed the storm to worsen so the event would be called off before any of my classmates saw me, and God or whoever it was who controlled such things heard at least that prayer if He didn't hear any other. There was no separation between the flash of lightning and the bellow of thunder, which turned the marrow in my bones into jelly. My sister, brother, and I screamed and the car swerved into the opposite lane, the tires kicking up gravel. For a moment, we were perpendicular in the road and I saw the pine tree that was struck had collapsed, breaking apart as if it had been made of sand. The hairs on my arm stood on end and the car smelled of ozone.

My older brother, Robbie, rubbed the top of his head where it struck the roof. He decided several weeks ago fourteen was too old to celebrate Halloween and so did not wear a costume. But, his heart wasn't in it, and I often caught him frowning at my Jack-o'-lantern bucket. Amber, two years my senior, was much more interested in the candy aspect of Halloween, and so threw her costume together only twenty minutes prior, pairing a pacifier with a novelty big kid's onesie and declaring herself a baby.

Bernie wrenched the car back into the right lane then hit the brakes until the tank of a car skidded to a stop. The stereo returned to life, with a syrupy steel guitar dripping its notes between a woman's haunting, mournful singing. In the space of a few seconds we seemed to have lost several hours in the day. Above the tops of trees to the west the sky was cotton candy pink, and there were already constellations pinned to the midnight blue behind. For twenty seconds or so it was just the woman's voice, the guitar, and our rapid breaths.

And as the skies turn gloomy,

Night winds whisper to me,

I'm lonesome as I can be...

"Is everyone okay?" Mama asked.

I looked for the fallen tree behind, but it was too dark to see. There were headlights in the distance, though, and Bernie gently pressed the gas pedal, the engine and its seldom-accessed power rumbling like a far-off stampede of bison. The neighborhood felt different, darker.

"Must have knocked the power out," Mama said, likely noticing the absence of porchlights.

But, the storm was over. It was gone. The only evidence of rain at that moment was plastered to the windows of our car. There were no clouds. There was no thunder. There was only the bubblegum-colored sky ahead and the starry night behind.

"W-what happened?" Amber asked, her face hidden behind her hands.

"Lightning. Just lightning," Bernie answered flatly even as his eyes scrutinized the now empty sky.

The song ended and a faster number took its place. Perhaps not realizing he was doing so, my stepfather lowered the volume until the music was inaudible.

"But where's the storm now?" Robbie asked, his voice cracking from confusion.

"I-I don't know, Robbie," Bernie said.

Mama freed one of Bernie's hands and held it, the ivory of her skin sinking into the chocolate of his. Her other hand rested on the swell of her belly, where my then unnamed little sister was marinating. We were a blended family, my older siblings white like my mother, representatives of an alcoholic father they had not seen in nearly a decade. I was the prize of my mother's subsequent marriage to my father, who was of Mexican descent and the first generation of the family to speak English. The dissolution of their marriage was more complicated, but he was at least still welcomed in the house on the rare occasions he visited me.

The Air Force brought Bernie and my mother together, rewarding his nearly thirty years of service with a final duty station in Montgomery, Alabama. Mama was also in the Air Force, mid-career at that time, and Alabama was just one of many stops along the way. We moved twenty minutes away to Prattville for its schools and relative safety.

Though he would not turn out to be the man of her dreams he was the man and the stability she needed then. And, we were happy. Not every minute of the day, but more often than not. We were also a curiosity in 1991. A black man, white woman, two white kids, and me with my raven hair and olive skin. Out there in the suburbs, the curiosity had a sharp edge to it. Our mailbox had a habit of dislodging itself from the post, always at night. Within days of our arrival in the neighborhood, Old Glory banners disappeared and the Confederate battle flag took their place.

Bernie collected himself with a long, forced breath as we crawled toward the stop sign by Highway 82. He flexed his fingers as if deciding what to do next. Headlights reflected in his eyes and he adjusted the rearview mirror, then drove across the highway aiming for the shortcut that would lead us downtown. The car shuddered as it dipped into a grass median.

"Shit!" he hissed as the spinning tires fought for purchase.

There was no grass median there, or at least there hadn't been in the four months we called the area home. It was asphalt, allowing northbound travelers to turn left into our neighborhood and permitting us access into the northbound lanes. The car's undercarriage screeched as it recovered from its brief voyage into the earthen culvert, and we headed north at a slow speed.

"Where was the…" Mama began, craning her neck to see.

"I don't know," Bernie answered, checking his mirrors.

He removed his cowboy hat and wiped sweat from his brow with the back of his hand. During his travels with the Air Force he lived in Texas on three different occasions, and adapted a western style that often added to the confusion outsiders experienced upon encountering our family for the first time.

The shortcut was up ahead on the right less than a quarter mile, not enough distance to build significant speed. In the backseat we volleyed a look of utter befuddlement amongst ourselves, which persisted when the shortcut did not reveal itself.

"Did we miss it?" Mama asked.

We hadn't. Though the light was low I saw only trees and kudzu vines. There was no shortcut.

We drove in silence.

I think each of us was trying to understand what happened, how the stormy early evening metamorphosed into a cloudless early night, how a strip of asphalt we had accessed one hundred times by then became a grass median, and the right turn, including the signs to indicate its presence, similarly vanished. Perhaps out of a sense of helplessness, Bernie controlled the one thing he could, the radio.

That was Patsy Cline and don't you just get the sense that's going to be a classic? My what a voice on that young woman from Virginia…

He cut the volume and cleared his throat, the steering wheel squeaking under his fingers as he squeezed it. There was a lone streetlight up ahead and a sign for an upcoming turn.

"We'll just see where this takes us," Bernie said.

"Are you sure?" Mama asked.

"I don't know what else to do."

All thoughts of candy, of trunk or treating, of my classmates seeing me in my sister's pantyhose were gone then. The puzzle pieces were there, but my eight year old brain could not assemble them.

Bernie made the turn, which put us on the familiar road to old downtown, but about a mile further north than normal. A scattering of

266

brake lights was ahead of us and a hazy, phosphorescent glow from the city. It was then I detected the scent I so often associated with the season, of fires burning. We followed the brake lights toward downtown.

The sign welcoming visitors was brightly illuminated. I was accustomed to a small sign with white lettering over a green background. There were at least six ways into the Prattville, and the lone *fancy* sign overlooked Highway 31, the road that connected the city to Montgomery. This sign was new, but looked old fashioned, with block letters carved in wood arching over a relief rendering of the Prattville Creek. There was an additional, smaller sign off to the right but angled toward the road.

"Whites only after dark…" Mama read.

Bernie glanced in the rearview and saw a pair of headlights gaining ground with more behind.

"Shit," he whispered.

Before the bridge there should have been a small trailer park, a place he could turn the car around. Bernie's eyes darted that direction but there were only blue-gray trees losing color to the night.

"Just drive through," Mama said nodding toward downtown.

He nodded his head and licked his lips, likely debating throwing the car in reverse right there in the middle of the road. Once we were on the bridge, however, there was no turning back. There was a commotion up ahead, a person standing in the road revealed only by his moon-yellow flashlight. The cars ahead of us slowed and threw on their blinkers indicating they were turning right toward Main Street, our original destination. Bernie grasped the window crank, but hesitated when he recognized the man holding the flashlight was a police officer.

"Parade traffic that way! Through traffic to Northington!" he

267

yelled, waving his flashlight in concert with the directions.

Bernie followed the cars heading for the brightly lit downtown, but I'm not sure he was conscious of the decision. In the backseat, the candy I secretly ate an hour before contorted in my belly as if the sour worms were actual worms.

"What's happening?" Robbie whispered.

Amber twisted her fingers into knots and stared at her knees.

"I don't know, but I'm scared," she mumbled.

"It's like we went…" Robbie began, but did not finish the thought.

The downtown lights were ablaze, from store windows to streetlamps and floodlights positioned on sidewalks to either side of Main Street. And they revealed a downtown I did not recognize. The cars were similar to Bernie's Thunderbird, but with sharper angles and more chrome. Some reminded me of black and white gangster movies he sometimes watched. The studio where I practiced karate had transformed into a hardware store. Mama's salon, which was right next to it, was a bustling diner.

The store windows were painted with Halloween scenes, and kids darted up and down the sidewalk as ghosts, clowns, and versions of Superman who had not discovered spandex. There were adults in lawn chairs, young men in jeans and white shirts with the sleeves rolled, and young women in flared skirts with those black and white shoes I never learned the name of. Music occupied the unclaimed air in the car, but it was disorganized, like several musicians playing different songs at the same time. And the tinge of burning was stronger, enough so that I could taste it in the back of my throat.

The cars in front of ours were also convertibles, tops down with riders sitting on the trunks, some in costume and some not. Little girls, miniature versions of their teenage sisters, waved at the car in front of us, where a young woman with a sparkling dress, tiara, and a silk sash sat. Her hand moved as if it was underwater as she returned the wave, and the girls collapsed into bashful giggles. It felt like Halloween. Despite the confusion, the implications of the sign I did not understand at the time, I smiled and sank into the wonder of the moment.

Each of us jolted at the tap on the window. Bernie and Mama shared a look before he rolled it down. From my place in the backseat I saw only the badge and the name tag, *Gillespie.*

"Evenin' folks. What organization you with?" he said, the Alabama twang moderately thick.

"I'm sorry?" Bernie said.

Bernie was a Vietnam War vet, and though he never saw combat he was privy to its effects in an intimate way. He prepared the bodies for return to American soil. He saw the worst of it. The missing limbs, eviscerations, skin burnt into black pixels. He knew the smell of decay. He knew the absolute destruction of war. He was not a harsh man, but he *was* stoic. Prior to that moment, I had never heard fear in his voice.

The man at the window retreated a step.

"Say, what year is this? She's a beauty!"

Bernie's mouth opened but no words tumbled out. He looked to Mama, who held both hands over her belly then, and pressed her back into the car door as if hoping she could melt through it and appear on the other side. She shrugged and I could not see her face, but I can guess it mirrored the terror he felt.

"It's, uh, it's the latest," Bernie said, his voice barely audible over the crash of cymbals and the blaring of brass instruments.

"How's that?"

"The latest model. Just picked her up," Bernie lied, eyes trained on the convertible in front of us.

"You're a lucky man, then. I'd love to take one of these down to the Gulf, you know? Say, what organization you with again? We gotta announce the names during the parade," he said, plucking a small notebook from his pocket.

Bernie fidgeted his fingers and shook his head slightly.

"I'm, uh, with the Air Force," he said.

Then I saw the man's face just to the right of Bernie's cowboy hat.

His eyes were hidden in the shadows. From the backseat they appeared as two black ovals. He gripped the car door, his long, thin fingers breaching the sanctity of our vehicle. His mouth was a razor slice, the hollows of his cheeks pulsing as he clenched his teeth. My sister's hand found mine and she squeezed so hard I had to clench my own teeth to keep from screaming.

Bernie looked straight ahead. There were kids in the street and only a foot or so between us and the next car. The pickup truck behind kissed our bumper. There was nowhere for him to go.

"Well, would you look at that," Officer Gillespie said, a sense of calm astonishment in his voice.

Bernie stiffened, his hat grazing the convertible top.

"A black cowboy," he continued, finishing the thought.

He used a different word, though.

There was another aspect to this story I did not notice at the time, and it only made sense twenty or so minutes later. The officer flickered, as if viewed through whirring fan blades. There was so much stimulation, music and shouting children, idling engines, that I did not think about it in the moment. It just happened.

The shadows around the officer's mouth parted as he smiled, revealing teeth speckled with chewing tobacco. He reached his hand inside the car, and Bernie shrunk away from it.

"You know," he began, bringing his face to within a few inches of my stepfather's, "That's some get-up you got. Looks damn real!"

Bernie's cowboy hat quivered as he nodded. The man squeezed Bernie's shoulder with his reed-like fingers and clapped him on the back.

The officer glanced behind, then whispered, "Better wipe off that make-up before you get too far from Main Street. Hate for someone to get the wrong idea 'bout you. Won't make it through the night in Prattville lookin' like that."

Bernie nodded. His knuckles looked like overripe plums threatening to burst through the skin as he squeezed the steering wheel.

The officer stood and scribbled something on the pad.

"Make sure you put the top down before the parade starts. They're gonna love you. What's your family's name again?"

Bernie cleared his throat and adjusted himself in the seat.

"Uh, Smith. We're the Smith family."

We were not. At that time there were two surnames in our family and neither was Smith.

The officer wrote on his notepad.

"Smith family. Air Force. Got it," the officer said, then pivoted his body toward the vehicle behind us.

A slow, shaky breath passed between Bernie's lips as the officer began to walk away.

"Oh, one more thing! Make sure the mayor sees you. He's gonna get a kick out of it! And put that top down!" the man barked as he walked away.

At the sound of the seatbelt unbuckling, my mother said, "You're not going to…"

"If I don't it just gives him a reason to come back," Bernie said.

Time and circumstances. At a different time or under different circumstances it would not have been an act of bravery to open that car door, to step out into the night. But at that time, and under those circumstances, it was the bravest act I had ever witnessed. He moved quickly and made it back to his seat just as the car in front of us shifted into drive and eased forward.

The discordant music coalesced into the sound of a marching band. Car and truck horns blared and headlights flashed. There was a boy dressed as a scarecrow outside my window. He was bent at the waist with both fingers jammed in his ears to block out the noise. As with the officer, he appeared to flicker in and out of existence for a couple of seconds, like one of those little animated flipbooks.

A tall figure dressed as a ghost grabbed him by the elbow and jerked so hard the straw hat fell onto the sidewalk.

"Oh my God," Mama whispered.

"Jesus," Bernie said.

It was not a man in a ghost costume. It was a different sort of costume entirely, more dangerous and terrifying than any specter could have been. The robe was so white it nearly glowed, and the hood with its pointed tip made him appear taller than he was.

Welcome to the Prattville Halloween parade! We've got a great line-up for you folks, but first I'd like to highlight our sponsors, beginning with the Sons of Confederate Veterans local chapter…

The boy squatted to retrieve his hat and was jerked roughly back to his feet. He extended an arm, grasping for the hat, which caught a gust of wind and rolled like a tumbleweed down the sidewalk.

Okay, let's kick this thing off our very own Prattville Lions marching band!

We began to move. Mama put two fingers to her lips and closed her eyes. Amber curled into a ball as my brother stared at his folded hands. The marching band music was only slightly improved in its organized form.

"It's okay. They think it's a costume," Bernie said, maybe more to himself than Mama.

"Okay," she said.

"We'll just drive through town and then keep going. We can go back h-h-…" he trailed off, not believing his own lie.

"Can we go to the base?" I asked.

Bernie made eye contact with me in the rearview mirror.

"Yes, Paul, that's a good idea. We can go to the base."

Let's give the band one more round of applause folks! Kids, get your bags ready! Up next is Don Moore with Don Moore Ford. Folks, if you're looking for a Ford you don't need to go to Montgomery to get a deal. Just come down and see your old friend Don!

The road curved to the left. On the right was the fountain that would, in 1991, be the centerpiece of many family photo shoots. Beyond the fountain was the dam and the cotton gin I only knew to be in a state of near collapse. But then it was brightly lit, silhouettes of night shift workers standing in the windows watching the parade pass.

There was a street vendor selling funnel cakes, a line of children waiting for their chance to bob for apples. There was a ring toss game and a bean bag game. But the longest line was for a dunk tank. The still dry person hovering above the water was an unflattering caricature of a black man, with oversized tomato-red lips.

273

I think Bernie was too focused on the road ahead to notice. As we moved into the brighter lights of Main Street, though, he began to attract attention, mostly from the adults in their lawn chairs. Fingers were pointed. Cameras flashed.

…and next we have Ms. Autauga County! You may know her as Laverne Rockwell and, yes, her daddy is the owner of Rockwell Vacuums…

Officer Gillespie was in the crowd to the left, shaking hands and patting shoulders as he had done with Bernie moments ago.

And, I am told that is a brand new Thunderbird just off the train from Michigan! Wow, that thing looks fast! Let's welcome the Smith family representing the Air Force! Would you get a look at that costume! You are a brave man Mr. Smith. Or is it Colonel Smith? Thanks for joining us and for serving our country!

We had no candy to throw, and so we waved. Crowds began to form to both sides. A few more camera flashes. Bernie nodded and doffed his hat as children dashed to and from his door trying to get a better look. It felt like a nightmare, the fading marching band music, the ill-fitting costumes, most of which looked homemade, and the joy on every face. Mostly that. Each face not hidden by a mask was smiling.

Officer Gillespie pointed to our vehicle. We were in the brightest part of Main Street by then, with floodlights crisscrossing in the sky above us. But, for a moment he appeared to be conversing with a shadow, one that shimmered with reflected light. The shadow peeled free from the conversation, and the pit that formed in my stomach found a new, deeper center. It *was* a shadow, in a sense. A shadow of the past. But right then it was walking toward Bernie as the car trickled down Main Street.

"Smith?" the man said, voice muffled by his black, satin hood.

"Yes?" Bernie said, pretending to be interested in the traffic.

274

"Boy, Gil was right! That's some get-up!"

Bernie nodded.

He leaned in close so that I could see his eyes. When he spoke it might have been intended just for Bernie, but I heard it clearly, "Tell you what, come on down to the next meeting at the lodge. We gotta couple of your folks with us. Air Force I mean. Things are getting pretty thick over in Montgomery, and it's a great time to be a knight. Tell 'em Mayor Will sent you."

His white, gloved hand appeared, intended for Bernie to shake. And though my stepfather did shake it, he kept looking forward. The man in the black robes did not release his hold but held it for a moment. He rubbed his thumb across the back of Bernie's hand and then inspected his glove.

"Oh my," he said then slowly retreated from the vehicle.

He walked backwards, eyes once again hidden by his hood.

"Shit, he knows," Bernie whispered.

"What?" Mama asked, sitting up in her seat.

A kid dressed as a cowboy ran up to the car and brandished his plastic gun.

"Bang! You're dead!" he shouted, then ran back to the sidewalk.

The man in black robes stood beside Officer Gillespie, offering his unblemished glove for inspection. The officer looked from the glove to our car, and then his hand found the butt of his service pistol.

"He knows it's not make-up. He knows," Bernie said.

Let's hear it for Principal Waldo and the rest of the Prattville High School staff!

275

276

Almost no applause followed. To our left, there was now a handful of men clustered around Officer Gillespie and Mayor Will. The glove had been removed at some point and was passed around the group.

"Come on. Come on," Bernie whispered.

"Just go!" Robbie said.

Bernie shook his head, "Kids in the road."

"Well honk the horn!" Mama said.

Amber sobbed beside me and I felt like doing the same.

The men, maybe half a dozen of them, began to walk in our direction. I saw at least one pistol aimed at the street. They spread out, moving aside the kids still picking up candy tossed out by parade vehicles.

"They're coming," Robbie said.

Up ahead, Main Street shifted into a residential area, and the parade traffic began to turn right into the parking lot of the First Baptist Church. Beyond the church, the street was much darker. At the rate we were traveling we only needed about another minute to reach it.

"Just go!" Mama said.

Bernie checked his mirrors and shook his head again, "Still kids in the street."

"They're coming!" Robbie yelled.

There were ten or more now, in plain clothes, costumes, and uniforms. The crowd seemed to sense the shift in the air, from celebration to predation. Men who likely had no idea what was happening joined the group. The eyes of the whole town were on us. As before, everything blipped out of existence, this time for a couple of seconds. Maybe I saw Prattville as it was in 1991, or maybe I just wished it was so. But, then I was back.

277

Many things happened in the next several seconds. I do not remember the proper order of them. The crowd in the road had thinned out as most of the children were in the middle of Main Street where the highest concentration of candy was. But, there was a small group on our left. They stood over a brutalized, black effigy, which was likely hung from the now frayed rope dangling from a streetlamp. They picked through the cotton stuffing searching for hidden candy. There was no sign designating this a game. It was just there.

The gunshot was like the crack of a whip. The driver's side mirror snapped but did not sever. The next thing I heard was the screech of spinning tires and the roar of the Thunderbird's engine. There were screams and shouts, the sound of grating metal as we clipped the car in front of us. Ms. Autauga County lost her tiara and rolled off the back of the car. I do not remember further gunshots, however. Our proximity to scattering children likely saved us.

I do remember the engine, all those restrained bison suddenly released. I remember the wind on my face, and Bernie's cowboy hat sailing into the night air. There were lights and sounds, all of it compressed into a single feeling of desperation. Much of my knowledge of that night was subsequently colored by what I learned as an adult, of the era and the South in particular. At eight years old I only knew there were men with guns chasing us. There was a fire burning in the Baptist Church parking lot to the right, so big and bright I felt the heat of it as we passed. Beyond that there were a few porchlights and then the refuge of darkness.

Engines came to life behind, the cavalry assembling to correct the indignity and embarrassment of our family's presence in their city. But Bernie's Thunderbird was hungry for asphalt.

"We're getting away!" Mama said.

Our eyes met as she peered over her headrest. I could not see the speedometer, but by the sound of the Thunderbird's engine it did not have much more to give. More flickering, this time the entire block and for several seconds. We rumbled through the neighborhood, the lights and sounds of downtown fading. There wasn't a car or truck in Prattville that would catch Bernie's Thunderbird that night. The world went dark on either side of us, no porchlights. Highway 31, which ran all the way to the base, was less than a mile ahead.

Everything flickered again, night peeling back a few hours, the empty fields to the left and right replaced with dollar stores and gas stations. It was the way the town looked in 1991.

"We made it!" Mama said, but too soon.

Bernie shifted the car down just as we returned to the Main Street of the past. Flashing red lights blocked our access to Highway 31 ahead, and the cars behind were suddenly much closer. Bernie swung the Thunderbird to the right and we were on a dirt road, seatbelts cutting into our bellies as we bounced in the backseat.

Another flicker between the past and present. The dirt turned to asphalt and back to dirt again. Headlights behind us, there and gone again.

"Oh my God!" Mama screamed as a locked gate appeared before us.

The Thunderbird fishtailed as Bernie slammed the brakes. I waited for the sound of car doors or possibly gunfire. But neither came. I blinked at the relative brightness and saw we were in a familiar place, the parking lot of the YMCA, which was thankfully empty. No one spoke as we waited for an abrupt return trip through time, but that was the end of it.

After a few minutes in which we assessed our physical health, knowing we were mentally deflated, we drove home. We took the long way, bypassing Main Street.

The tree that was struck by lightning in our neighborhood was moved aside by then. There were a few trick-or-treaters out, but it wasn't a popular place for it considering the distance between houses.

At home we recounted the night's events, which already seemed less real. There was no Internet then, and so we could only guess what happened. The term *time slip* had not entered my lexicon, but it did later on in life. I don't know if the term fits. But, there was a tension that seemed to build the further we got from the place where lightning struck.

Sleep came quickly. My body was exhausted from the waves of adrenaline. I woke some time during the night and saw a band of light beneath my door. I left my bed to investigate.

"What are you doing, Bernie?" I asked.

He was out of breath and had a baseball bat in his hands.

"Nothing. Just getting some energy out," he said, and mussed my hair.

The next morning, as I took the trash out, I saw a familiar mailbox in the bin, one I passed when walking our dogs through the neighborhood. It was dented, some of the black and gold stickers with the letters of the owner's last name missing, but the G was hanging on. I knew the name. And I knew the man. He sat on his porch most mornings, cigarette in one hand and a cup for tobacco juice in the other.

I learned not to wave at him as he never waved back, though he was friendly with other kids. We had no reason to drive past his house, as there was nothing beyond it other than the cul-de-sac at the end of the street. After that night, though Bernie made a habit of it. Always wearing his cowboy hat, in the Thunderbird, with the top down, just like *he* asked for all those years ago.

The first time we passed, maybe it was just out of surprise or confusion, he waved. It was a distant memory for him, an image that crawled out of his dreams and into reality. I remember him standing on his lawn, cigarette pasted to his dry lip, his gaze alternating between our Thunderbird and the now empty post where his mailbox had been.

Afterbirth

The house was alive with activity, doors opening and closing, a constant tattoo of shoes upon the wooden steps, which screeched like a surprised barn owl. It was a beehive, or perhaps a hornet's nest. To Agnus, it was all very exciting. At four years old he did not understand many things, but he knew this day was different, the influx of smiling faces, the endless stroking of the peach fuzz lining his cherub cheeks by hands both familiar and not.

With each new arrival came a fresh gust of autumn through the front door. Eddies of smoke-tinted air escorted flurries of sun-colored leaves into the foyer like spiders escaping the cold. It was Halloween, but trick-or-treating was not on the table this year.

He understood today he was to become something new, something he had never been before. His father crouched to eye level and brushed aside a swoop of dusty blond hair, "Big day for my little man. Big day for our family. Don't worry about that Halloween stuff. It's not real."

The priest from church, a man so tall Agnus knew the structure of his chin better than his face, placed a hand on his father's shoulder.

"A very important day for you, Agnus. For all of us."

Agnus thought the man had the most unusual voice, as if the inside of his throat was made of tree bark, the thin and peely kind. It made him shudder, like the time he bit into a packing peanut, not knowing what it was.

Father Paul patted his head once, then clasped his hands together behind his back in his typical manner. He stomped up the stairs as if his actual destination was the basement, and his manner of reaching it was pulverizing the wood beneath this boots.

That's where Mommy was. In the special room.

Although many church members made the same journey that day, to the special room, Agnus was not permitted. He asked his father why this was so.

"She doesn't want you to see her in pain. It's just not the right time, buddy."

"But the other people…"

His father mussed his hair, "Oh, they don't matter, buddy. Not the way you do. Just wait, buddy. You're going to be the star of the show."

Agnus sat on the stiff couch in the living room with the family bible on his lap. He could not read more than his own name but enjoyed the pictures and how the book binding felt cool to the skin of his bare legs. It was beginning to warm in the house with so many bodies moving in and out. He flipped through the pages as that word repeated in his mind like a new heartbeat.

Brother

Brother

Brother

Some church ladies descended the stairs, dabbing at their wet eyes with tissue, mascara like rivers of smoke caressing their cheeks. The mixture of happiness and tears was confusing to Agnus, and he had witnessed this exercise repeated throughout the day. Visitors, all of them from church, were ushered upstairs. Once, he thought he heard his mother murmuring amid the other soft voices speaking just above a whisper. After a few minutes they returned, sometimes loitering in the entryway. Occasionally, they strayed into the living room to brush a finger across Agnus' cheek.

Agnus accepted the affection, but trained his eyes on the staircase, hoping to see the smiling face of his father beckoning him to the place Mommy was. But, it was never his father's face, just the folks from church. Some dressed like they were going to a Halloween party right after. The boy avoided even the brush of a finger from these. They got to see his mommy and celebrate Halloween and he was stuck downstairs with a book he could not read.

A man Agnus did not recognize approached, his thumbs hooked inside his belt loops. The stream of visitors had slowed as the afternoon progressed. Agnus wasn't sure, but believed it was just his parents and the priest upstairs and this stranger in the living room.

"What do you have there, son?" the man asked, nodding at Agnus' lap.

Agnus frowned.

This man was not his father.

He hovered over the boy and flipped the book over to expose the cover.

"Your parents taught you well. That book – it's all you need in life, son."

Agnus squirmed at the word *son*.

He raked his long fingers through Agnus' hair, the skin tingling along the path traced by his fingernails. The sensation began at the scalp and terminated as a pile of cold salamanders in his stomach. There was a shriek from upstairs. His mother, in pain. Agnus attempted to stand but was held in place.

"Not the time, son."

The stranger stalked across the living room, moving as if he was underwater. He paused at the base of the stairs and nodded to Agnus.

"It's okay to feel left out, son. But, you have the most important job of all."

Brother

Brother

Brother

Agnus glared and said nothing, his scalp still fizzing where the stranger touched him. This was becoming a Halloween to forget. If being a *brother* was so important why was he trapped downstairs with a book he could not read? Daddy said he would need to help the little brother grow, that it was an awesome responsibility and only he could do it. Agnus smiled at that and flipped open the bible again. Though he could not read the words he enjoyed the pictures.

Hours later, the daylight leaked from the living room and Agnus wondered if his father had forgotten about him. He placed the book on the coffee table and tip-toed to the stairs. Men's voices mixed with the sound of his mother moaning. He recognized his father's, a steady drone seldom rising or falling in pitch. Often louder was the voice of the priest. He sounded like he did at church. It was so hard to fall asleep in church when that man was yelling.

When a door creaked open, Agnus sprinted back to the couch, retrieving the bible and setting it on his lap.

"Sorry, buddy," his father said, turning the living room light on, chasing the long shadows away.

He was wearing his church outfit. The one he only wore sometimes

286

on special days. Sweat dappled his forehead and soaked the scooped neck of his robe. He eyed the book on Agnus' lap and smiled, noting that it was upside down.

"Come on, big brother, let's have a bite."

Agnus followed his father into the kitchen. It had been a long day, but he had not been forgotten.

"What would you eat if you could eat anything?" his father asked, smiling so broadly Agnus felt warmth blossom in his chest.

"Anything?"

His father pursed his lips, "Anything in the house. The stuff Mommy and me tell you not to have, the stuff only for after you've eaten all of your vegetables. That kind of stuff."

Agnus pictured the pantry and then the refrigerator.

Pudding?

No, he sometimes got that even when he didn't eat his vegetables.

Peanut butter and jelly?

It was his favorite, but not special enough.

He mentally opened drawers and cabinets.

"Ice-cream!" he said, finally.

"For dinner?"

Agnus nodded.

"Ice-cream for dinner it is! And you know what? You don't even need a bowl, just a spoon."

Agnus clambered up the bar stool at the kitchen island as his father rummaged through the freezer. He emerged with a carton of ice-cream Agnus instantly recognized as his favorite.

"Don't tell Mom!" he whisper-shouted as he placed the ice-cream in the microwave, "Otherwise we have to wait for it to soften. You know,

I bet your brother will like ice-cream, too. What do you think?"

"Really?"

He set the microwave for fifteen seconds, "Not right away. Right now he needs food to help him grow, but when he's older maybe."

Despite the tension in his belly, Agnus smiled. By the time he reached the bottom of the carton it was mostly a puddle of sweet cream, but still delicious. Agnus abandoned his spoon, pressed the carton to his lips, and slurped.

"Wow, that was impressive!"

Agnus smiled and wiped his mouth with the back of his arm.

"Is it almost time, Daddy?" he asked.

The numbers on the microwave clock were blurry. It was well past his bedtime.

His father nodded, "If all goes well, Agnus. It's almost time."

The man did not look at his son as he said this. Instead he looked out the window to the fat, orange moon, its façade pixelated by the naked, trembling branches of the oak tree in the backyard.

"That reminds me!" his father said, rubbing his hands together.

He glided across the kitchen and squeezed Agnus' shoulder as he passed.

In his absence Agnus realized his mother's wail was both louder and more persistent.

"A fancy new outfit on your special day, big brother."

Agnus hopped off the stool and sprinted to reach his father.

"For me?"

"For you!"

It was a miniature version of the clothes his father wore, the special

288

clothes.

Only, his robe was white instead of black.

His father kneeled, "Now, and this is the silly part, you have to be all the way naked to put it on."

Agnus was halfway out of his clothes before his father finished the sentence. The robe was cool, almost cold against his skin.

"Perfect! Now, let me go check on Mommy and I'll be right back."

Agnus twirled in his new outfit, laughing at his reflection in the glass of the oven door. Upstairs, the cries grew louder and louder, Father Paul's leathery voice rising in concert. Agnus returned to the stairs, the ice-cream in his belly feeling sour then. He wanted to race to his mother's side, to take the pain away from her.

Last night, she stayed in his bedroom long after she finished reading his favorite book. She happy-cried, her sweet breath tickling the fine hairs of his ear as she whispered lullabies to him. Agnus was a bit old for lullabies, but it meant something to his mother, and so he did not fight.

Good children gather near and far

To dance beneath the Morning Star...

He fell into sleep with his mother's words in his mind, and had the most wonderful dreams.

The noise upstairs reached a crescendo, too many sounds at once and all of them terrible. Agnus sat on the bottom step, tracing his finger along the symbols carved into the black vellum of the family bible. Many of the symbols adorned the walls of the house, though Agnus did not understand their meaning.

Agnus did not want to be a big brother. He felt foolish in his white robes, the hem already speckled with dust from the floor. He felt forgotten, the house still reeking of the odors of the dozens of people who passed through it earlier in the day. Had there been such a procession for his birth? Agnus did not think so. In between outbursts he heard the happy chatter of trick-or-treaters outside, and occupied his time rushing to the window to watch them pass. There were all kinds, zombies and vampires, skeletons and princesses. Agnus giggled as two friends dressed as Chinese food passed in front of his house, one limping and grimacing at his shoes.

The upstairs door creaked open, and only then did Agnus realize the house was still again. No screaming. No cries of pain. The blinds snapped back into place as he raced to the bottom of the stairs.

"Agnus?" his father said, followed by creaks of his descent down the stairs.

Agnus quickly stood and smoothed his robe, brushing aside the dust bunnies that collected along the bottom. His father appeared on the landing carrying a bucket, which appeared to hold substantial weight.

"Careful I don't splash this on ya, little man," he said as he walked down the stairs.

Agnus followed him into the kitchen, his nose scrunching at the acidic odor. His father did not go to the sink, as Agnus would have guessed, but to the stove, where a large pot sat on a burner.

"What's that?" Agnus asked.

His father thumbed sweat from his brow.

"That?" he said, nodding at the bucket "That's for leftovers."

His father sucked in an exaggerated breath and mouthed the word *stinky* as he waved his hand in front of his face.

"Well, little man, it's time."

"It is? I get to see Mommy?"

"And…"

"And my brother…"

"That's right! You gotta potty or anything?"

Agnus shook his head.

"You sure? Last chance…" his father offered.

Agnus shook his head again.

"Okay, head up to the door. I'll catch up."

Agnus pressed his knuckles to the door, but did not knock. There were soft sounds coming from the room, pleasant sounds. No more shouting. He had not heard his father scale the steps but he was suddenly behind, placing a hand to the small of Agnus' back.

"It's okay," he said.

Agnus turned the knob and allowed the door to open on its own. The room was very dark, the only source of light a cluster of candles above the headboard. Shadows stretched and shrank as the flames flickered.

"Go on. It's your big day," his father whispered.

Agnus crossed the boundary into the room and shivered, his breath billowing in misty puffs. He did not hear the door close, or the thud of the deadbolt sliding home. He stepped toward the light and did not hear the crinkling of plastic behind him, or his father humming as he went about his task.

His mother was as beautiful as ever, but she was not alone in the room. The priest stood at the window, his eyes fixed on the moon. The stranger from earlier, the one who called Agnus *son* sat in the far corner. Almost no light reached him, but there was enough of a residual glow for Agnus to notice he looked different, larger somehow. And, though it should not have been possible, Agnus could still see his eyes even though no light shined upon them.

"Agnus, come meet him," his mother said, her voice hoarse but kind.

The boy hesitated, fidgeting in his new, white robe.

"It's okay, buddy. This is what you're here for," his father said.

Agnus watched him for a moment as he smoothed the clear, plastic tarp on the floor. The man gave a thumbs up, which Agnus quickly mirrored. He scurried the remaining distance and stood at his mother's side.

"Isn't he beautiful?"

She pulled back the blanket, revealing the back of the head.

His hair is black like Mommy and Daddy's.

Agnus frowned.

The hair was black, but there was too much of it. His mother adjusted the bundle so it faced Agnus.

"He looks just like his father," she said, her fingers – the same fingers that traced lazy patterns across Agnus' back only the night before, smoothed the fine down of his face.

"Daddy?" Agnus said, looking to his father.

He now wore the hood with the little holes for eyes. He shook his head and lifted his arm, pointing to the corner of the room where the other man sat.

"He's going to do so many important things, Agnus, so many important things for the world. And you get to help," his mother said.

"I do?"

"Yes, right now you have the most important job of all."

The priest turned away from the window and rolled up his sleeves. He cleared his throat and loosened the top button of his shirt.

The creature resting on his mother's chest opened its eyes. They were black and glossy, little fires twinkling in their inky depths like distant nebulae. The plastic crinkled again as the priest joined Agnus' father on the tarp. In the far corner, the other man stood, the floorboards beneath him groaning. His eyes, the only part of him Agnus could see clearly, hovered near the ceiling.

"What is it?" Agnus asked.

He wondered what the neighborhood kids would think of his little brother. Would they make fun of him for his looks? Agnus would have to protect him. He was a big brother now, after all. He stood a little taller. He had been told many times that day that his was the most important job.

His mother lifted her hand from the baby's fur and stroked Agnus' cheek. She smiled once, then directed her gaze to her husband and nodded.

"Why, you get to be the first to feed him."

Beyond the Valley – Jess

For a time, she was nowhere. She drifted, pulled in one direction and then another. Jess felt none of it. She was no longer Jess. She was pure, sparkling energy, the essence of humanity on a jet stream of interdimensional ether.

She woke with a tune in her head, something she might have heard at a carnival as a child. She inhaled the air and was surprised to find it did not smell of popcorn and funnel cakes. It smelled of wet grass and ozone. There was a rumble in her ears, gentle, like the crash of ocean waves heard from a great distance. She sat up, blinking beneath an evening sun. The memories of the Valley floated through her mind like embers, cooling and expiring before meaning was gleaned.

"6-6-4-7-5…" she uttered, smacking her lips.

There was grass to the left and right as far as she could see, cumulonimbus clouds chasing darkness ahead of her. Her spine stiffened as she sensed something behind. One of the embers was a snapshot of an inky pool dotted with starlight. She seized it. At once, the memory of the Valley, her friends, the radio with its secret broadcast, and the void rushed at her.

She scooted forward, feeling as though a hand, or tendril, might reach through at any moment.

"Derek?" she croaked, crab-walking forward.

295

"Gabe? Russell?"

Jess stopped and craned her neck behind to see the void, fading so that it was nearly transparent.

"Wait!" she shouted, scrambling like a beetle set free from a glass jar prison.

But it was faded, nearly gone, and with the void gone she was stuck here. Alone. Wherever here was.

She stood, wiping off her hands and stepped toward the dwindling aura. As she extended a hand the void evaporated, and she was left reaching for the setting sun. For a moment she stayed that way, hand extended as the images of the Valley churned through her mind.

Gabe.

My God, what happened to Gabe?

And the mysterious stranger, Stan? Dan?

The grass was wet with the rain and it lashed around her exposed arms. She turned, searching the horizon for something orient herself. There were no buildings, city lights, no structures. It was a sea of dewy grass, robbed of its color in the fading light.

Jess squinted into the sun, just a smoldering wedge then, and saw its light was obscured. Something was in front of it. It might have been a tree, but it was something. She staggered forward, the wet grass snaking around her ankles.

As the sun dipped fully beneath the horizon she caught a glimpse of straight lines, of some sort of architecture. It was not a tree. Maybe a billboard, which also meant a road. The puddle of leftover sunlight splattered in the sky was too feeble. The structure vanished with the last of the light as she strained to uncover its anatomy.

The journey took half an hour during which Jess had ample time to consider where she'd been and where she was. She searched her memory for anything of value Dan might have imparted, anything to help her understand what happened to her. But, despite the volume of his words he did not *say* all that much. Jess decided his sole purpose had been to lead her group of friends to the void.

The sky above was dusted with stars, constellations she thought she recognized. A half-moon emerged from the departing thunderheads, though its light was inconsequential. It looked the same as the moon she had known her whole life. Perhaps she was simply transported to somewhere on Earth, the Great Plains of North America or the sprawling fields of Ukraine.

That possibility didn't *feel* right to her.

It was totally, oppressively silent.

There were no sounds of people, engines, doors slamming, nothing. There were no bird songs or crickets chirping. The light breeze in the air failed to stimulate the heavy grass to movement. She was the only source of sound, labored breaths as she cast aside the wet grass.

"6-6-4-7-5," Jess muttered again.

What did it even mean? Nothing, most likely. It was a ruse, an element of the void's effort to capture her. It *felt* meaningful when she stood before its quivering depths and heard it speak the numbers to her.

"Maybe it was just a reflection," she whispered, shuddering at the thought.

Suddenly, she was free of the constricting grass. She stood on an overgrown lawn, a farmhouse off to her right, its white paint barely detectable in the darkness. The windows were dark and there was no noise coming from the house, no air conditioning unit running.

"Hello?" Jess called.

Hands held out in front of her, she stumbled over debris on the lawn hidden by the grass.

"Damnit!" she shouted, hopping on one foot.

The metal tricycle she accidentally kicked was already tipped on its side. She limped forward a few feet before settling into her normal gait.

"Excuse me? Is anyone home?"

She scaled the steps to the porch and opened the screen door. There were a few wicker chairs on the porch, a table in between that might have once held glasses of lemonade on a hot summer day. She stood on the welcome mat and tapped the metal door frame.

"Hello?" she said.

It felt incredibly intimate there, at the entrance to a stranger's home. By all appearances it was abandoned, but that did not lessen her unease. What if the owners returned from an evening movie to find this college-aged kid on their porch? She could not present the events of the past two days without seeming crazy in the effort.

She grabbed the doorknob and twisted.

"Hello?" she said again as the door opened on angry hinges.

What little light there was outside dissipated within. There were no ambient sources, the green glow of a microwave clock, the blinking lights of a router. She was in absolute darkness. There was no difference in the world she saw with her eyes closed. Jess searched the space in front of her and shuffled forward with tiny steps.

If there were no people what was her purpose here? There was no electricity, no phone service. She touched a hard, cool surface her fingers told her might be the granite-top of a kitchen island. Although she could not recall the last time she ate, probably trail mix in the Valley, her stomach had gone dormant. She was thirsty, but it could wait.

The kitchen led to a laundry room, she determined by the feel of the washer and dryer. There was a long rectangle of moonlight, a door to the backyard. Jess retraced her steps and found another passage through the kitchen.

The kitchen and laundry room were both tiled, but the adjoining room was not. The floorboards responded to her weight with creaks and an occasional POP that sounded like bones snapping. Jess passed through a dining room, brushing dust off the tops of chairs. There was a slight step down into the living room where she felt her way around a couch and recliner. The couch would do for the night. The world would make a lot more sense in the morning. But, what if the void brought her here, to this home in particular, intentionally?

She continued to explore, touching photographs on the wall, knocking a couple of them free from their nails. The house felt as if it was occupied by an elderly couple. The television had a wooden housing and rabbit ears on top. She guessed it had likely not moved from its place on the living room floor for decades.

There were competing smells in the house.

Dust. Mildew. Wet places in hidden corners.

Jess sneezed continually, eyes permanently watered. She grasped a banister and ascended the stairs without thinking. The wood seemed to sag beneath her weight, as if it was made from cloth. In the back of her mind throughout her blind exploration of the house, the calliope music played, followed by the robotic recitation of the series of numbers that meant nothing to her.

She followed the banister to the right and uttered a mouse squeak of surprise when she stepped on air, anticipating an additional stair. Jess touched the wallpaper with her fingertips. Strips had wilted free from the wall, leaving behind a slightly gummy residue. This detail, more than any she encountered to that point, indicated the house was not only abandoned, but likely had been for some time.

Jess encountered a doorframe, found a knob and twisted it. The room glowed faintly with moonlight, the shape of a sink and toilet barely visible. The mildew scent was stronger here and triggered a short outburst of sneezes.

She dabbed at her nostrils and closed the door. There was a closet a few feet past the bathroom. Jess touched the items within, eventually withdrawing a blanket and tucking it under her arm. The house was just shy of chilly, but she imagined it would cross that threshold during the night.

The floorboards reacted to a shifting of weight somewhere nearby on the second floor. Air exploded from Jess' mouth as if she'd been punched in the gut. Maybe she was not alone.

She steadied herself against the wall and stepped backwards toward the stairs. She held her breath until she saw stars floating in the darkness. Ten seconds stretched into half a minute.

"H-Hello?" she chirped.

Her tongue felt like a strip of leather in her mouth as she attempted to swallow.

There was no response and the house remained still and silent, save for the sound of her breaths. It was an old house, she thought. Had likely been vacant for years by the state of disrepair. Without air conditioning the floorboards probably warped. As the house settled there were bound to be noises.

She talked herself into opening another door, this time the opposite side of the hall. The air was a few degrees cooler and smelled different than the rest of the house. Her nostrils flared. She tasted it on the back of her throat, a natural scent reminiscent of earth and avocados. The smell stirred her empty stomach back to life and she cradled it as she entered the room.

There was no residual light as with the bathroom, no haze of moonlight leaking through the slats of blinds. Jess imagined the floor in front of her was gone, the wood rotted away. She would not know until she began to fall, plummeting to the first floor of the house. Instead of stepping forward she slid as well as her boots allowed. Had the lights in the house suddenly come on she would have presented quite the sight, eyes like hard-boiled eggs, quivering in their sockets, one arm swiping at the air as the other clutched a moth-eaten blanket.

Her fingertips grazed a bedpost and she pressed her body against it. A fit of sneezing overtook her again, the smell in the room so distinct but evasive. Still anchored to the bedpost, she explored the new territory with pats of her hand. As she moved further up the bed she felt lumps beneath the comforter.

Jess relinquished the blanket for a moment to reclaim full use of her hands. She squeezed and prodded, the hidden shapes forming a mental picture in her mind.

"Oh, fuck," she whispered.

It was a body. She gripped the tibias of either leg, confirming her guess upon discovering the kneecaps.

She swallowed the bile creeping up the back of her throat and breathed through her mouth, unable to contend with the odor. She had to know before she left.

Jess sidestepped, hand hovering above where she thought the heart would be. She swallowed again, and pursed her lips as she attempted to steady her breaths.

It was all because of that damned radio. Derek said they might be the first people in that part of the Valley for hundreds of years. The presence-appearance of a semi-modern and still functioning radio did not make sense.

But, little in the Valley made sense. She recalled Russell digging in his ears with his long, elegant fingers. The blood on his fingertips.

Fingertips. There was something beneath her fingertips. Not a beating heart. Not a corpse. It felt like…

She didn't know. There was a disconnect between the textures reported by her fingertips and any correlation in her memory. It was a ticklish sensation, like a filament, or the barbs of a feather. How did it relate, whatever it was, to the body on the bed?

Jess bumped a nightstand with her hip and abandoned the mystery beneath her fingertips momentarily. She searched the surface of the nightstand, knocking over a glass. She knew the cold metal was a gun the instant she touched it. Jess jumped at the realization and backpedaled a few paces.

Her boots slid over grit on the floor, and she lost her balance. She fell, but not to the floor.

"What the hell…"

She rested on her knees and patted the obstacle, which shifted beneath her fingers. It was dirt. Soil. A pile of it in a dead person's bedroom.

Jess had her fill of mysteries for one night. She retreated to the first floor and lay on the couch, which was damp to the touch but a better option than anything she might find on the second floor. She waited for sleep to come, and it might have at some point. In pure, absolute darkness she drifted between dreams and vision.

When she traveled through the void she saw nothing with her eyes but sensed the stretching and thinning of her essence. In that space between worlds, on the periphery of reality, she might have existed for ten seconds or ten thousand lifetimes. She saw Gabe as he was in the end, the thin white worms bursting free from his flesh as he perambulated, zombie-like, toward the black pool. Had he survived the journey through the void? Where was Derek? Where was Russell?

In the dark, reenacting her role, Jess rebelled against the call of the void. She smashed the radio against the walls of the cave, its strange signal severing and restoring clarity to her muddled brain.

She roused in the dusky light of dawn.

There was a weight on her chest, a familiar feeling. Her boxer, Ivy, often waited until Jess was asleep before climbing into bed with her. She rested her velvety head on Jess' chest and joined her in dreams, warming her face with bursts of dog breath.

But, Ivy was dead. Had been for five years by then. Jess blinked a few times, the shape on her chest rising and falling with her breaths. There was too little light in the room to make it out clearly. Jess reclaimed the hand that had been stroking it.

It stood and arched its back. Jess sat up, which prompted the shape to warble a brief protest and perch upon the arm of the sofa. The silhouette was familiar but not right. Jess wiped the sleep from her eyes and leaned forward to close the distance between her and it.

Sunlight from the kitchen began to fill the living room like a slowly rising tide. The shape tolerated the light for a moment, just long enough for Jess to understand how wrong it was.

It would not be accurate to call it a cat. It retained certain qualities of a cat, but it was no longer a cat. There was little fur left, just a few stubborn patches. The rest was bare skin, though not entirely featureless. Narrow stalks, extending a couple of inches from the creature, lined its entire body. Some of the stalks terminated in little bulbs. Its face was a ruin. One eye socket was wholly overtaken by the peduncles, a cluster of bleached strands like spaghetti noodles. The remaining eye hovered several inches from the face, supported by a single stalk the thickness of an index finger.

Jess plugged her mouth with three fingers, the scream muffled to a yip. The eye, more a pouch of gray pulp, fixed on her. It opened its corrupted mouth, flashing quivering strands where its teeth should have been. It howled with tainted vocal cords, the sound wet and reedy, and sprang off the couch.

Two of its legs crumbled from the impact, the remaining bones splintering into a dozen spongy shards. It hobbled from the room, the intact bones and sinew quivering under the new weight. Jess gagged as digestive juices sprayed the back of her throat.

She cast aside the blanket and took in her surroundings for the first time. There were school pictures on the wall, a few bleached spots where she knocked them free during her blind exploration of the house. The television was as she imagined it beneath her fingertips, a wooden goliath with a thick pelt of dust. The couch she slept on was spotted with mold, a pattern of magnolias beneath.

She grabbed a magazine off the coffee table and blew the dust off. She squinted at the address label on the bottom corner.

"D. Heller, Lebanon Tennessee," she read.

It was time to go.

Except for one thing. She placed both magazines on the table and walked around the couch. There were gaps in stairs where the wood completely rotted away. Had she stepped there last night her entire leg would have gone through. She held the banister in a death grip, leaning some of her weight upon it.

There was more light in the house then. Jess reached the second story and was surprised at how short the hallway was. Her baby steps the night before made it feel as if it was a much larger space. All doors were closed except for the one she left open last night. She would just peek inside. She just needed to see it. It might help make sense of what had happened to this world.

She stood outside the door for a moment, feeling as if she should knock for some reason. he did, a gentle rap of the knuckles, and pushed the door open.

It was darker in the room than the hallway. The sun glowed through crisscrossed boards nailed over the single window. She stepped inside, coughing at the tang in the air.

Gauzy shadows disguised the body on the bed. She inched closer to it, glancing over her shoulder as if the door might close of its own accord.

The stalks had grown to a length of six inches or so, but were wilted. They bloomed from the man's torso. From the dry soil in his belly. The fungi that had grown through the skin of his face were withered, leaving behind a fine gray down. His lips were pulled back to reveal a desiccated mouth, yellowed teeth stained with dirt.

Jess looked at her fingers, recalling how she felt the fungi bloom in the dark. She wiped her hands on her jeans and retreated.

A hand grasped her ankle and Jess screamed. Her instinct was to

306

pull away, the momentum of the action propelling her onto the body on the bed. The corpse collapsed beneath her, the old porous bones snapping with muted cracks. She scrambled over the bed and landed on the floor.

Panting, Jess whispered, "The cat. It was the fucking cat."

She peered over the bed but only saw the body.

"Kitty?"

She only heard the thumping of her heart. It was something else. Not the cat. The cat could barely crawl out of the room. It was a shoe. Had to be a shoe.

Jess stood. What she saw did not make sense for a moment. There was a pile of dirt on the floor. She remembered touching it the night before just before leaving the room. The soil shifted.

The hand that grabbed her ankle began to rise. Dirt spilled free and a figure emerged, sitting upright.

"Oh my God," Jess whispered into the comforter.

The figure stood in a series of mechanical iterations. Clods of dirt fell from the nude body, revealing the sex. The pendulous breasts hung like old gym socks, bits of flesh missing here and there, tubules vibrating from the motion of her efforts. The bloom above the delta of her sex was particularly vigorous, perhaps hundreds of fungi there.

"Sweetie?" she croaked with shredded vocal chords.

Jess bit the comforter. She was not afraid of being seen. Both eyes were gone, replaced by pale strands terminating in kidney bean-shaped growths.

"Sweetie, it's so dark. Sweetie?"

Jess stood and took a step to the side. The floorboard squeaked and the old woman turned her ear toward the sound. The growth there looked like a floret of cauliflower.

"Sweetie? I can't see you, love. I-I'm so thirsty. I'm hungry, too," she said, clutching her midsection.

Jess sidestepped as she spoke, using the voice as cover. She was at the foot of the bed then, eyeing the half-opened door.

The woman, D. Heller, Jess guessed, sniffed the air.

"I'm thirsty, sweetie. And, it's so hot in here."

She pivoted, more soil falling to the floor, then sniffed, bending over. Jess grasped the door handle. The woman kneeled to the floor and plunged her hands into the soil that had been her hiding place. She held it to her mouth, the stalks dancing on her tongue seeming to thrum with anticipation.

She shoved the dirt into her mouth and moaned with pleasure, her stalks stiffening. Jess closed the door as she left the room, her stomach twisted into knots.

It was warm outside, clouds frozen in place in the sky, but never seeming to obscure the sun. She walked down the gravel road and hoped it would lead her to food eventually.

Jess heard it before she saw it.

The calliope music playing so faintly it might have been a dream. The tune was a persistent feature of her imagination. The radio, the very same model as in the Valley, was in the middle of the road.

It felt like an old friend in her arms. She whistled its tune and repeated the number pattern.

3-7-4-1-5

6-6-4-7-5

She reached a crossroads, no road signs present. With nothing else to guide her, she decided to turn north.

Jess rubbed her eye, which had begun to itch.

A black goat emerged from a cornfield that had grown wild, years of unharvested crops littering the ground. It watched her pass, only its strange, hourglass eyes moving.

"3-7-4-1-5," Jess said.

The goat nodded to the north, the direction she was headed.

The void spoke to her.

"6-6-4-7-5."

Maybe it would return her to her friends. She rubbed her eyes again. She was itchy all over, but it felt concentrated there. She followed the road. Hopefully it would take her somewhere cool and dark.

Acknowledgements

First, thank you to my family, who are my unpaid alpha/beta readers. I often run up against a deadline and take you along with me. Thanks for not pushing back too hard. I would also like to acknowledge The NoSleep Podcast team, including David for helming a platform for these stories, which might otherwise have ended up trapped in a sad folder on my computer collecting digital dust. Thank you to Olivia for your friendship and encouragement with this project and others. Thank you to Jessica McEvoy for introducing the NoSleep Book Club to my firstborn, warts and all. A special shout out to my Facebook NoSleep Mom, who always understood that joke. Thank you to the producers and voice actors for your exceptional talent with both my work and the work of others. And, thank you to the NoSleep Podcast community.

As well, thank you to my writing friends/NoSleep Podcast fellows: Adam Davies, Scott Savino, Nick Botic, Billy Stuart, Marcus Damanda, S.H. Cooper, and Mr. Michael Squid among others in a much longer list.

Thank you to Richard Thomas. I submitted *Comancheria* (then *Palo Duro)* to your Twitter contest and was elated at your feedback. Life, the military, and COVID interrupted my journey with Storyville, but I do reference the materials and it has improved my writing.

Thank you to Brett Bullion, who responded to an unprompted DM and has spent the last 2+ years with these stories invading his likely otherwise pleasant existence. You may not have known you were the first person to read at least a couple of these stories!

The following artists accompanied me as I wrote: Between the Buried and Me, Conjurer, Cult of Luna, The Dillinger Escape Plan, Fires in the Distance, Flor de Toloache, Gojira, Harm's Way, Insomnium, Jinjer, Katatonia, Knocked Loose, Metallica, Ne Obliviscaris, Norma Jean, Opeth, Persefone, Rivers of Nihil, Rorcal, Spiritbox, Swallow the Sun, TOOL, and **BRANDON BOONE**

About The Author

LP Hernandez was born into a military family and has lived all over the world. His love for horror began with Goosebumps, Are You Afraid of the Dark?, and a version of Stephen King's *Carrie* with a blood splattered Sissy Spacek on the cover. His work has been included in several anthologies including If I Die Before I Wake vol 5, Black Rainbow, Sirens at Midnight, Lockdown Horror, and Tavistock Galleria among others. His stories have also been adapted as audio dramas on the NoSleep Podcast, including several featured in this collection. When he is not writing he serves as a Medical Service Corps officer in the United States Air Force. He loves his family, heavy metal, and a crisp high five.

About The Illustrator

Brett Bullion is a dark fantasy illustrator residing in Austin, TX with his lovely wife, brilliant son, dog, turtle, and polar bear. He was raised on a healthy diet of 80s horror, 90s anime, and games of all kinds (currently D&D). You can find more of his work online at www.BrettBullionArt.com

Made in the USA
Las Vegas, NV
13 November 2021

34309908R10177